A
HOLOGRAM
FOR THE
KING

A
HOLOGRAM

FOR THE

KING

A NOVEL

DAVE EGGERS

HAMISH HAMILTON
an imprint of
PENGUIN BOOKS

HAMISH HAMILTON

Published by the Penguin Group
Penguin Books Ltd, 80 Strand, London WC2R 0RL, England
Penguin Group (USA) Inc., 375 Hudson Street, New York, New York 10014, USA
Penguin Group (Canada), 90 Eglinton Avenue East, Suite 700, Toronto, Ontario, Canada M4P 2Y3
(a division of Pearson Penguin Canada Inc.)
Penguin Ireland, 25 St Stephen's Green, Dublin 2, Ireland (a division of Penguin Books Ltd)
Penguin Group (Australia), 707 Collins Street, Melbourne, Victoria 3008, Australia
(a division of Pearson Australia Group Pty Ltd)
Penguin Books India Pvt Ltd, 11 Community Centre,
Panchsheel Park, New Delhi – 110 017, India
Penguin Group (NZ), 67 Apollo Drive, Rosedale, Auckland 0632, New Zealand
(a division of Pearson New Zealand Ltd)
Penguin Books (South Africa) (Pty) Ltd, Block D, Rosebank Office Park,
181 Jan Smuts Avenue, Parktown North, Gauteng 2193, South Africa

Penguin Books Ltd, Registered Offices: 80 Strand, London WC2R 0RL, England

www.penguin.com

First published in the United States of America by McSweeney's 2012
First published in Great Britain by Hamish Hamilton 2013
001

Printed in Great Britain by Clays Ltd, St Ives plc

A CIP catalogue record for this book is available from the British Library

ISBN: 978–0–241–14585–2

www.greenpenguin.co.uk

MIX
Paper from
responsible sources
FSC
www.fsc.org   FSC™ C018179

Penguin Books is committed to a sustainable
future for our business, our readers and our planet.
This book is made from Forest Stewardship
Council™ certified paper.

ALWAYS LEARNING   **PEARSON**

For Daniel McSweeney, Ron Hadley,
and Paul Vida, great men all

It is not every day that we are needed.
—Samuel Beckett

I.

ALAN CLAY WOKE up in Jeddah, Saudi Arabia. It was May 30, 2010. He had spent two days on planes to get there.

In Nairobi he had met a woman. They sat next to each other while they waited for their flights. She was tall, curvy, with tiny gold earrings. She had ruddy skin and a lilting voice. Alan liked her more than many of the people in his life, people he saw every day. She said she lived in upstate New York. Not that far away from his home in suburban Boston.

If he had courage he would have found a way to spend more time with her. But instead he got on his flight and he flew to Riyadh and then to Jeddah. A man picked him up at the airport and drove him to the Hilton.

With a click, Alan entered his room at the Hilton at 1:12 a.m. He quickly prepared to go to bed. He needed to sleep. He had to travel an hour north at seven for an eight o'clock arrival at the King Abdullah

Economic City. There he and his team would set up a holographic tele-conference system and would wait to present it to King Abdullah himself. If Abdullah was impressed, he would award the IT contract for the entire city to Reliant, and Alan's commission, in the mid-six figures, would fix everything that ailed him.

So he needed to feel rested. To feel prepared. But instead he had spent four hours in bed not sleeping.

He thought of his daughter Kit, who was in college, a very good and expensive college. He did not have the money to pay her tuition for the fall. He could not pay her tuition because he had made a series of foolish decisions in his life. He had not planned well. He had not had courage when he needed it.

His decisions had been short sighted.
The decisions of his peers had been short sighted.
These decisions had been foolish and expedient.

But he hadn't known at the time that his decisions were short sighted, foolish or expedient. He and his peers did not know they were making decisions that would leave them, leave Alan, as he now was — virtually broke, nearly unemployed, the proprietor of a one-man consulting firm run out of his home office.

He was divorced from Kit's mother Ruby. They had now been apart longer than they had been together. Ruby was an unholy pain in the ass who now lived in California and contributed nothing financially to Kit's finances. College is *your* thing, she told him. Be a man about it, she said.

Now Kit would not be in college in the fall. Alan had put his house on the market but it had not yet sold. Otherwise he was out of options. He owed money to many people, including $18k to a pair of bicycle designers who had built him a prototype for a new bicycle he thought he could manufacture in the Boston area. For this he was called an idiot. He owed money to Jim Wong, who had loaned him $45k to pay for materials and the first and last on a warehouse lease. He owed another $65k or so to a half-dozen friends and would-be partners.

So he was broke. And when he realized he could not pay Kit's tuition, it was too late to apply for any other aid. Too late to transfer.

Was it a tragedy that a healthy young woman like Kit would take a semester off of college? No, it was not a tragedy. The long, tortured history of the world would take no notice of a missed semester of college for a smart and capable young woman like Kit. She would survive. It was no tragedy. Nothing like tragedy.

They said it was a tragedy what had happened to Charlie Fallon. Charlie Fallon froze to death in the lake near Alan's house. The lake next to Alan's house.

Alan was thinking of Charlie Fallon while not sleeping in the room at the Jeddah Hilton. Alan had seen Charlie step into the lake that day. Alan was driving away, on his way to the quarry. It had not seemed normal that a man like Charlie Fallon would be stepping into the shimmering black lake in September, but neither was it extraordinary.

Charlie Fallon had been sending Alan pages from books. He had been doing this for two years. Charlie had discovered the Transcendentalists late in life and felt a kinship with them. He had seen that Brook Farm was not far from where he and Alan lived, and he thought it meant something. He traced his Boston ancestry, hoping to find a connection, but found none. Still, he sent Alan pages, with passages highlighted.

The workings of a privileged mind, Alan thought. Don't send me more of that shit, he told Charlie. But Charlie grinned and sent more.

So when Alan saw Charlie stepping into the lake at noon on a Saturday he saw it as a logical extension of the man's new passion for the land. He was only ankle-deep when Alan passed him that day.

II.

WHEN ALAN WOKE in the Jeddah Hilton he was already late. It was 8:15. He had fallen asleep just after five.

He was expected at the King Abdullah Economic City at eight. It was at least an hour away. After he showered and dressed and got a car to the site it would be ten. He would be two hours late on the first day of his assignment here. He was a fool. He was more a fool every year.

He tried Cayley's cellphone. She answered, her husky voice. In another lifetime, a different spin of the wheel wherein he was younger and she older and both of them stupid enough to attempt it, he and Cayley would have been something terrible.

—Hello Alan! It's beautiful here. Well, maybe not beautiful. But you're not here.

He explained. He did not lie. He could no longer muster the energy, the creativity required.

—Well, don't worry, she said, with a small laugh — that voice of hers implied the possibility of, celebrated the existence of a fantastic life of abiding sensuality — we're just setting up. But you'll have to get your own ride. Any of you know how Alan will get a ride out here?

She seemed to be yelling to the rest of the team. The space sounded cavernous. He pictured a dark and hollow place, three young people holding candles, waiting for him and his lantern.

—He can't rent a car, she said to them.

And now to him: —Can you rent a car, Alan?

—I'll figure it out, he said.

He called the lobby.

—Hello. Alan Clay here. What's your name?

He asked names. A habit Joe Trivole instilled back in the Fuller Brush days. Ask names, repeat names. You remember people's names, they remember you.

The clerk said his name was Edward.

—Edward?

—Yes sir. My name is Edward. Can I help you?

—Where are you from, Edward?

—Jakarta, Indonesia, sir.

—Ah, Jakarta, Alan said. Then realized he had nothing to say about Jakarta. He knew nothing about Jakarta.

—Edward, what do you think of me renting a car through the hotel?

—Do you have an international driver's license?

—No.

—Then no, I don't think you should do this.

Alan called the concierge. He explained he needed a driver to take him to the King Abdullah Economic City.

—This will take a few minutes, the concierge said. His accent was not Saudi. There were apparently no Saudis working at this Saudi hotel. Alan had assumed as much. There were few Saudis working anywhere, he'd been told. They imported their labor in all sectors. We must find someone appropriate to drive you, the concierge said.
—You can't just call a taxi?
—Not exactly, sir.

Alan's blood went hot, but this was a mess of his making. He thanked the man and hung up. He knew you couldn't just call a taxi in Jeddah or Riyadh — or so said the guidebooks, all of which were overwrought when it came to elucidating the dangers of the Kingdom of Saudi Arabia to foreign travelers. The State Department had Saudi on the highest alert. Kidnapping was not unlikely. Alan might be sold to al-Qaeda, ransomed, transported across borders. But Alan had never felt in danger anywhere, and his assignments had taken him to Juarez in the nineties, Guatemala in the eighties.

The phone rang.
—We have a driver for you. When would you like him?
—As soon as possible.
—He'll be here in twelve minutes.

Alan showered and shaved his mottled neck. He put on his undershirt, his white button-down, khakis, loafers, tan socks. Just dress like an American businessman, he'd been told. There were the cautionary tales of overzealous Westerners wearing thobes, headdresses. Trying to blend in, making an effort. This effort was not appreciated.

While fixing the collar of his shirt, Alan felt the lump on his neck that he'd first discovered a month earlier. It was the size of a golf ball, protruding from his spine, feeling like cartilage. Some days he figured it was part of his spine, because what else could it be?

It could be a tumor.

There on his spine, a lump like that — it had to be invasive and deadly. Lately he'd been cloudy of thought and clumsy of gait, and it made a perfect and terrible sense that there was something growing there, eating away at him, sapping him of vitality, squeezing away all acuity and purpose.

He'd planned to see someone about it, but then had not. A doctor could not operate on something like that. Alan didn't want radiation, didn't want to go bald. No, the trick was to touch it occasionally, track attendant symptoms, touch it some more, then do nothing.

In twelve minutes Alan was ready.

He called Cayley.

—I'm leaving the hotel now.

—Good. We'll be all set up by the time you get here.

The team could get there without him, the team could set up without him. And so why was he there at all? The reasons were specious but

10

had gotten him here. The first was that he was older than the other members of the team, all of them children, really, none beyond thirty. Second, Alan had once known King Abdullah's nephew when they had been part of a plastics venture in the mid-nineties, and Eric Ingvall, the Reliant VP in New York, felt that this was a good enough connection that it would get the attention of the King. Probably not true, but Alan had chosen not to change their minds.

Alan was happy for the work. He needed the work. The eighteen months or so before the call from Ingvall had been humbling. Filing a tax return for $22,350 in taxable income was an experience he hadn't expected to have at his age. He'd been home consulting for seven years, each year with dwindling revenue. No one was spending. Even five years ago business had been good; old friends threw him work, and he was useful to them. He'd connect them with vendors he knew, pull favors, cut deals, cut fat. He'd felt worthwhile.

Now he was fifty-four years old and was as intriguing to corporate America as an airplane built from mud. He could not find work, could not sign clients. He had moved from Schwinn to Huffy to Frontier Manufacturing Partners to Alan Clay Consulting to sitting at home watching DVDs of the Red Sox winning the Series in '04 and '07. The game when they hit four consecutive home runs against the Yankees. April 22, 2007. He'd watched those four and a half minutes a hundred times and each viewing brought him something like joy. A sense of rightness, of order. It was a victory that could never be taken away.

Alan called the concierge.
—Is the car there?

—I'm sorry, he will be late.

—Is this the guy from Jakarta?

—It is.

—Edward.

—Yes.

—Hi again, Edward. How late will the car be?

—Twenty more minutes. Can I send some food up to you?

Alan went to the window and looked out. The Red Sea was calm, unremarkable from this height. A six-lane highway ran just alongside it. A trio of men in white fished at the pier.

Alan looked at the balcony next to his. He could see his reflection in the glass. He looked like an average man. When shaved and dressed, he passed for legitimate. But something had darkened under his brow. His eyes had retreated and people were noticing. At his last high school reunion, a man, a former football player whom Alan had despised, said, Alan Clay, you've got a thousand-mile stare. What happened to you?

A gust of wind came from the sea. In the distance, a container ship moved across the water. Here and there a few other boats, tiny as toys.

There had been a man next to him on the flight from Boston to London. He was drinking gin and tonics and monologuing.

It was good for a while, right? he'd said. What was it, thirty years or so? Maybe twenty, twenty-two? But it was over, without a doubt it was, and now we had to be ready to join western Europe in an era of tourism and shopkeeping. Wasn't that the gist of what that man on the plane had said? Something like that.

He wouldn't shut up, and the drinks kept coming.

We've become a nation of indoor cats, he'd said. A nation of doubters, worriers, overthinkers. Thank God these weren't the kind of Americans who settled this country. They were a different breed! They crossed the country in wagons with wooden wheels! People croaked along the way, and they barely stopped. Back then, you buried your dead and kept moving.

The man, who was drunk and maybe unhinged, too, was, like Alan, born into manufacturing and somewhere later got lost in worlds tangential to the making of things. He was soaking himself in gin and tonics and was finished with it all. He was on his way to France, to retire near Nice, in a small house his father had built after WWII. That was that.

Alan had humored the man, and they had compared some thoughts about China, Korea, about making clothes in Vietnam, the rise and fall of the garment industry in Haiti, the price of a good room in Hyderabad. Alan had spent a few decades with bikes, then bounced around between a dozen or so other stints, consulting, helping companies compete through ruthless efficiency, robots, lean manufacturing, that kind of thing. And yet year by year, there was less work for a guy like him. People were done manufacturing on American soil. How could he or anyone argue for spending five to ten times what it cost in Asia? And when Asian wages rose to untenable levels — $5 an hour, say — there was Africa. The Chinese were already making sneakers in Nigeria. Jack Welch said manufacturing should be on a perpetual barge, circling the globe for the cheapest conditions possible, and it seemed the world had taken him at his word. The man on the plane wailed in protest: It should *matter* where something was made!

But Alan did not want to despair, and did not want to be dragged down with his seatmate's malaise. Alan was optimistic, wasn't he? He said he was. *Malaise.* That was the word the man used again and again. It's the black humor that really does it. The jokes! the man wailed. I used to hear them in France, England, Spain. And Russia! People grumbling about their hopeless governments, about the elemental and irreversible dysfunction of their countries. And Italy! The sourness, the presumption of decline. It was everywhere, and now it's with us, too. That dark sarcasm. It's the killer, I swear to God. That's the sign you're down and can't get up!

Alan had heard it before and he didn't want to hear it anymore. He put on his headphones and watched movies the rest of the flight.

Alan left the balcony and returned to the dark cool of the room.

He thought of his home. He wondered who was in his home at the moment. Who might be passing through, touching things, leaving.

His house was for sale, had been for four months. Is that the lake where the guy froze to death?

The only thing Ruby called about was the house. Was it sold yet? She needed the money and thought Alan would sell the house and somehow keep the sale secret. You will know when it's sold, he told her. There is also the internet, he said. He hung up when she began yelling.

A woman had staged Alan's house. There are people who do this. They come into your house and make it more appealing than you ever could. They brighten the darkness you have brought into it with your human mess.

Then, until it's sold, you live in a version of your house, a better version. There is more yellow. There are flowers and tables made of reclaimed wood. Your own belongings are in storage.

Her name was Renee, with wispy hair swept upward like cotton candy. Start by eliminating clutter, she said. You'll need to box up and remove ninety percent of all this, she said, sweeping her arm over all he had accumulated in twenty years.

He packed it up. He removed, removed. He left the furniture, but when she returned she said, Now we replace the furniture. Do you want to buy it or rent it?

He removed his furniture. There were two couches in the living room and he gave them both away. One to a friend of Kit's. One to Chuy who cut his lawn. Renee rented artwork. Noncommittal abstractions, she called them. They were in every room, canvases with agreeable colors, vague shapes signifying nothing.

That was four months ago. He had been living in the house all the while, evacuating when the realtors wanted to show it. Sometimes he stayed. Sometimes he stayed locked in his home office as the visitors walked through his home, commenting. Low ceilings, they would say. Small bedrooms. Are these the original floors? There's a musty smell. Are the occupants older people?

Sometimes he watched the potential buyers come in, leave. He peeked through his office window like an imbecile. One couple stayed so long that Alan had to urinate in a coffee cup. One visitor, a professional woman in a long leather coat, saw him through the window as she was walking away, down the driveway. She turned to the realtor and said, I think I just saw a ghost.

Alan watched the waves break gently against the shore. Who knew Saudi Arabia had a vast and pristine coast? Alan had not known this. He looked at a few dozen palm trees below, planted in the courtyard of either his hotel or the one next door, the Red Sea beyond. He thought of staying here. He could assume a new name. He could abandon all debts. Send Kit money somehow, leave the crushing vise of his life in America behind. He had done fifty-four years of it. Wasn't that enough?

But no. He was more than that. Some days he was more than that. Some days he could encompass the world. Some days he could see for miles. Some days he climbed over the foothills of indifference to see the landscape of his life and future for what it was: mappable, traversable, achievable. Everything he wanted to do had been done before, so why couldn't he do it again? He could. If only he could engage on a continual basis. If only he could draw up a plan and execute it. He could! He had to believe he could. Of course he did.

This Abdullah deal seemed like a given. No one could compete with Reliant's size, and now they had a goddamned hologram. Alan would close this up, get his cut, pay back everyone in Boston, then get going. Open a small factory, start with a thousand bikes a year, then ramp up from there. Pay Kit's tuition with pocket change. Send away the realtors, pay what's left on his house, stride the world, a colossus, enough money to say fuck *you*, and *you*, and *you*.

A knock at the door. His breakfast had arrived. Hash browns to his room in five minutes. Impossible unless he was eating food prepared for someone else. Which he realized he was. He didn't mind. He let the waiter set everything up on a table on the balcony, and with a flourish Alan signed the bill while seated ten stories up, squinting into the wind. He felt, momentarily, that this was him. That he was worthy of this. He needed to adopt an air of ownership, of belonging. Maybe if he was the sort of man who could eat someone else's hash browns, who the hotel wanted to impress so much they sent him someone else's breakfast, maybe then he was the sort of man who could get an audience with the King.

III.

THE PHONE RANG.

—We had a problem with the first driver. We called a second one. He's on his way. He should be here in twenty minutes.

—Thank you, Alan said, and hung up.

He sat, breathing carefully until he felt calm again. He was an American businessman. He was not ashamed. He could muster something today. He could be better than a fool.

They had given Alan no guarantees. The King is very busy, they told him repeatedly in emails and phone calls. Of course he is, Alan said again and again, and reiterated that he was willing to meet anywhere, at the time of His Majesty's choosing. But it was not simple like that; it was not just that the King was busy, but that his schedule changed quickly and often. It had to change often and quickly, given there were many who might wish to do the King harm. So not only does the King's schedule change often, given the demands of state, but it must change often, for the sake of king and kingdom. Alan was told that Reliant, along with a number of other vendors interested in providing services to the King Abdullah Economic City, were to prepare their wares and present them at a site to be determined, somewhere at the coastal heart of the burgeoning city, and that they would be notified shortly before the King would arrive. It could be any day, and it could be any time, Alan was told.

—So days, weeks? he asked.

—Yes, they said.

And so Alan had arranged this trip. He'd done this kind of thing before — kiss the ring, present the wares, cut a deal. Not an impossible task, usually, if you had the right fixers and kept your head down. And working for Reliant, the largest IT supplier in the world, was not challenging. Abdullah, presumably, wanted the best, and Reliant considered themselves the best, certainly the biggest, twice as big as their closest U.S. competitor.

I know your nephew Jalawi, Alan would say.

Maybe *I'm close with your nephew Jalawi.*

Jalawi, your nephew, is an old friend.

Elsewhere, relationships no longer mattered, Alan knew this. They did not matter in America, they did not matter much of anywhere, but here, among the royals, he hoped that friendship had meaning.

There were three others from Reliant along on the trip, two engineers and a marketing director — Brad, Cayley, and Rachel. They would demonstrate the capabilities of Reliant, and Alan would rough out the numbers. Providing IT for KAEC would mean at least a few hundred million for Reliant right away, and with more to come, and more crucially, a life of comfort for Alan. Maybe not a life of comfort. But he could dodge potential bankruptcy, would have something to retire with, and Kit would stay at the college of her choosing and would be that much less disappointed in life and in her father.

He left the room. The door closed like cannon fire. He walked down the orange hall.

They had built the hotel to bear no evidence of its existence within the Kingdom of Saudi Arabia. The whole complex, fortressed from the road and sea, was free of content or context, devoid of even a pattern or two of Arabic origin. This place, all palm trees and adobe, could have been in Arizona, in Orlando, anywhere.

Alan peered down into the atrium, ten stories below, where dozens of men milled about, all in traditional Saudi dress. Alan had to remember the terminology: the long white tunics were thobes. The cloth covering the hair and neck was the gutra, held in place by the black round rope, the iqal. Alan watched the men mill about, the thobes giving their movements a kind of weightlessness. A convention of spirits.

At the end of the hall he spotted an elevator door closing. He jogged to it and thrust his hand into the gap. The doors jerked back, startled and apologetic. In the glass elevator were four men, all in thobes and gutras. A few glanced up at Alan but quickly returned their eyes to a new tablet computer held between them. The owner was demonstrating the keypad feature, and was turning the device round and round, the buttons dutifully reconfiguring, and this was giving great pleasure to his friends.

The glass container that held them all fell down through the atrium to the lobby, silent as snow, and the doors opened to a wall of fake rock. The smell of chlorine.

Alan held the door for the Saudis, none of them thanking him. He followed. Fountains threw water into the air without reason or rhythm.

He sat down at a small cast-iron table in the lobby. A waiter appeared. Alan ordered coffee.

Nearby, two men, one black and one white, sat together, dressed in identical white thobes. Alan's guidebook told him there was a pronounced, even naked, racism in Saudi Arabia, but here was this. Perhaps not evidence of societal harmony, but still. He could not think of an instance when a custom or dictum described in a guidebook had ever been borne out in practice. Conveying cultural norms was like reporting traffic conditions. By the time you published them they were irrelevant.

Now someone was standing near Alan. Alan looked up to see a chubby man smoking a very thin white cigarette. He held up a hand, as if to wave. Alan waved, confused.

—Alan? Are you Alan Clay?

—I am.

The man stubbed his cigarette into a glass ashtray and gave his hand to Alan. His fingers were long and thin, soft as chamois.

—You're the driver? Alan asked.

—Driver, guide, hero. Yousef, the man said.

Alan stood. Yousef was short, his cream-white thobe giving his stout frame the silhouette of a penguin. He was young, not much older than Kit. His face was round, unlined, with the wispy mustache of a teenager.

—Having some coffee?
—Yes.
—Did you want to finish?
—No, that's okay.
—Good. This way, then.

They walked outside. The heat was alive, predatory.
—Over here, Yousef said, and they hurried across the small parking lot to an ancient Chevy Caprice, puddle-brown. This is my love, he said, presenting it as a magician would a bouquet of fake flowers.
The car was a wreck.
—You ready? You don't have a bag or anything?
Alan did not. He used to carry a briefcase, legal pads, but he'd not once looked at the notes he took in any meeting. Now he sat in meetings and wrote nothing, and this practice had become a source of strength. People assumed great mental acuity from someone who took no notes.

Alan opened the back door.
—No, no, Yousef said. I'm not a chauffer. Sit in front.

Alan obeyed. The seat released a small cloud of dust.
—You sure this thing will get us there? Alan asked.
—I drive this to Riyadh all the time, Yousef said. It's never failed.

Yousef got in and turned the ignition. The engine was mute.

—Oh wait, he said, and got out, opened the hood, and disappeared behind it. After a moment, he closed the hood, got in again, and started the car. It coughed awake, sounding like the past.

—Engine problem? Alan asked.

—No, no. I had to disconnect the engine before I went into the lobby. I just have to make sure no one wires it.

—Wires it? Alan asked. To explode?

— It's nothing terroristic, Yousef said. It's just this guy who thinks I'm screwing his wife.

Yousef put the car in reverse and backed up.

—He might be trying to kill me, he said. Here we go.

They left the hotel roundabout. At the exit they drove past a desert-colored Humvee, a machine gun mounted on top. A Saudi soldier was sitting next to it, in a beach chair, his feet soaking in an inflatable pool.

—So I'm in a car that might explode?

—No, not now. I just checked. You saw me.

—You're serious about this? Someone's trying to kill you?

—Could be, Yousef said, and pulled onto the main highway, parallel to the Red Sea. But you never know for sure till it happens, am I right?

—I waited an hour to get a driver whose car might blow up.

—No, no, Yousef said, now distracted. He was trying to activate his iPod, an older model, which was reclining in the drink holder between them. Something was wrong with the connection between the iPod and the car stereo.

—It's nothing to worry about. I don't think he knows how to wire a car that way. He's not a tough guy. He's just rich. It would only be possible if he hired someone.

Alan stared at Yousef until the young man added it up: a rich man very well might hire someone to wire the car of the man screwing his wife.

—Fuuuck, Yousef said, turning to Alan. Now you've got *me* scared.

Alan considered opening the door and rolling out of the car. It seemed a more prudent course of action than riding with this man.

Meanwhile, Yousef removed another thin cigarette from a white package and lit it, squinting at the road ahead. They were passing a long series of huge, candy-colored sculptures.

—Terrible, right? Yousef said. He took a long drag, and any concern about hitmen seemed to disappear. So Alan. Where are you from?

Something about Yousef's blasé demeanor rubbed off on Alan, and he stopped worrying. With his penguin shape and thin cigarettes and Chevy Caprice, he was not the type of man who would interest assassins.

—Boston, Alan said.

—Boston. Boston, Yousef said, tapping the steering wheel. I've been to Alabama. One year of college.

Against his better judgment, Alan continued talking to this lunatic.

—You studied in Alabama? Why Alabama?

—You mean, because I was the only Arab for a few thousand miles? I got a scholarship for a year. This was Birmingham. Pretty different from Boston, I'm guessing?

Alan liked Birmingham and said so. He had friends in Birmingham.

Yousef smiled. —That big statue of Vulcan, right? Scary.

—That's right. I love that statue, Alan said.

The Alabama stint explained Yousef's American English. He spoke with only the faintest Saudi accent. He was wearing handmade sandals and Oakley sunglasses.

They sped through Jeddah and it all looked very new, not unlike Los Angeles. *Los Angeles with burqas*, Angie Healy had once said to him. They had worked together at Trek for a while. He missed her. Another dead woman in his life. There were too many, girlfriends who became old friends, then *old* friends, girlfriends who got married, who aged a bit, whose kids were now grown. And then there were the dead. Dead of aneurysms, breast cancer, non-Hodgkin's lymphoma. It was madness. His daughter was twenty now, and soon would be thirty, and soon after, the afflictions came like rain.

—So are you screwing this guy's wife or what? Alan asked.

—No, no. This is the woman I was supposed to marry. Like ten years ago. She and I were totally in love, but her father...

He looked to Alan to gauge his reaction so far.

—It sounds like a soap opera, I know. Anyway, I wasn't good enough for the father. So he forbids her to marry me, blah blah, and she goes and marries another guy. Now she's bored and she texts me all the time. She writes me on Facebook, everywhere. The husband knows this and he thinks we're having an affair. You want something to eat?

—You mean, should we stop and eat?

—We could go to a place in the Old City.

—No, I just ate. We're late, remember?

—Oh. We're in a hurry? They didn't tell me that. We shouldn't be going this way if we're late.

Yousef made a U-turn and sped up.

IV.

MAYBE KIT WAS better off staying home a year. Her college roommate was a strange bird, a rail-thin girl from Manhattan, a noticer. The roommate would notice that Kit was restless in her sleep, and she had some opinions about what it meant, how it could be treated, the deep-seated causes of such behavior. Her noticings were followed by questions, suspicions about the various problems Kit might have. She noticed tiny bruises on Kit's arms, and demanded to know what man had done this to her. She noticed Kit's voice was high, a bit small, almost childlike, and this, the roommate explained, was frequently a sign of childhood sexual abuse, the victim's voice frozen at the age of the trauma. Did you ever notice your voice was like a child's? she asked.

—You do this a lot? Alan asked.
—Drive people around? It's a side thing. I'm a student.
—Of what?
—A student of life! Yousef said, then laughed. No, I'm fucking with

you. Business, marketing. That kind of thing. I have no idea why.

They passed a vast playground, and for the first time, Alan saw children. Seven or eight of them, hanging on the monkey bars and climbing on the slides. And with them were three women in burqas, charcoal black. He had been among burqas before, but to see these shadows moving through the playground, following the children — it gave Alan a chill. Was it not something from a nightmare, to be chased by a flowing figure in black, hands outstretched? But Alan knew nothing and said nothing.

—How long is the drive? Alan asked.
—To the King Abdullah Economic City? That where we're going?
Alan said nothing. Yousef was smiling. This time he was kidding.
—About an hour. Maybe a little more. When were you supposed to be there?
—Eight. Eight thirty.
—Well, you'll be there at noon.

—You like Fleetwood Mac? Yousef asked. He'd gotten the iPod to work — it looked like it had been buried in the sand for centuries and then unearthed — and was now scrolling through his songs.
They left the city and were soon on a straight-shot highway that cut through raw desert. This was not beautiful desert. There were no dunes. This was an unrelenting flat. An ugly highway cut through it. Yousef's car passed tankers, freight trucks. Occasionally, off in the distance, there was a small village of grey cement, a labyrinth of walls and electrical wires.

Alan and Ruby had once driven across the United States, from

Boston to Oregon, for a wedding of a friend. The kind of ludicrous option available before children. They had fought repeatedly, explosively, mostly about their exes. Ruby wanted to talk about hers, in great detail. She wanted Alan to know why she'd left them and chosen him, and Alan wanted none of it. Was a clean slate too much to ask for? Please stop, he begged. She continued, glorying in her history. Stop stop stop, he finally roared, and no words were spoken between Salt Lake City and Oregon. Each silent mile gave him more strength and, he imagined, bolstered her respect for him. His only weapons against her were silence, truculence; he cultivated an occasional brooding intensity. He had never been as stubborn as he was with her. This was the version of himself who spent six years with her. This version of Alan was fiery, jealous, always on his heels. He had never felt more vital.

Yousef lit another cigarette.

—Not the most masculine brand, Alan noted.

Yousef laughed. —I'm trying to quit, so I went from regular size to these. They're half the width. Less nicotine.

—But more dainty.

—Dainty. Dainty. I like that. Yes, they are dainty.

One of Yousef's two front teeth was at a diagonal, crossing its twin. It gave his smile a special sort of madness.

—Even the box, Alan said. Look at it.

It was silver and white and tiny, like a miniature Cadillac driven by an insect pimp.

Yousef opened the glove compartment and dropped the box in.

—Better? he said.

Alan laughed. —Thank you.

For ten minutes, they said nothing.

Alan debated whether this man was taking him to the King Abdullah Economic City at all. Whether he was a charming kidnapper.

—You like jokes? Alan asked.

—You mean, like, jokes that you remember and tell?

—Yes, Alan said. Jokes that you remember and tell.

—It's not a Saudi thing, these kinds of jokes, Yousef said. But I've heard them. A British guy told me the one about the Queen and the big dick.

Ruby hated the jokes. —So embarrassing, she said after any evening out when he'd told one or ten. Alan knew a thousand and everyone who knew Alan knew that he knew a thousand.

He'd been tested, even — a group of friends, a few years ago, had made him tell jokes for two hours straight. They thought he'd run through all that he knew by then, but he'd only begun. Why he remembered so many he'd never know. But whenever one was wrapping up, another appeared before him. Never failed. Each joke was tied to the next, like a magician's string of scarves.

—Don't be such a cornball, Ruby said to him. You sound like some vaudevillian. No one tells jokes like that anymore.

—I do.

—People tell jokes when they have nothing to say, she said.

—People tell jokes when there's nothing left to say, he said.

He didn't actually say that. He thought of it many years later but by then he and Ruby weren't talking.

Yousef tapped the steering wheel.

—Okay, Alan said. A woman's husband has been sick. He's been slipping in and out of a coma for several months, but she's been staying by his bedside every single day. When he wakes up, he motions for her to come nearer. She comes over, sits next to him. His voice is weak. He holds her hand. 'You know what?' he says. 'You've been with me all through the bad times. When I got fired, you were there to support me. When my business went sour, you were there. When we lost the house, you gave me support. When my health started failing, you were still by my side... You know what?' 'What, dear?' she asks gently. 'I think you bring me bad luck!'

Yousef snorted, coughed. He had to stub out his cigarette.
—That's good. I didn't see that coming. You have more?
Alan was so grateful. He had not told a joke to an appreciative young person for many years.

—I do, Alan said. Let's see... Oh, this one's good. Okay, there was this man named Odd. John Odd. And he hated his last name. People constantly made fun of it, called him and his wife 'the Odd couple,' named him 'the Odd man out' wherever he went, all that. So he's getting older and writes out his will. And in the will he says when he dies he doesn't want his name on the gravestone. He just wants to be buried in an unmarked grave with a plain headstone, no name, nothing. So he dies, and his wife respects his wishes. So there he is, in this unmarked grave, but every time someone walks by the cemetery and sees the unmarked grave they say, 'Look, isn't that Odd?'

Yousef laughed, had to wipe his eyes.

Alan loved this guy. Even his own daughter, Kit, shook her head, No, please no, whenever he tried to set a joke up.

Alan continued. —Okay. Here's a question. What do you call a guy who knows forty-eight ways of making love but doesn't know any girls?

Yousef shrugged.

—A consultant.

Yousef smiled. —Not bad, he said. A consultant. That's you.

—That's me, Alan said. For a while at least.

They passed a small amusement park, brightly painted though seeming abandoned. A Ferris wheel, pink and yellow, stood alone, wanting children.

Alan thought of another joke.

—Okay, this one's better. There's a policeman. And he's just pulled up to the scene of a horrible car accident. There are parts of the victims everywhere, an arm here, a leg there. He's taking it all down when he comes across a head. He writes in his notebook: 'Head on bullevard' but he spells it b-u-l-l, and he knows he's spelled it wrong. So he crosses it out, tries again. 'Head on bouelevard.' Again he spells it wrong, too many 'e's. So scratch scratch. He tries again. 'Head on boolevard,' b-o-o-l. 'Damn!' he says. He looks around and sees that no one is looking. He nudges the head a little bit with his foot, takes out his pencil again. 'Head on curb.'"

—That's good, Yousef said, though he hadn't laughed.

They drove in silence for a mile or two. The landscape was flat and blank. Anything built here, an unrelenting desert, was an act of sheer will imposed on territory unsuited for habitation.

Charlie's body, when they pulled it from the lake, looked like debris. He was wearing a black windbreaker, and the first thing Alan thought was that it was a pile of leaves wrapped in a tarp. Only his hands were visibly human.

—Do you need anything from me? Alan asked the police.

They didn't need anything. They'd seen the whole thing. Fourteen police and firemen watched Charlie Fallon die in that lake over the course of five hours.

V.

—So why are you going here?

—Where?

—KAEC.

Yousef pronounced it like *cake*. Good to know, Alan thought.

—Work, Alan said.

—You in construction?

—No. Why?

—I thought maybe you'd help get it started. There's nothing happening there. No building at all.

—You've been there?

Alan assumed the answer would be yes. It had to be the biggest
thing anywhere near Jeddah. So of course Yousef had seen it.

—No, he said.

—Why not?

—There's nothing there.

—Not yet, Alan corrected.

—Not *ever*.

—Not *ever*?

—It won't happen, Yousef said. It's already dead.

—What? It's not dead. I've been researching this for months. I'm presenting there. They're full steam ahead.

Yousef turned to Alan and smiled, a huge grin, monumentally amused. Wait till we get there, he said. He lit another cigarette.

—Full steam ahead? he said. Jesus.

On cue, a billboard came into view, advertising the development. A family was arranged outside on a deck, an unconvincing sunset behind them. The man was Saudi, a businessman, a cellphone in one hand, a newspaper in the other. The woman, serving breakfast to the husband and two eager children, wore a hijab, a modest blouse and pants. Below the photo was written KING ABDULLAH ECONOMIC CITY: ONE MAN'S VISION, ONE NATION'S HOPE.

Alan pointed to it. —You don't think that'll happen?

—What do I know? I just know they haven't done anything yet.

—What about Dubai? That happened.

—This isn't Dubai.

—It can't be Dubai?

—It won't be Dubai. What women want to come here? No one moves to Saudi Arabia if they don't have to, even with the pink condos by the sea.

—The woman on the billboard seems a step forward, Alan said.

Yousef sighed. —That's the idea, they say. Or they don't say it, but they're hinting that at KAEC, the women will have more freedoms. That they'll be able to mix more freely with the men and drive. That kind of thing.

—And isn't that good?

—If it happens, maybe. But it won't happen. It might have happened at one time, but there's no more money. Emaar's a bust. They're going broke in Dubai. Everything was overvalued and now they're busted. They owe money all over the planet, and now KAEC's dead. Everything's dead. You'll see. You have any more jokes?

Alan was alarmed, but tried not to take Yousef's pronouncement too seriously. He knew there were detractors in Saudi and elsewhere. Emaar, the global developer that built much of Dubai, was in trouble, victim of the bubble, and everyone knew that without King Abdullah's personal involvement and his own cash, KAEC was in trouble. But of course the King would put his money in. Of course he would ensure that it moved forward. It had his name on it. It was his legacy. King Abdullah's pride would not allow him to let the whole thing fail. Alan made all these assertions to Yousef, trying to convince himself, too.

—But what if he dies? Yousef asked. He's eighty-five. What then?

Alan had no answer. He wanted to believe that this kind of thing, a city rising from dust, could happen. The architectural renderings he'd seen were magnificent. Gleaming towers, tree-lined public spaces and promenades, a series of canals allowing commuters to get almost anywhere by boat. The city was futuristic and romantic, but also practical. It could be made with extant technology and a lot of money, but money Abdullah certainly had. Why he didn't just put the money up himself, without Emaar, was a mystery. The man had enough money to raise the city overnight — so why didn't he? Sometimes a king had to be a king.

The exit ahead said King Abdullah Economic City. Yousef turned to Alan, raised his eyebrows in mock drama.

—Here we go. Full steam ahead!

They exited the highway and drove toward the sea.

—You sure this is the right way? Alan asked.

—This is where you wanted to go, Yousef said.

Alan saw no sign of a city-to-be.

—Whatever it is, it's there, Yousef said, pointing in front of them. The road was new, but it cut through absolutely nothing. They drove a mile before they arrived at a modest gate, a pair of stone arches over the road, a great dome atop it all. It was as if someone had built a road through unrepentant desert, and then erected a gate somewhere in the middle, to imply the end of one thing and the beginning of another. It was hopeful but unconvincing.

Yousef stopped and rolled down his window. A pair of guards in blue fatigues, rifles draped loosely over their shoulders, approached cautiously and circled the car. They seemed surprised to see anyone, let alone two men in a thirty-year-old Chevy.

Yousef spoke to them, mentioning his passenger with a rightward nod of his chin. The guards leaned down to see the American in the passenger seat. Alan smiled professionally. One of the guards said something to Yousef, and Yousef turned to Alan.

—Your ID.

Alan handed him his passport. The guard disappeared into his office. He returned and handed the passport back to Yousef and waved them through.

Beyond the checkpoint, the road split into two lanes. The median was covered in grass, burnt and struggling, kept alive by a pair of men in red jumpsuits who were watering it with a hose.

—I'm guessing these aren't union men, Alan said.

Yousef smiled grimly. —I heard a guy in my dad's shop the other day. He said, 'We don't have unions here. We have Filipinos.'

They drove on. A row of palm trees began in the median grass, all of them newly planted, some still wrapped in burlap. Interspersed every ten trees or so were banners attached to lampposts, bearing images of what the city would look like once finished. One featured a man in a thobe getting off a yacht, briefcase in hand, being greeted by two men in black suits and sunglasses. In another, a man was swinging a golf club at dawn, a caddy next to him — another South Asian, presumably. There was an airbrushed rendering of a fabulous new stadium. An aerial rendering of a beachfront lined with resorts. A photo of a woman helping her son use a laptop computer. She was wearing a hijab, but was otherwise dressed in Western clothing, everything lavender.

—Why would they advertise those kinds of freedoms if they weren't sincere? Alan asked. The risk Abdullah's taking in pissing off the conservatives is pretty big.

Yousef shrugged.

—Who knows? It impresses guys like you, so maybe it's working.

The road straightened out and again cut through desert without feature or form. Streetlights were placed every twenty feet or so, but otherwise there was nothing at all, the whole thing like a recently abandoned development on the moon.

They drove another mile toward the sea until the trees appeared again. Groups of workers, some in hardhats, some wearing scarves on their heads, huddled under the palms. In the distance, the road ended a few hundred yards from the water, where a handful of buildings stood, looking like old gravestones.

—This is it, basically, Yousef said.

The desert wind was strong, and the dust came over the street like fog. Still, two men were sweeping the road.

Yousef pointed and laughed. —This is where the money's going. They're sweeping the sand in a desert.

VI.

THE ENTIRETY OF the new city thus far comprised three buildings. There was a pastel-pink condominium, which was more or less finished but seemed empty. There was a two-story welcome center, vaguely Mediterranean in style, surrounded by fountains, most of which were dry. And there was a glass office building of about ten stories, squat and square and black. A sign attached to the facade read 7/24/60.

Yousef was dismissive. —That means they're open for business every day, every hour, every minute. Which I doubt.

They parked in front of the low welcome center, located just off the beach. It was adorned with various small domes and minarets. They got out of the car, the heat profound. It was 110 degrees.

—You want to come with? Alan asked.

Yousef stood before the building, as if deciding if anything within could be worth his time.

—Add it to my bill, Alan said.

Yousef shrugged. —Could be funny.

The doors opened outward, automatically, and a man emerged, in a gleaming white thobe.

—Mr. Clay! We have been expecting you. I am Sayed.

His face was thin, his mustache wide. He had small, laughing eyes.

—I'm sorry you missed the shuttle, he said. I understand the hotel had some trouble waking you.

—I'm sorry to be late, Alan said, his eyes steady.

Sayed smiled warmly. —The King won't be coming today, so your tardiness is inconsequential. Will you come inside?

They entered the building, dark and cool.

—Alan looked around. Is the Reliant team in here, or...

—They're in the presentation area, Sayed said, waving in the general direction of the beach. His accent was British. All these high-level functionaries in the Kingdom, Alan had been told, had been educated in the Ivy League and U.K. With this guy, Alan guessed St. Andrews.

—But I thought maybe I would give you the tour, Sayed said. Does that hold appeal for you?

Alan felt like he should at least check in with the team, but did not say so. The tour seemed harmless and was likely quick.

—Sure. Let's do it.

—Excellent. Some juice?

Alan nodded. Sayed turned, and another helper handed him a glass of orange juice, which he handed to Alan. The glass was crystal, something like a chalice. Alan took it and followed them through the lobby, full of arches and images of the city-to-be, into a large room where an enormous architectural model, waist-high, dominated.

—This is my associate, Mujaddid, Sayed said, indicating another man, who stood by the wall in a black business suit. Mujaddid was about forty, sturdily built, clean-shaven. He nodded.

—This is the city at full completion, Sayed said.

Now Mujaddid took over. —Mr. Clay, I give you the dream of King Abdullah.

The model's tiny buildings, each as big as a thumb, were all cream-colored, with white roads winding throughout, curving gently. There were skyscrapers, factories and trees, bridges and waterways, thousands of homes.

Alan had always been a sucker for a model like this, vision like this, a thirty-year plan, something rising from nothing — though his own experiences with bringing such a vision to fruition had not been so successful.

He'd commissioned a model once. The thought of it brought a twinge of regret. That factory in Budapest was not his idea, but he'd leapt upon the task, thinking it was a step to greater things. But converting a Soviet-era factory to a Schwinn-owned, capitalist model of efficiency—this had been madness. He'd been sent to Hungary to tackle the project, to bring American bicycle manufacturing to eastern Europe, to open up the whole continent to Schwinn.

Alan had commissioned a scale model, he'd had a grand opening, there were high hopes all around. Maybe they could send the Hungarian bikes beyond Europe. Maybe back to the U.S. The labor costs would be nothing, the craftsmanship high. Those were the assumptions.

But it fell apart. The factory never worked to capacity, the workers couldn't be trained, they were inefficient, and Schwinn didn't have the capital to properly modernize the machinery. A colossal failure, and from then on Alan's days at Schwinn, as a man who could get things done, were numbered.

And yet looking at this model now, Alan had a sense that this city might really happen, that with Abdullah's money it *would* happen. Sayed and Mujaddid were staring at it with him, seeming just as fascinated as he was as they explained the various stages of construction. The city, they said, would be complete by 2025, with a population of a million-five.

—Very impressive, Alan said. He looked for Yousef, who was roaming the lobby. Alan caught his eye, urged him into the room, but Yousef shook his head quickly, dismissing the thought.

—This is where we are right now, Mujaddid said.

Mujaddid nodded to a building directly below his nose, which looked precisely like the one he was standing in, though this one was the size of a grape. On the model, it stood on a long promenade running along the waterfront. Suddenly a laser's red dot appeared on its second story, as if a spacecraft had targeted it for disintegration.

Alan finished his juice, and then had nowhere to put his glass. There was no table, and the man with the platter had disappeared. With his sleeve, he dried the bottom of his glass and placed it on the surface of what he took to be the Red Sea, about a half mile from shore. Sayed smiled politely, took the glass, and left the room.

Mujaddid smiled grimly. —Should we see a film?

Alan and Yousef were led into a high-ceilinged ballroom, bright with mirrors and gold leaf, where a series of yellow couches, arranged in rows, faced a giant screen covering one full wall. They sat down and the room darkened.

A woman's voice began speaking in a clipped British accent.

'Inspired by the exemplary leadership and far-reaching vision of King Abdullah...' A computer-generated version of the city model appeared, now animated and glowing at night. The camera swooped down and over a gorgeous mountain range of black glass and lights. 'We present the dawn of the world's next great economic city...'

Alan looked to Yousef. He wanted Yousef to be impressed. The movie must have cost millions. Yousef was scrolling through messages on his phone.

'...to diversify the Middle East's largest economy...'

Soon it was daytime at KAEC, at street level, and there were speed-boats careening through the canals, businessmen shaking hands by the water, container ships arriving at the ports, presumably sending out the many products manufactured at KAEC.

'Inter-Arab financial cooperation...'

A series of flags appeared, representing Jordan, Syria, Lebanon, the UAE. There was a segment on the mosque that would be built, one that could accommodate two hundred thousand worshipers at once. A brief shot of a college lecture hall, women on one side of the classroom and men on the other.

'A twenty-four-hour city...'

A port that could process ten million containers annually. A dedicated hajj terminal that could process three hundred thousand pilgrims a season. A giant sports complex that would open like a clamshell.

Now Yousef was interested. He leaned over to Alan. —A stadium shaped like a vagina. Not bad.

Alan wasn't laughing. He was sold. The film was spectacular. It looked like the greatest city since Paris. Alan saw Reliant's role in it all: data transport, video, phones, networked transportation, RFID tagging for shipping containers, technology in the hospitals, schools, court-rooms. The possibilities were endless, beyond even what he or Ingvall or anyone else had even imagined. Finally the film reached its crescendo, the camera lifting skyward to reveal the whole of the King Abdullah Economic City at night, glittering, fireworks blooming over it all.

The lights came up.

Again they were in a showroom of mirrors and yellow couches.

—Not bad? Mujaddid said.

—Not bad at all, Alan said.

He looked to Yousef, whose expression was blank. If he had a joke to make, doubts to express, and it seemed he did, he knew better than to do so now, in this room, with the lights on.

—Let's see the model of the industrial district, Sayed said.

They were soon in a room filled with drawings of factories, ware-houses, trucks being loaded and unloaded. The idea, Sayed explained, was that they would be manufacturing things that used Saudi oil — plastics, toys, even diapers — and shipping them all over the Middle East. Maybe Europe and the United States too.

—I understand you were in manufacturing for a time? Sayed asked.

Alan was at a loss.

—We do our research, Mr. Clay. And I owned a Schwinn as a kid. I lived in New Jersey for about five years. When I was in business school, Schwinn was one of our case studies.

Always the case studies. Alan had participated in a few of them, but after a while it was too depressing. The questions from those wise-ass students masquerading as earnest young go-getters. Why didn't you anticipate the popularity of BMX bikes? And what about mountain bikes? You got murdered there. Was it a mistake to have shopped out all the labor to China? This coming from kids whose experience with business was summer lawn-cutting. How did your suppliers become your competitors? That was a rhetorical question. You want your unit cost down, you manufacture in Asia, but pretty soon the suppliers don't need you, do they? Teach a man to fish. Now the Chinese know how to fish, and ninety-nine percent of all bicycles are being made there, in one province.

—It was interesting for a period, though, wasn't it, Sayed said, when you had the Schwinns made in Chicago, the Raleighs made in England, the Italian bikes, the French… For a time you had real international competition, where you were choosing between very different products with very different heritages, sensibilities, manufacturing techniques…

Alan remembered. Those were bright days. In the morning he'd be at the West Side factory, watching the bikes, hundreds of them, loaded onto trucks, gleaming in the sun in a dozen ice-cream colors. He'd get in his car, head downstate, and in the afternoon he could be in Mattoon or Rantoul or Alton, checking on a dealership. He'd see a family walk in, Mom and Dad getting their ten-year-old daughter a World Sport, the kid touching the bike like it was some holy thing. Alan knew, and the retailer knew, and the family knew, that that bike had been made by hand a few hundred miles north, by a dizzying array of workers, most of them immigrants — Germans, Italians, Swedes, Irish, plenty of Japanese and of course a slew of Poles — and that that bike would last more or less forever. Why did this matter? Why did it matter that they had been made just up Highway 57? It was hard to say. But Alan was good at his job. Not such a difficult job, to sell something like that, something solid that would be integral to a thousand childhood memories.

—Well, that's gone, Alan said, hoping to be finished with it.

Sayed was not finished.

—Now it's a matter of putting different stickers on the same bikes. They're all built in the same handful of factories — every brand you can think of.

Alan didn't have much to say. He agreed with Sayed. He wanted to continue the tour, but the business student in Sayed was deep in his case study.

—Do you ever feel like you might have done it differently?

—Me? Personally?

—Well, whatever part you might have played. Might it have worked out differently? Was there a way Schwinn might have survived?

Might have. Might have. Alan parsed the words. He would bludgeon the man if he used these words again.

Sayed was waiting for an answer.

—It was complicated, Alan mumbled.

Alan had gotten this before, too. People felt nostalgic about Schwinn. They thought that somehow it must have all been squandered by a bunch of imbeciles running the brand, imbeciles like him. How could a company like Schwinn, which owned the majority of the U.S. market for about eighty years, have gone bankrupt, sold to Trek for next to nothing? How was it possible? Well, how was it not possible? The men behind Schwinn had tried to continue making bikes in the U.S.

According to some, that was mistake No. 1. They hung on in Chicago till 1983. Alan wanted to shake this MBA prick. Do you know how hard it was to hold out even that long? To try to make bicycles, very complicated and labor-intensive machines, on the West Side of Chicago, in a hundred-year-old factory, until 1983?

—Alan?

Alan looked up. It was Yousef.

—The tour's moving on. You want to come? *Might* you want to come?

Sayed was standing at the end of the hall.

—Let's go upstairs, he said.

Two flights of steps and they found themselves above the city-in-the-making. The observation room afforded 360-degree views, and Alan paced along the windows. It was raw, yes, but from this vantage point the city was beautiful. Now it made sense. The Red Sea was turquoise, a light ripple from a gentle wind bringing the tide in. The sand was almost white, very fine. A tiled promenade snaked into the distance, dividing the oceanfront from the pink condominium and what Alan could now see were the foundations for at least a few more. Palm trees were planted throughout the development, and lined the nearest canal, sky-blue and clean, taking in water from the sea and cutting through the city, heading east. What had seemed like utter failure from the road into the city seemed, now, entirely on target. The place was bustling, workers everywhere in their primary-colored jumpsuits, the place getting built. Any investors seeing the project from this vantage point would be convinced that it was being completed with great taste and with what Alan, at least, saw as admirable speed.

—You like it? Mujaddid asked.

—I do, Alan said. Look at that. All cities need rivers.

—Indeed, Mujaddid said.

Yousef was looking through the glass, too, his face stripped of cynicism. He seemed to be enjoying the sight without guile.

Sayed and Mujaddid led Alan and Yousef to an elevator. They dropped down two floors, and when the doors opened, they were in an underground garage.

—This way.

Sayed led him to an SUV. They stepped in. It smelled new. They drove up a ramp and into the light again. A hard left took them toward the water, and seconds later, the car stopped.

—Here we are, Mujaddid said.

They had driven two hundred yards. Before them was an enormous tent, white and taut, the kind used for weddings and festivals.

—Thank you, Alan said, stepping back into the heat.

—So we'll see you at 3 p.m.? Sayed said.

At some point there must have been some mention of an appointment.

—Yes, Alan said. In the main building, or the welcome center?

—It will be in the main building, Sayed said. With Karim al-Ahmad. He is your primary contact.

Alan stood before the tent, puzzled. There was a vinyl door.

—My people are in there? he asked.

—Yes, Mujaddid said, his face without doubt or apology.

—In a tent, Alan said.

It seemed impossible. Alan was sure there had been a mistake.

—Yes, Mujaddid said. Your presentation will be made in the presentation tent. I trust you will find everything you need inside.

And he closed the door to the car, and was off.

Alan turned to Yousef.

—I'm sure you can leave now.

—You have a way to get home?

—Yeah, there's a van or something.

They settled on a price, and Alan paid him. Yousef wrote a string of digits down on a business card.

—In case you miss the shuttle again, he said.

They shook hands.

Yousef raised his eyebrows at the tent.

—Full steam ahead, he said, and was gone.

VII.

IN THE TENT, Alan saw no one. The space was vast and empty, smelling of sweat and plastic. The floor was covered with Persian rugs, dozens of them overlapping. About thirty folding chairs were spread around as if there had been a wedding here and the guests had just left. A stage stood on one end of the tent, where Alan's team would assemble the speakers and projectors.

In a far corner of the tent, shadowy and crouching, he could make out three figures, each staring into the grey screens of their laptops. He walked toward them.

—There he is! a voice boomed.

It was Brad. He was in khakis and a crisp white shirt, his sleeves rolled up. He stood to shake Alan's hand, and did his best to bend the bones within. With his short, stocky build, legs almost bowed, he looked like a wrestling coach.

—Hey Brad. Good to see you.

Rachel and Cayley rose. They had shed their abayas, and they greeted

Alan barefoot, in shorts and tank tops. The tent was air-conditioned but had not reached anything like a comfortable level. All three young people were glistening.

They waited for Alan to say something. He had no idea what would be expected. He knew these young people only glancingly. They had met briefly, three months ago, in Boston, at the insistence of Eric Ingvall. Plans were made, and duties explained, timelines and goals. They had been given papers to sign, waivers required by the Kingdom, stating that they would all abide by the rules of the KSA, and that if they broke a law and were convicted, they were subject to the same punishments as anyone else. The waiver pointedly listed execution among the outcomes for certain crimes, including adultery, and they had all signed with a certain giddiness.

—You guys doing okay out here? Alan asked.

He could manage nothing better. He was still trying to process the fact that they were all in a tent.

—It's fine, but we can't get a wi-fi signal, Cayley said.

—We get a faint one from the Black Box, Brad added, throwing his head toward the 7/24/60 office building that stood on higher ground. They'd already devised a nickname for it.

—Who put you in the tent? Alan asked.

Cayley answered. —When we got here, they said the presentations would be made here.

—In a tent.

—I guess so.

—Did they say anything to you, Rachel ventured, about why, you know, we're out here? As opposed to in the actual main building?

—Not to me they didn't, Alan said. Maybe all the vendors will be out here.

Alan had expected a dozen or so other companies, busy with preparations, frenzied activity in anticipation of a royal visit. But to be out here, alone, in a dark tent — Alan couldn't figure it out.

—I guess that makes sense, Rachel said, chewing the inside of her mouth. But we're the only ones here.

—Maybe we're just first, Alan said, trying to maintain some levity.

—Just weird being Reliant and being out here, right? Brad wondered. He was a company man, a thoroughly competent young person who had likely never, in his life thus far, had to depart from the playbook he'd been given and had memorized.

—This is a new city. Uncharted territory, right? Alan said. You ask anyone about the wi-fi? he asked.

—Not yet, Cayley said. We figured we'd wait for you.

—And we did have a decent signal for a while, Rachel added. With that, she floated back to the far end of the tent, as if suspecting that the signal, now that it was being talked about, would reappear.

Alan looked at Cayley's computer, saw the signal's concentric curves, most of them gray, not black. For a holographic presentation they needed a hard line, and if not that, a massive signal, nothing faint or poached.

—Well, I guess I'll have to ask about this. You start on setting up the rest of the equipment?

—No, not yet, Brad said, wincing. We were kind of hoping that this was a temporary situation. The presentation won't work nearly as well out here.

—You've been here just looking for a signal?

—So far, Cayley said, now seeming to realize that they might have been doing more.

From the darkness at the other end, Rachel chimed in. —We did have a decent one for a while.

—Right. About an hour ago, Cayley added.

VIII.

THERE HAD TO BE some reason Alan was here. Why he was in a tent a hundred miles from Jeddah, yes, but also why he was alive on Earth? Very often the meaning was obscured. Very often it required some digging. The meaning of his life was an elusive seam of water hundreds of feet below the surface, and he would periodically drop a bucket down the well, fill it, bring it up and drink from it. But this did not sustain him for long.

Charlie Fallon's death made the news all over the country. He stepped into the lake in the morning, fully clothed. Alan saw him only ankle-deep and thought not much of it. The Transcendentalist was getting muddy.

Alan drove on.

But Charlie stepped in deeper. He did it slowly. Other neighbors saw him up to his knees, his waist. No one said anything.

Finally he was standing with the water at his chest and Lynn Maggliano called the police. They came, and the fire department came, too. They stood on the shore and they yelled to him. They told him to come back. But no one went to get him.

Later the police and firemen said that due to budget cuts, they hadn't been trained for rescues like this. If they went in after him, it would have been a big liability issue. And besides, they said, the man was standing up. He seemed fine.

Finally a high school girl paddled out in an innertube. When she reached Charlie Fallon, he was was blue and unresponsive.

She screamed. The police and firemen got their tools and dragged him in. They worked on his chest but he was dead.

—Alan?

Brad was looking at him, concerned.

—Yes, Alan said. Let's have a look outside.

He walked toward the entrance. Rachel and Cayley made a move to follow, but Brad stopped them.

—You shouldn't be seen outside dressed the way you are, he said.

They said they were happy to stay inside, where it was cool.

Alan and Brad walked out together. They squinted into the sun and heat, looking around for any evidence of a tower or cable apparatus.

—Over there, Brad said, pointing to the pink condominium, a small satellite dish attached to its side.

They walked to it.

—What are we looking for here? Alan asked.

Brad was the engineer, so Alan hoped to defer to him in matters of technology.

—I guess to see if it's plugged in? Brad said.

Alan glanced at Brad, to see if he was serious. He was.

It seemed to be plugged in. But it was about thirty yards from the tent and thus probably useless to them. Again they stood, squinted, looked around. They saw clusters of workers in jumpsuits, purple and red, installing bricks in the promenade or sweeping sand from it.

—Is that a tower? Alan asked. There was a two-story metal structure, something between an oil derrick and a weathervane, in the middle of the promenade. They walked to it, and saw no wires extending from it. Whether or not this meant anything to them was unclear. They walked back to the tent, no smarter than they were before.

Inside, Rachel and Cayley were now in opposite dark corners, again crouched over their screens, like mothers tending to infants.

—Anything? Brad asked them.

—Not really, Cayley said. Comes and goes.

—You get an email out? Brad asked.

—Not yet, Rachel said.

Alan needed to recover for a few minutes from the heat, so he took a folding chair and sat in it. Brad took the seat next to him.

—We've been trying to email Karim, our contact over here, Brad said.

—Where is he? Alan asked.

—Supposedly here at KAEC.

—In the building? The Black Box?

—I think so.

—You try walking over there?

—Not yet. I'm not going back out in that heat if I don't have to.

And so they continued to sit in the tent.

IX.

ERIC INGVALL AND HIS stupid face. Sitting there at that long granite table, reading Alan's report with those ugly lips pursed. Alan had wanted to punch that face. Punch his smarmy face till it showed him some respect.

—I really need you to be organized on this one, Ingvall had said.

Ingvall was a renowned anal-retentive. When things were not presented the way he liked, his face cinched into a tortured pout. He was dissatisfied with Alan's report on KAEC. Alan had been asked to prepare something before the trip, a look at KAEC, what Reliant's prospects were, and Alan had done so. The report was finished early and was far longer and more detailed than Ingvall had asked for.

—But you leave so many questions unanswered, Ingvall said, his face pained. And that makes me uncomfortable.

Alan chuckled and said there were questions unanswered in the report because he hadn't been to Saudi yet and couldn't presume to know the lay of the land — much less the state of Abdullah's mind.

—This is sales, Alan said, smiling. You make estimates, you make a plan, then you go there, everything changes, but you make the sale.

Ingvall did not smile and did not agree.

—I need reassurance that you're the right man to send on this, Ingvall said. You've been on the sidelines for a while, and I need to know you're sharp. That you're a gamer.

Alan glanced outside, at the harbor below.

Alan's people had come to America from Ireland during the famine. Three brothers left from County Cork and landed in Boston in 1850. They started manufacturing brass buttons, and the buttons led to a foundry in South Boston, doing wide-ranging work in tubing, valves, boilers and radiators. They hired other Irishmen, and then Germans and Poles and Italians. The business boomed. The brothers built second homes on the coast. They hired tutors for their children, and their children learned Latin and Greek. Their names were all over buildings in Boston. Churches and hospital wings. Then there was the Depression, and everyone started over. Alan's father had no second home in Chatham. He was a foreman at the Stride Rite factory in Roxbury. He did fine, and saved enough for his son, Alan, to go to college. But Alan dropped out of college to sell Fuller Brush products, and then sold bicycles, and did fine, extremely well for a while there, until he and others decided to have other people, ten thousand miles away, build the things they sold, and soon left himself with nothing to sell, and now he was in this conference room overlooking the harbor, and he was staring at this pinched-face Eric Ingvall, who owned him and who knew it.

—I think it's a slam dunk, Alan had said.

—See, that's what worries me, Ingvall had said. Your overconfidence does not reassure me.

X.

CAYLEY PULLED UP a chair. —So. How many people do you think he'll bring with him?

—Who? Alan asked.

—The King, she said.

—I don't know. I guess about a dozen. Maybe more.

—You think he has sole discretion to make the decisions on IT here?

—I would expect so, sure. The city has his name on it.

Now Rachel joined them. —Have you met him? she asked.

—Me? No. I knew his nephew about twenty years ago.

—Was he a prince?

—He was. He still is.

—And will he be here?

—No, no. He's in Monaco. He doesn't get himself involved in business much anymore. He flies around, gives money to causes.

Alan pictured Abdullah's nephew, Jalawi. His peculiar face. His mouth was lopsided, as if drawn by a shaky hand, and this gave him a wry, mocking look. But he was very sincere, very curious, and quick to cry. He cried all the time. Widows, orphans, any story brought on the tears and opened his wallet. Jalawi had been advised to limit his exposure to people. Everyone he met he became involved with and tried to transform. Word was he was dying of bone cancer.

—Anyway, Alan said. King Abdullah won't be here today. You should relax.

They sat in silence for a moment. It was obvious that Rachel and Cayley wanted to get back to their laptops, but their manners demanded they engage Alan, the senior member of the team, a man of mysterious provenance and presumed importance.

—You see much of Jeddah? Rachel asked him.

—No, not much yet, he said.

—You get some sleep? Cayley asked.

Alan told her the truth, that he'd been awake for almost sixty hours and had finally, at six or so that morning, fallen asleep. They all urged him to go back to the hotel, to rest. They could handle things for the rest of the day.

—Do you have some kind of sleep aid? Cayley asked.

—No. I figured I'd be executed at customs. You?

None of them did.

—I had an idea, Brad said. He looked to Alan, as if testing the very notion of having an idea. Alan tried to look encouraging.

—Well, I wanted your opinion before doing it, Brad ventured, but I was thinking we call corporate and let them know that conditions here are less than satisfactory.

Alan looked at Brad for a long moment. How would he tell him that this was a terrible idea? He tried to think of a way.

—Good thought, he said. But let's table it for now.

—All right then, Brad said.

—My appointment with Karim al-Ahmad is at 3 p.m., Alan said. I'm sure that'll clear everything up.

The young people nodded, and they sat together, silent, for a spell. It was just after noon. It seemed, already, that they'd been in the tent for days.

—Do we know where we eat? Cayley asked.

—I don't know, Alan said. But I'll find out.

As if trying to rescue a souring mood, Rachel leaned forward. —I have to say, she said, I think this is all pretty amazing. Did you see the health club at the hotel?

Brad had, Cayley had not.

—It has a thighmaster, Rachel said. A Nautilus one.

And so twenty minutes passed this way, discussing the ways that their situation was new and strange and ideal or not so much so. They wondered if food would be brought to them. They wondered if they should go to the Black Box to get it themselves. They wondered if they had been expected to bring their own.

Cayley talked about a new phone she'd gotten, and showed it to everyone. She said she'd looked for a while at the site for a place to toss her old one, and in the end had just thrown it on a mound of debris.

Alan soon lost the thread. He drifted off and found himself looking outside. The tent had a series of plastic windows that gave a gauzy impression of the sand and sea beyond. Alan wanted to be out there, in the light and heat.

He stood.

—Time to see what the hell's happening, he said, straightening his shirt. He promised that he would take care of the food question, the wi-fi signal question, the question of just why they were in a vinyl tent by the sea.

XI.

ALAN LEFT THE TENT, the heat a brief assault, and walked toward the Black Box. He followed the promenade to the glass building, dodging unfinished areas, piles of dirt or stacks of stones, clusters of tools. He leapt over a palm tree waiting to be planted, crossed the street and stood before the office building. There were about forty steps up to the front door, and by the time he reached it, he'd soaked through his shirt.

The lobby was bright, burnished, air-conditioned, the floors a blond wood. It looked like a Scandinavian airport.

—Can I help you?

A young woman, wearing a headscarf loosely, was sitting to his right at a half-moon desk of black marble.

—Hello, Alan said. What's your name?

—My name is Maha, she said. Black eyes, an aquiline nose.

—Hi Maha. My name is Alan Clay from Reliant Systems. I have an appointment at three o'clock to see Karim al-Ahmad, and—

—Oh, you're early. It's just past two.

—Yes, I know. But I'm with Reliant, and we're out in that tent down there by the beach, and we can't get a wi-fi signal, which is essential to our presentation.

—Oh, I don't know anything about the wi-fi down there. I can't imagine that they have a wi-fi signal in the tent.

—See, that's the problem. Is there someone I can talk to about this?

Maha nodded vigorously. —Yes, I think Mr. al-Ahmad would be the one. He's in charge of the vendors presenting in the tent.

—Great. Is he in?

—No, I'm afraid not. He'll probably be arriving here just before your meeting. He spends much of the day in Jeddah.

Arguing the point seemed useless. Alan's meeting with al-Ahmad was only an hour away.

—Thank you, Maha, he said, and left.

But he couldn't go back to the tent. He had no news for the young people, and had the idea that if he could stay away until the meeting, then it would seem to them that all the while he'd been engaged in a lengthy sit-down with al-Ahmad, during which all the issues had been solved.

As soon as he passed again into the heat and light, he remembered the food. He hadn't asked about the food. But he couldn't go back to the Black Box now. It would look pathetic, this sweating man with his many needling questions, and now having forgotten the central issue of food. No, he would ask all the questions at three o'clock. Until then the young people would make do.

He walked down the promenade, a bending design of inlaid bricks, thinking it all through. He was fifty-four years old. He was dressed in a white shirt and khakis and was walking along what might someday be a seaside path. He had just left his team, three young people tasked with setting up and demonstrating holographic communications technology for a king. But there was no king, and they were in a tent, alone, and there seemed to be no knowing when any of this would be rectified.

He lurched forward. His foot had dropped into a hole where bricks had yet to be laid. He righted himself, but he'd twisted his ankle and the pain was acute. He stood and tried to shake the pain away.

His body was scarred everywhere from the accidents of his last five years. He'd become clumsy. He was hitting his head on cabinets. Crushing his hands in car doors. He'd fallen in an icy parking lot and walked for months like a man made of wood. He was no longer elegant. Someone called him that, *elegant*, decades earlier. It was summer, a warm wind, and he had been dancing. The woman was elderly, a stranger, but the word had lodged within him, had given him solace. Did it mean anything that an old woman had once thought him elegant?

He thought of Joe Trivole. That first day together, at the first door they approached, he'd told Alan to let the woman inside know they were there. Alan instinctively had reached for the doorbell.

—No, no, Trivole said, and then knocked on the door, a quick and happy musical riff. He turned to Alan. A stranger rings, a friend knocks, he said. The door opened.

A woman stood behind the screen, looking confused. She was about fifty, wild grey hair, glasses hung by a copper chain. Alan looked to Trivole, who was grinning as if he'd stumbled upon his favorite grade-school teacher.

—Hello! How are you today?

—I'm fine. Who are you? she asked.

—We are representatives from the Fuller Brush Company, based in East Hartford, Connecticut. Have you heard of Fuller Brush?

The woman was amused. —Of course. But I haven't seen one of you guys in years. You're still out there, huh?

—Indeed we are, ma'am. And I appreciate you giving us a few seconds on a wonderful day like this.

Trivole turned to survey the yard, the trees, the blue sky above. And then he turned back to the door and began wiping his feet. Instinctively, the woman took a few steps back and opened the door wider. She had not asked Trivole and Alan in, but now she was making way for them — simply because Trivole had begun wiping his feet. Suddenly Alan had the same feeling he had while watching a hypnotist or magician — that there were people in the world for whom the world and its people were subjects on which to cast spells.

Alan continued down the makeshift walkway. He was approaching the pink condominium. Up close, it resembled something he'd seen a few hundred times along various Florida coasts. It was undistinguished, enormous; its wide flat face looked to the sea with dull resistance. There were likely three hundred units in the building.

Looking in the windows he saw something plausible. The first floor was built for retail and dining, and some of the future tenants had staked out their spots. Pizzeria Uno, Wolfgang Puck. Maybe there would be people here someday, eating and laughing and seeming alive.

He could still do this. He thought of his silver bike, the prototype he'd had made. It was so beautiful. Everything was silver and chrome, even the gears, even the seat. Had anyone ever made a more beautiful object? You could see it from space it was so bright and shone so defiantly.

He'd brought Kit to see the prototype.

—You built this? she asked.

—Well, I had it built. I helped design it.

—It's stunning, she said. Can you ride it?

—Anyone can ride it.

She touched it, stood back, taking it in, reassessing.

—This is *very good*, Dad.

When he got back to the hotel he would write Kit a letter. She'd written him a humdinger a few days before, six pages in her orderly hand, most of it condemning her mother, Ruby, wanting nothing more to do with her. Now Alan found himself in the odd position of having to defend a woman who had tunneled through him so many times and so recklessly that he felt lucky to appear, from a distance, whole. Kit's letter was denunciatory and final, a document marking, justifying, celebrating, the end of her relations with her mother.

Alan couldn't have it. He had to repair the damage. Alan didn't want to be the only parent. And he worried — or rather he knew — that if Kit could find her mother unworthy, then using the same tools of reassessment, she would find Alan unacceptable, too. He needed to draw a line. He needed to prop Ruby up.

He and Kit had been sending each other letters for years. The first was after Ruby's DWI. He wanted to put it all in context for Kit. Nice letter, Dad, she'd said after the first one. Since then, Alan had been putting his thoughts on paper for Kit, letters of three or four pages, and they had some impact. She returned to them in times of doubt, she told him. They cooled her exasperation, brought her back from various ledges. Usually she wanted to leave her mother, to sever ties entirely. They were constitutionally different, it was obvious now, Kit having more of Alan's stolidity — Ruby would call it bourgeois — but in any case Kit was tired of the spirals, was exhausted by the deep cleaning Ruby tried to do every time they talked.

First, though, Kit needed strategies for cordoning off the chaos. To circumscribe contact. Alan hadn't figured out how to do that himself until recently. Email had been the key. He and Ruby had agreed to limit their communication to messages pertaining to Kit, and nothing over three lines. It had worked. Alan hadn't spoken to Ruby on the phone for two years and the break in battle had allowed his nerves to strengthen, his mind some respite. He no longer jumped at the sound of loud voices.

—Alan!
He turned. It was Brad. Alan was startled, but feigned calm.
—How're things going back there? he asked.
—Fine, Brad said. But it's almost three. You heading to the office?
Brad tossed his chin over his shoulder, toward the Black Box.

Alan looked at his watch. It was 2:52.
—Yup, Alan said. Just running through my pitch.

He followed Brad back along the promenade.

—Don't worry about the food, Brad said. Rachel had some crackers in her bag. So we're all set there.

Faint sarcasm. He did not like Brad.

When they passed the tent, Brad stopped. —Good luck, he said. His face was full of worry and wonder. Alan knew at that moment what it would be like, decades later, when he was feeble, unable to take care of himself, when Kit would first catch him soiling his pants and drooling. The look she would give him was this, the one Brad was giving him now — that of gazing upon a human who was more burden than boon, more harm than good, irrelevant, superfluous to the forward progress of the world.

XII.

Maha was sipping an iced tea.

—Oh, hello again, Mr. Clay.

—Hello Maha. Is Karim al-Ahmad in?

—No, I'm afraid he's not.

—Should I wait here? We have an appointment at 3 p.m.

—Yes, I know. But he won't be able to make it today. I'm sorry to say that he's stuck in Jeddah.

—He's stuck all day in Jeddah?

—Yes sir. But he said he will be here tomorrow. All day, and you can name the time you want to meet.

—Are you sure there's no one else here I should talk to in the mean-time? Just about the wi-fi and the food, things like that?

—I think Mr. al-Ahmad is your best contact for all those things. And anytime tomorrow will be fine. It will all get sorted, I'm sure.

Alan returned to the tent, where he found the team in their separate corners with their laptops. Rachel was watching a DVD, something involving cooking, a bearded chef. Alan told them all that Mr. al-Ahmad was not in that day.

The ride back to Jeddah passed quickly, the young people chattering throughout like summer campers. Alan watched the road, half awake, his ankle aching. When he got to his room, he couldn't remember if he'd said goodbye to anyone. He did remember entering the dark lobby, smelling the chlorine.

He'd been in the sun too long and was grateful for the dark, for the cool, for the manmade and ugly. But when the heavy door to his room punctuated the end of the day, he felt trapped and alone. There was no bar in the hotel, no diversion that would satisfy his needs, whatever they were. It was just past six o'clock and there was nothing to do.

He thought of calling one of the three young people, but asking them to dine would not work. Not appropriate. He could not call either of the women. Lecherous. He could call Brad but he did not like Brad. If they were all eating, and he was invited, he would eat. If they called he would come. By seven, though, no one had called. He ordered room service and ate a chicken breast and salad.

He showered. He rubbed the knob on his neck.
He got into bed and hoped for sleep.

Alan could not sleep. He opened his eyes and turned on the TV. There was a story about the BP leak. Still no discernible progress. They had attempted a top kill, something involving dumping cement on top of the hole. Alan couldn't watch. The leak devastated him. It had been unstoppable for weeks, and all he and everyone else could do was watch the plumes of oil shooting into the ocean. Alan favored every extreme method of putting an end to it. When he heard the idea, proposed by a Navy man, of sending a nuke down there, he thought, Yes, yes, do that, you fuckwads. Just end it, please. Everyone's watching.

He turned off the TV.

He looked to the ceiling. He looked to the wall.

Alan thought of Trivole.

—Everything can be sold using one of four angles, he'd said.

Nine in the morning and they were standing on the street, in front of a dilapidated house. It was only a few blocks from the home where Alan had been raised, but he'd never given this right-leaning house a glance or thought.

—First thing you have to do is analyze the customer, okay?

Trivole was wearing a double-breasted tweed suit. It was early September and far too hot for such a garment, but he didn't seem to be sweating. Alan never saw him perspire.

—Each customer requires a specific approach, a specific appeal, Trivole said. There are four. The first one is Money. This one is simple. Appeal to their thrift. Fuller products will save them money by preserving their investments — their wood furniture, their fine china, their linoleum floors. You can tell immediately if someone is practical. You see a simple, well-kept home, a practical dress, an apron, someone who does their own cooking and cleaning, you go with this first strategy.

—Second is Romance. Here you sell the dream. You put the Fuller products in among their aspirations. Right there next to the vacations and yachts. 'Champagne!' I like to say. With the foot spray, I get them to take off their shoe, and I say, 'Champagne!'

Alan didn't understand that one. —Just 'Champagne!' out of no-where? he asked.

—Yes, and when I say it, they feel like Cinderella.

Trivole wiped his dry brow with a silk handkerchief.

—Third is Self-Preservation. You see fear in their eyes, you sell them Self-Preservation. This one's easy. If they're afraid to let you in, if they talk to you through the window or something, you go with this way. These products will keep you healthy, safe from germs, diseases, you tell her. Got it?

—Yes.

—Good. The last one is Recognition. She wants to buy what every-one else is buying. You pick the four or five names of the most respected neighbors, you tell her those folks already bought the products. 'I just came from Mrs. Gladstone's house and she insisted I come here next.'

—That's it?

—That's it.

Alan became a good salesman, and quickly. He needed the money to move out of his parents' house, which he did a month later. Six months after that, he had a new car and more cash than he could spend. Money, Romance, Self-Preservation, Recognition: he'd applied the cat-egories to everything. When he left Fuller and went to work for Schwinn, he brought the same lessons to bike sales. All the principles applied: the bikes were practical (Money); they were beautiful, glittering things (Romance); they were safe and durable (Self-Preservation); and they were status symbols for any family (Recognition). And so he'd moved up quickly at Schwinn, too, from retail sales in downstate Illinois to the regional sales office, to a place at the table with the execs in Chicago, planning strategy and expansion. And then the union-busting. Then Hungary, Taiwan, China, divorce, this.

He turned the TV on again. Some news story about the Space Shuttle. One of the last flights. Alan turned the TV off. He didn't want to see that, either.

He found himself dialing his father's number. International long-distance, it would cost a fortune. But the Shuttle had him thinking of Ron, and that had him thinking of calling him.

It was a mistake. He knew it was a mistake the second the phone started ringing.

He pictured his father in his New Hampshire farmhouse. The last time Alan had seen him, about a year back, he'd seemed stronger than he had in decades. His face was ruddy, his eyes gloriously alive.

—Look at that mutt, Ron said that day.

They would be on the porch, drinking Scotch, watching Ron's dogs, three of them, all garrulous and filthy. His favorite was an Australian sheepherding type who never stopped moving.

—*That* is a mutt for all ages, Ron said.

Ron lived on a farm near White River Junction. He kept pigs, goats, chickens and two horses, one that he rode and another he boarded for a friend. Ron knew nothing about farming, but after he retired, and after Alan's mother died, he bought 120 acres in a soggy valley near town. He complained about it constantly — *This fucking place will kill me* — but by all accounts it was keeping him alive.

Alan had grown slower with time, was patched up and scarred, but his father had somehow become stronger. Alan wanted a less adversarial relationship, and was that too much to ask? He could do without the taunts. Alan, you *hungry*? He loved to needle him about the Hungary debacle. Ron had been a union man. They made fifty thousand shoes a day at Stride Rite! he'd say. In Roxbury! You couldn't get Ron to shut up about the place, all of its innovations. First company to provide day-care to its workers. Then eldercare, too! He'd retired with a full pension. But that was before the company ditched the unions and moved production to Kentucky. That was 1992. Five years later they moved all production to Thailand and China. All this made Alan's role at Schwinn even more disagreeable to Ron. That Alan had been management, had helped scout a new, non-union location for Schwinn, had met with suppliers in China and Taiwan, had contributed *not insignificantly* — Ron's words — to all that undid Schwinn and the 1,200 workers employed there, well, it made communication difficult. Most subjects led to their differing ideas of what ailed the nation and thus were off-limits. So they talked about dogs and swimming.

There was a small lake that Ron had dug and in which he swam every day, from April to October. The water was cold and full of algae and Ron smelled of it always. *The bog man*, Alan called him, though Ron hadn't smiled.

—You want to help me kill a pig? he'd asked.

Alan declined.

—Fresh bacon, kid, he said.

Alan wanted to go into town for a real meal. Ron was playacting, to some extent, all this Farmer Ron stuff. He knew a good deal about French food, wine, and now he was pulling this meat-and-potatoes schtick. In town, Ron leered at women on the street. —Look at that one! Bet she's got a great snatch.

This was all new, acting the part of caveman. Alan's mother never would have stood for such barbarity. But who was the real Ron? Maybe this was him, the man he was before his wife, Alan's mother, refined him, improved him? He had settled back to his natural form.

The phone stopped ringing.

—Hello?

—Hey Dad.

—Hello?

—Dad. It's Alan.

—Alan? You sound like you're on the moon.

—I'm in Saudi Arabia.

What had Alan expected? Astonishment? Praise?

There was silence.

—I was thinking of the Shuttle, Alan said. That trip we took to see the launch.

—What're you doing in Saudi Arabia?

It sounded like an opening, an invitation to brag a bit, so Alan gave it a shot.

—Well, it's pretty interesting, Dad. I'm here with Reliant, and we're pitching an IT system to King Abdullah. We've got this remarkable teleconferencing equipment, and we'll be doing a presentation to the King himself, a three-dimensional holographic meeting. One of our reps will be in London but it will look like he's in the room, with Abdullah—

Silence.

Then: —You know what I'm watching on TV here, Alan?

—No. What are you watching?

—I'm watching this thing about how a gigantic new bridge in Oakland, California, is being made in China. Can you imagine? Now they're making our goddamned bridges, Alan. I got to say, I saw everything else coming. When they closed down Stride Rite, I saw it coming. When you start shopping out the bikes over there in Taiwan, I saw it coming. I saw the rest of it coming — toys, electronics, furniture. Makes sense if you're some shitass bloodthirsty executive hellbent on hollowing out the economy for his own gain. All that makes sense. Nature of the beast. But the bridges I did not see coming. By God, we're having other people make our *bridges*. And now you're in Saudi Arabia, selling a hologram to the pharoahs. That takes the *cake*!

Alan contemplated hanging up. Why couldn't he?

He walked to the deck and looked out over the sea, a few tiny lights in the distance. The air was so warm.

Ron was still talking. —Every day, Alan, all over Asia, hundreds of container ships are leaving their ports, full of every kind of consumer good. Talk about *three-dimensional*, Alan. These are actual *things*. They're making actual *things* over there, and we're making websites and holograms. Every day our people are making their websites and holograms, while sitting in chairs made in China, working on computers made in China, driving over bridges made in China. Does this sound sustainable to you, Alan?

Alan rubbed the knob on the back of his neck.

—Alan, you getting this down?

Hell, he could pretend it was a mistake. Alan pressed a button on his phone and hung up.

XIII.

AT EIGHT O'CLOCK in the morning, Alan was on the shuttle again, with the same young people. They chirped about the hotel, and things they had done the night before.

—I swam in the pool, Cayley said.

—I ate a whole pie, Rachel said.

Alan had not slept. A circus of worries kept his mind darting all night long, taking in the action. By the end it was almost funny. When the sun broke over the sea, his face heavy on the pillow, he'd chuckled to himself. Goddamn, goddamn, goddamn.

When they got to the new city, there was a note on the tent door: *Reliant: welcome back to the King Abdullah Economic City. King Abdullah welcomes you. Please make yourselves at home and we will be in contact after the lunch hour.*

Inside the tent, all was the same. There were the many white chairs amid the gloom. Nothing had been touched.

—They left us some water, Rachel said, pointing to a half-dozen plastic bottles, lined up on the rug like artillery.

Alan and the team sat in the dark cool tent. The young people had brought food from the hotel. They sat around one of their laptops and they watched a movie most of the morning.

After lunch, no one from the Black Box arrived.

—Should we go up to see them? Cayley asked.

—I don't know, Brad said. Is that customary?

—Is what customary? Alan asked.

—Is it customary to show up uninvited like that? Maybe we should just wait here.

Alan left the tent and walked up to the Black Box. He was soaked when he arrived, and again he was greeted by Maha.

—Hello Mr. Clay.

—Hello Maha. Any chance of seeing Mr. al-Ahmad today?

—I wish I could say yes. But he is in Riyadh today.

—Yesterday you said he'd be here all day.

—I know. But his plans changed last night. I'm so sorry.

—Let me ask you something, Maha. Are you absolutely sure that we shouldn't be meeting with anyone else here?

—Anyone else?

—Anyone else who might be able to help us with the wi-fi, and might be able to give us some prognosis about what will happen in terms of the King, our presentation?

—I'm afraid not, Mr. Clay. Mr. al-Ahmad really is your primary contact. I'm sure he's very anxious to meet you, but has been unavoidably delayed. He will be back tomorrow. He has guaranteed it.

Alan walked back down to the tent, his ankle aching.
He sat in the darkness on a white chair.
The young people were watching another movie.
—Should we be doing something else? Cayley asked.
Alan couldn't think of anything else to do.
—No, he said. What you're doing is fine.

After an hour, Alan stood and went to the plastic window.
—To hell with it, he said.
He left the tent, was struck dumb by the heat, recovered, and walked to the Black Box, soaked in sweat.
When he arrived, he did not see Maha. There was no one at the reception desk. Good, Alan thought to himself, and strode quickly across the vast lobby.
He took the elevator up, the doors parted, and he was in the middle of what appeared to be a very busy workplace. Men in suits walked past him, carrying papers. Women in abayas, heads uncovered, hurried by.
He walked down the hallway, seeing no numbers or nameplates.
Alan hadn't thought of exactly what he'd say if he came upon a decision maker here. There was the nephew. Mention the nephew. And of course Reliant being the largest in the world, a company built for a job like this. Money. Romance. Self-Preservation. Recognition.

—You look new.

89

A female voice, deep and sonorous. He looked up. A caucasian woman, blond, about forty-five, stood before him. Her head was uncovered. With the black gown dropping from her shoulders like a curtain, she looked like a judge.

—I'm supposed to meet someone, he said.
—Are you Alan Clay?
That voice. It was tremulous, as if someone had strummed the low strings of a harp. An accent from Northern Europe.
—Yes.
—You're supposed to meet with Karim al-Ahmad?
—I am.
—He won't be here today. I work in the office next to him. He told me to look out for you.

Alan assembled himself and put on a glossy smile. —No, no. I'm just surprised. I understand completely. Busy times here, I'm sure.
She said her name was Hanne. She had an accent. Alan guessed Dutch. Her eyes were ice blue, her hair cut with a slashing severity.
—I was about to have a smoke, she said. Join me?

Alan followed her through a glass door and onto a wide balcony, where other KAEC employees and consultants were smoking, talking, drinking tea and coffee.
—Watch the step, she said, but it was too late. He'd tripped on the runner below the door, and his arms flew forward as if attempting flight. A dozen pairs of eyes saw it happen, and a dozen mouths smiled. It was not a simple trip. It was comical, wild, theatrical. The sweating man

entering, his arms shooting everywhere, yanked by invisible puppeteers.

Hanne smiled sympathetically and motioned for him to sit across from her, on a low couch of black leather. Her eyes seemed almost flirtatious, but that was impossible. Not so soon after he'd embarrassed himself. Probably not ever.

—You're from Reliant? she asked.

—Recently, yes.

Alan rubbed his ankle. He'd twisted it further.

—And you're here to present?

—The idea is to supply the city with IT, yes.

They went on this way for a bit as he glanced around. None of the women, Saudi or not, were covered. There was a black plastic barrier on either side of the balcony that prevented them from seeing anything but the sea ahead. And, he assumed, prevented anyone below from glimpsing the world, egalitarian and free from restrictions, within the Black Box. This was the cat-and-mouse game being played in the Kingdom. Its people were forced into the role of teenagers hiding their vices and proclivities from a shadowy army of parents.

—So how are things at Reliant? she asked.

He told her what he knew, which was very little. He mentioned a few projects, a few innovations, but she knew it all anyway. She knew everything, it turned out, that he did, about his business and all others related to his. In a few minutes of introductions, of assessing where their paths might have crossed, they covered a handful of consulting firms, the plastics business in Taiwan, the fall of Andersen Consulting, the rise of Accenture.

—So you're here to get the lay of the land, she said, putting out her cigarette and lighting another.

—I'm really just trying to get an idea of the timeline. When we could expect to have some news about the King, that kind of thing.

—What were you told? I hope they didn't make a promise to you.

—No, no, he said. They explained things pretty clearly. But I've been holding out hope that it might be soon. I was led to believe that our chairman knew the King somehow. That this was something between the two of them and would be, you know, fast-tracked.

Her eyes registered new information. —Well, that would be good for us all. The King hasn't been here in a while.

—How long is a while?

—Well, I've been here eighteen months, and he hasn't been here yet.

XIV.

Hanne noticed what must have been the visible decline and fall of Alan's face.

—But listen, she said. You're with Reliant. I'm sure your people know more than I do. I'm just a consultant. I do payroll. I'm sure your presentation is the reason he's coming soon, right? Even if the King were coming tomorrow, I wouldn't be high on the list of those in the know.

She stubbed out her second cigarette and stood. —Shall we?

She led him inside. They passed through the lobby and into a hall-way lined with glass-box offices and conference rooms. A few dozen men and women whisked by in various directions, equally split between those in Western business attire and local garb. The offices and cubicles were almost entirely blank, free of all signs of anyone taking root or assuming longevity. Some desks were bare but for a monitor, the computer having been disconnected and removed. There were phones with no owners, projectors pointing at windows. The whole thing had the look of a start-up, which perhaps it was.

Hanne's office was a ten-by-twelve glass cube and looked as if she'd moved in minutes before. There was a cheap desk of particle board and walnut veneer, two silver file cabinets. Nothing on the walls but a piece of paper taped behind her desk with the words STE CONSULTING. Reading his thoughts, she said, —I work with employment contracts, all the contractor salaries. I can't have paperwork lying about.

There were no pictures of any kind of family, any human attachments at all. When she sat down, her hands clasped before her, the look of a judge was complete.

—So is everything okay out there? she nodded toward the window, and now Alan could see the tent, far in the distance.

—Yeah, I wanted to ask about that. Why does the King want these presentations in a tent? Wouldn't this...

—Well, this building has only so many finished rooms, and we can't have the presenters occupying them for the time it might take. If you were to set up in one of the conference rooms, then we couldn't use it for weeks or months.

—And the wi-fi? Our signal is weak to nonexistent.

—I'll definitely ask around.

—It's integral to the presentation.

—I understand. I'm sure it'll get worked out. This is your first day?

—Second.

—Been to Saudi before?

—No.

—Well, things work at a certain pace here. And on top of that, you're in the middle of nowhere. You've had a look around?

—I have.

—Wi-fi is the least of our problems.

Alan managed a smile. He had no idea if this whole thing was some elaborate joke on all of them.

—Should I come back later?

—Why would you do that?

—You said Karim al-Ahmad would be back later.

—Maybe, maybe not. Better just to check in tomorrow.

The idea seemed at once exasperating and alluring, knowing there was absolutely nothing he could do the rest of the day.

She smiled. —You're from the East Coast?

He nodded. He'd been trying to place her face and her accent and now he thought he had it. —You're Danish.

She squinted, tilted her head. A reevaluation.

—Not bad, she said. Have you adjusted yet? The time change?

—I haven't slept in sixty-two hours.

—Tragedy.

—I feel like a pane of glass that needs to be shattered.

—You have pills?

—No. Everyone's asking me that. I wish I did.

She blinked meaningfully at him. —I have something.

She retrieved a key, opened a drawer in her desk, and arranged something on the floor. With her foot, she pushed it till it met his shin.

—Don't look down.

But he had already glanced at it. Inside a book bag there appeared to be a thin green bottle, tall and with flat sides.

—Olive oil? he asked.

—Sure. That's what you tell anyone who asks. Just have a taste when you get back to the hotel. I'm pretty sure it will shatter your glass.

—Thank you.

She stood. The meeting was over.

—Here's my number, she said. Call if you need help with anything.

He returned to the tent and inside, he found the young people in three different corners. Each was sitting cross-legged, computers on their laps, checking their signals.

—Any news? Brad asked.

Alan tucked his bottle behind a fold in the tent.

—Nothing solid, he said.

He explained that their man al-Ahmad was not in that day, but would be the next. —Tomorrow all will be known, he said.

—Did you eat? Cayley asked. The tone of her voice implied that he, Alan, had just finished a wonderful meal in the Black Box, but had brought nothing back for those suffering in the tent.

He hadn't eaten since breakfast. The young people seemed satisfied that Alan was as powerless as they had previously assumed.

—So today, should we set up? Rachel asked.

Alan had no idea.

—Let's hold off till tomorrow, he said.

They seemed satisfied by this explanation, and went back to their various corners of the tent and to their screens. Alan stood in the middle of the tent, unsure of exactly what to do with himself. He didn't have any work in particular to do, or phone calls to make. He retreated to the remaining corner, sat down, and did nothing.

XV.

IT WAS SEVEN THIRTY when Alan figured it was time to knock himself out. He'd gotten back to the Hilton at six, had eaten, and now was ready to sleep for half a day. He opened the olive oil bottle. The smell was medicinal, toxic. He took a sip. An acid burn overtook his mouth, scorched his gums, his throat. Hanne had set him up. Was she trying to kill him?

He called her.

—What are you trying to do to me?

—Who's this?

—Alan. The guy you're trying to kill.

—Alan! What are you talking about?

—Is this gasoline?

—Are you calling from the hotel phone?

—Yes. Why?

—The connection's not so good. Call me from your cellphone.

—And he did.

Her voice was impatient. —Alan, that stuff isn't legal here. So you

97

shouldn't call me about it on the hotel phone.

—You really think they have people listening?

—No, I don't. But the people who do well in Saudi have learned to be careful, you know, avoid unnecessary risks.

—So it's not gasoline? Or poison?

—No. But it's not so different from grain alcohol.

Alan sniffed the top of the bottle.

—Sorry I doubted you.

—It's okay. I'm glad you called.

—I think I just need to sleep.

—Have a couple swigs and you'll sleep.

He hung up the phone and took another sip. His body shook. Every drop flayed his throat, but once it reached his stomach, there was a warmth that redeemed the pain.

He took the bottle and went to the balcony. There was no breeze from the shore. If anything, it had gotten hotter since he'd arrived at the hotel. He sat down and put his feet up on the railing. He took another sip from the bottle. He thought of Kit. He went back inside, found the hotel stationery and took three sheets back to the balcony.

He wrote on his lap, his feet on the rail.

'Dear Kit, You say that your mother has always been "emotionally unreliable," and still is that way. This is true to a certain extent, but who among us is the same in all seasons? I've personally been a moving target for years, wouldn't you agree?'

No, he needed to be more constructive.

'Kit, your mother is made of different stuff than you or me. More volatile and flammable materials.'

He crossed that out. The greatest tragedy about Ruby was that talking about her made him sound like a bastard. She had done him great harm, repeatedly — she'd torn him open, thrown all kinds of terrible ruinous stuff inside him, and then had sewn him back up — but Kit couldn't know that. He took another sip. A numbness overtook his face. He took another pull. My God, he thought. He'd had the equivalent of two shots and already he was feeling weightless.

Alan went inside and opened his laptop. He wanted to see his daughter. She'd emailed him a photo recently, of herself with two friends, all in business suits, attending some kind of summer job fair in Boston. She was still utterly a child, with a cherubic face that would remain young longer than was anyone's right. He opened his photos and found the one he was looking for. In it her face was pink, round, freckled and shining. Her friends, whose names he should know but could not conjure, were leaning into each other, their heads meeting — a pyramid of youthful hope and naïveté.

He was already in the photo program, the vast grid of his life in thumbnails, so he scanned backward. Everything was there, and it terrified him. For Alan's last birthday, Kit had taken a few dozen photo albums from his garage and sent them away to a service that scanned all the pictures within and put them on a disc. He'd dumped them all onto his laptop and now they were all there, photos from his own childhood, from his life with Ruby, from the birth and growth of Kit. Someone, Kit or the digitizers, had arranged them all more or less chronologically, and now he could, and too often did, scan through the thousand pictures, a record of his life, in minutes. All he had to do was keep his finger on the leftward arrow. It was too easy. It was not good. It kept him in a dangerous stasis of nostalgia and regret and horror.

Alan took another sip. He closed the computer and walked to the bathroom, where he considered shaving. He considered showering. He considered taking a bath. Instead he grabbed at the back of his neck. The growth was hard, rounded but halved, and it rose from his spine like a tiny fist.

He pushed on it and felt no pain. It was not part of him. There were no nerve endings there. It couldn't be serious. But then, what was it? He pushed harder, and now felt a pain shoot down his spine. It was connected. There was a tumor attached to his spinal cord, and soon it would send cancer up and down the nerve corridor, to his brain, to his feet, everywhere.

It all came together. A once-vital man was being hobbled by this, a slow-growing tumor that made him half the man he'd been. He needed a doctor.

He turned on the TV. Something on the news about a flotilla leaving Turkey, heading for Gaza. Humanitarian aid, they said. Disaster, he thought. He sipped again from the glass. The last few sips had, he realized, moved him from mellow to giddy. The numbness engulfed the area around his nose. He picked up his glass, loosened the last drop and sent it down his throat.

Ruby laughed loudly, and fought loudly. It was the sidewalks where she performed most fearlessly. *Don't you hit that child*, she said to a stranger as they were leaving a Toys 'R' Us. Kit was five. Ruby had never had an accent of any kind but she said those words with a twang, and Alan could only guess that she felt that feigning some country blood allowed her to interfere, would collapse the class distinctions between them.

Alan heard those words and left with Kit; he knew trouble was coming. He was soon in the car, Kit in her seatbelt, waiting in the parking lot. He knew, when passing the woman who was spanking her child, that Ruby would say something, and he knew that the woman would say something in return, and he didn't want to hear any of it. He had no idea it would go further than that, but when she got to the car Ruby was crying and her face was red. She'd been slapped. *Can you believe that bitch hit me?*

He could believe it. The woman had seemed exactly the type of woman who would hit someone. She was spanking her son, after all — not a stretch to hit a stranger scolding her for doing so. There were too many stories like this. Arguments at the grocery store over soft carrots led to screams, insults, a scene unforgettable to all in their little town. Soon they had to drive two miles further to a different supermarket. She would go from a simple exchange focused on the issue at hand to generalized statements about their lives and purpose. *You fucking losers! You hypocrites! You grocery-store fucking zombies!*

The growth on his neck beckoned him again. If it wasn't part of him, it wouldn't hurt to prick it. That was the only way to test it. To know. If it was him — if it was some part of his spine that was mal-formed — it would hurt if he lanced it with something sharp.

He took a long pull from the bottle and in seconds he was before the mirror, holding the serrated knife from dinner. He had a distant inkling that he would regret this. He struck a match and got as close to sterilizing the blade as he could. Then he took the knife and slowly twisted it into the growth. There was pain, but only the kind normally associated with puncturing the skin. When he reached the growth, and in seconds he knew he had, there was nothing extraordinary. Just pain. Standard, fascinating pain. The blood was minimal. He stanched it with a towel.

What had he discovered? That it was some kind of cyst, something without nerves. That it would not kill him. That he had not properly sterilized the knife.

That would be a problem. Still, pleased with his surgical skills, he walked to the balcony and looked out the window, at the highway and all its tiny travelers. The Red Sea lay beyond, inert, the whole thing doomed. The Saudis were sucking it dry to drink. In the seventies they'd drained a few billion gallons to desalinize and feed their wayward wheat industry — the whole project now abandoned. Now they were drinking that sea. My God, he thought, did people belong in this part of the world? The Earth is an animal that shakes off its fleas when they dig too deep, bite too hard. It shifts and our cities fall; it sighs and the coasts are overtaken. We really shouldn't be here at all.

'Dear Kit, The key thing is managed awareness of your role in the world and history. Think too much and you know you are nothing. Think just enough and you know you are small, but important to some. That's the best you can do.'

Oh shit, he thought. That would be unlikely to inspire her. He would not need to commit that to paper.

'Kit, you mentioned in your letter the time we picked your mom up from jail. I didn't know you knew.'

She had told Kit about the DWI.

'You were only six. We never talked about it after it happened. Yes, she got a DWI. She was found asleep in her car, after she'd driven it through a shop window. I'm not sure how you knew all this. Did she tell you?'

This was what Kit was fleeing. The overload. Her mother's constant and unfiltered unburdening.

'If she did tell you, she shouldn't have.'

Alan was asleep when the call had come. —Are you Alan Clay, husband of Ruby? She was in a jail in Newton. He had no choice but to pack Kit up in the car and drive to retrieve Ruby, who was still stoned when he collected her. Figures you'd come, she said to him. This was meant as some kind of reproach, some kind of diminishment. She said *Hi, Sweetie* to Kit and fell asleep on the ride home.

'Dear Kit, Wouldn't you rather have an exciting woman like your mom, over some kind of predictable—

Your mother is a rare breed. An exciting, high-performance—'

Now he was describing a sports car. Did children want sports cars for parents? No. They wanted Hondas. They wanted to know that the car would start in all seasons.

'Kit, you know the key to relating to your parents now? It's mercy. Children, when they become teenagers and then young adults, grow unforgiving. Anything but perfection is pathos. Children are judgmental on an Old Testament level. All errors are unforgivable, as if a contract of perfection has been broken. But what if one's parents are granted the same mercy, the same empathy as other humans? Children need more Jesus in them.'

Now there was something wet on his back, a rivulet swimming to his waist. He looked up, thinking of rain. Then he knew. Blood. He'd forgotten to clean up or bandage his surgery. He went back inside, took off his shirt and twisted before the mirror. Not as bad as he expected — a trio of crimson vines making their way to his waist. He dried them with another towel. He thought of the dry cleaners who would remove the blood from this white shirt. They would ask no questions.

We don't have unions. We have Filipinos.

It was time to refill the glass. No one could see him here. It was so good not to be seen. All day he'd been among the young team, intermittently visible, someone presumably to be looked up to, a senior. Even picking wax from his ear was an operation to be done with great delicacy and speed. But now there was this room. No one could see the blood he was dabbing from his back. No one knew of his secret surgery, his various discoveries. He loved this room. Could that be true? But he did love the room, and he touched the wall to prove it.

He poured another splash of the clear fluid into his glass. It was not so much. Not so much. The bottle was still half full. Taking another sip, he decided it was wonderful. It was all beyond wonderful. Being drunk was rewarding. He could see the appeal. He poured again. The fidgety tick of glass on glass. The anything-goes flood of the fluid into the cup.

He stood. The hotel room seemed to sway. His body was numb. The floor was a rope bridge, frayed and twisting. Was he about to be sick? No, no. What would the Saudis think of a man like him, vomiting in a room like this? He stumbled to the bed, righted himself and looked in the mirror. He was smiling. It was wonderful. It was like the day following a vivid dream — all day you had a sense of having done something extraordinary, and that the day was a needed and deserved rest from that adventure. It was an enrichment, a doubling of a life. And the way he felt at the moment was similar. He felt more than himself. He felt he was doing something extraordinary. It was a wonderful addition to the day, really, with the colors of the street pulsing, the floor shifting as it did.

The walls were his friends. There was something to this, to this drinking alone in one's room. Why hadn't he ever done this before? He could do all this and no one could say boo. All this was his. These beds were his. The desk, the walls, that big bathroom with the phone and the bidet. He walked over to his second bed and looked at his things, his electric razor and itinerary and binders and folders, spread out, ready.

He looked at the pillows at the head of the bed. You are so white, he thought. He liked the sound of that and wanted the pillow to hear it. —You are so white, he said. Now stop staring.

He downed the last swallow and refilled the glass. This is an adventure, he thought. The moonshine makes me an adventurer. And then he finally understood why people drink alone, and drink more than they should drink alone. An adventure every night! It made a hell of a lot of sense.

He had to call Kit. No, not Kit. Someone, though. He picked up his phone. There was one message on it. It had come in the last hour. Morning in Boston. He listened to the voice mail. The first was from Eric Ingvall. —Hey buddy. Haven't heard from you, so I assume all is good. Check in tomorrow if you get a chance. I need a status report.

The second message was from Kit. —Call me. It's nothing bad.

This made him want to call her all the more, but somewhere in the listening to her very sober and very small voice — she was diminutive and her voice was high, though always firm and always clear — he realized that he would not sound good tonight. He was tired, and he was drunk, he now knew unequivocally that he was drunk, and one should not call one's daughter in such a state, especially when trying to instill her with confidence about his ability to provide for her.

He sat at the desk and wrote.

'Dear Kit, Parenting is a test of endurance. You have to have the fortitude of a triathlete. People say, *It goes so fast. They grow up so fast.* But I don't remember it ever going fast. It was ten thousand days, Kit, requiring a military sense of order and precision. You were never late for

school, for practice, for anything. Think of it! It was an intricate archi-
tecture of daily meals, appointments, check-ups, rules enacted and en-
forced, sympathy begged for and granted, frustration felt, ruinously, and
stamped down. That's not to say it went slowly or seemed overlong.
Just that it wasn't fast.'

He would probably have to cut that part. It didn't sound right, any
way he put it. But it was true. The raising of a child is the building of
a cathedral. You can't cut corners.

'So can I get some latitude here? Cut us both some slack. I remember
when I realized my parents were hypocrites like everyone else. I was
eighteen. And after that I was high on the power brought by that realization. What did I know, though? I guess I'd realized that they lied
from time to time. And that my mom took pills, had been hooked on
morphine for a while when I was younger. And so I lorded it over them.
I was the perfected version of them, I thought. Makes you think of
Hitler Youth or the Khmer Rouge, right? The children, full of themselves and their purity, shooting the adults in the rice paddies.'

He put the pen down. He could barely see the page.
He stood and the ceiling whirled over him. He fell to the bed and
looked at the wall. He had underestimated the moonshine. Even when
he had realized its power he had underestimated it. Hanne, you devil!
he thought. I really love this world, he thought. The making of this
wall. I love the people who did it. They did good things here.

XVI.

ALAN OPENED HIS EYES. 10:08. He'd missed the shuttle again. He would call Yousef.

He threw his legs off the bed and stood in the dark room. Beyond the heavy curtains he knew the day was bright, too bright to be part of. There was an acute pain in the back of his neck. He made a mental note to investigate that in the shower.

He stood, found the mirror over the desk, and looked at himself. His face was wrecked, his cheeks sinking to his jowls, his jowls sinking, with some flourish, into his shirt.

In the shower he washed his hair and body and thought, Who is this man who could miss the shuttle not once but twice in three days? Who is this man who could again wake at 10 a.m., having no doubt missed calls to his cellphone, knocks on the door?

At that moment he had a clear recollection of a woman knocking, saying Alan? Alan? He'd barked at them, sending them away, thinking she was a maid. But now, he realized, a maid would not have been calling his name. It must have been Rachel or Cayley. It was Rachel. He knew it now.

He dried himself and picked up the hotel phone. It had been disconnected. When had he done that? Much about the previous night he remembered, but at a certain point it fell off a cliff. He found a dent in the bathroom door, at foot level. His laptop was under the bed. A flash of inspiration: Had his room been ransacked? Maybe Hanne's worries about the secret police were well-founded. The muttawa had been here. They'd heard their conversation and had come in to investigate while he slept. No. For starters, the moonshine was still there, half-full.

He called Yousef.

—You available?

—Alan? You sound terrible. Were you attacked?

—Can you drive me to KAEC?

—Of course. But I have to ask, are you missing these shuttles on purpose, to spend more time with Yousef, your guide and hero?

—You're using too many words, Alan said.

—I'll be there in twenty minutes.

Alan threaded his heavy arms through a clean shirt, feeling he was despoiling its immaculate cotton. As he buttoned it, the collar rubbed against his neck, and the pain was extreme. He went to the bathroom mirror and turned himself around, but could see nothing. He needed two mirrors held strategically to see what looked like a gunshot wound.

Or more like he'd been gnawed on by a rat, a rat trying to dig a hole into Alan's back. A faint recollection came swimming into view: had he taken a knife to the growth on his neck? Was that possible? And again the battle was on, between the responsible self he knew this morning, who would engage a driver at great cost to take him to his duties at the city-to-be in the desert by the sea, and the self who would carouse around the hotel room, stabbing phantom tumors, kicking doors and writing unsendable letters. Which among the selves was expendable? This was eternally the question.

Alan looked around the bathroom for something like a bandage or antiseptic. There was nothing. He buttoned his shirt and hoped no one would see what he'd done.

He went downstairs. He sat in the atrium, ordered coffee. By the concierge desk, there was an electronic sign announcing the events to be held that day at the hotel.
NEW FUTURES: Medina Room
ARABIAN TRADING SUPPLIES: Mezzanine Floor
PRINCIPLES OF BANKING: Hilton Hall
SUCCESS STEPS, PART I: 10 a.m.
SUCCESS STEPS, PART II: 11 a.m.
He could be successful by noon, here at the Hilton. Why, then, was he going to the tent by the sea?

Alan was taking his first sip of coffee when Yousef appeared.
—Alan.
—Alan tried to smile. Hello, he said.

—You look worse than I expected. What happened?

—Just a night of... Alan caught himself. As friendly as they were, he couldn't tell where Yousef stood on the subject of alcohol.

—Just jet lag. Never had it so bad.

Yousef smirked. —I went to college in Alabama. I know a hangover when I see one. Where'd you get the booze?

—I'd rather not say.

Yousef laughed. —You'd *rather not say?* What, you think you've come upon some rare commodity? That you might endanger your source?

—You think this is funny.

—I do.

—I made a promise.

—Not to tell?

—I don't break promises.

—Oh God. Fine. But listen: You don't have to go to KAEC. There's no way the King is coming today. He's in Yemen. Look.

Yousef took Alan's newspaper and showed him page 3: a photo of Abdullah on the tarmac of the Yemeni airport. Alan hadn't been told anything about this.

—I should go, though, for appearances.

—You want to get some food first? You're already late.

They walked outside, and the daylight, which Alan had dreaded, was diffuse, forgiving. He felt attended to, as if the sky and sun would cleanse him, might wash away last night's debauchery.

The bellhop, a huge man with a walrus mustache, was grinning at Yousef.

—Salaam, Yousef said to him, and shook his hand. He comes into my dad's shop, Yousef explained. He buys a lot of sandals.

Alan got in the car while Yousef searched under the hood. After a minute Alan got out again and came around to help.

—What are we looking for? Red sticks of dynamite?

—I'm not sure, Yousef said. Maybe some unusual wires?

Alan had been kidding. —You really don't know? he asked.

—How would I know? I watch the same TV shows as you.

Together the two men, neither of them having ever seen a bomb, looked at Yousef's engine to detect whether or not it contained one.

—I don't see anything, Alan said.

—I don't either.

They got in the car. Yousef put the key in the ignition.

—Ready?

—Don't make it more dramatic.

Yousef turned the key. The engine roared. Alan's heart was popping.

They drove away from the hotel, again passing the same Saudi soldier atop the Humvee, his face in the shadow of the beach umbrella above, his feet soaking in the baby pool.

—So your dad has a shop?

—In the old city. He sells sandals.

—Wait. Your dad sells shoes?

—Yup.

—My dad, too. That's incredible.

Alan looked over to Yousef, half expecting this to be a joke of some kind. The coincidence was too much.

—You don't believe me? Yousef said. I'll show you the shop while you're here. That's where I worked growing up. We all had to, my brothers and me. But my dad's a dictator. He won't listen to us. Especially me. I could help that place a lot, modernize it. But he's old now. He doesn't want to hear anything new.

Yousef's brothers had all gone into other professions. One brother was a doctor in Jordan. Another was an imam in Riyadh. The last one was in college in Bahrain.

They were on the highway now.

—Let's have a joke, Yousef said. For good luck.

—That a Saudi custom?

—I don't know. I never know about our customs. Or what people think our customs are. I'm not sure we have customs.

—I don't have any jokes today, Alan said.

But then one occurred to him.

—Okay. A husband and wife are getting ready for bed. The wife is standing in front of a full-length mirror taking a hard look at herself. 'You know, dear,' she says, 'I look in the mirror, and I see an old woman. My face is all wrinkled, my hair is grey, my shoulders are hunched over, I've got fat legs, and my arms are all flabby.' She turns to her husband and says, 'Tell me something positive to make me feel better about myself.' He studies her hard for a moment, thinking about it, and then says in a soft, thoughtful voice, 'Well, there's nothing wrong with your eyesight.'

Yousef laughed out loud. Too loud.

—Please be quiet.

—Your head hurts that much? Must have been some bad *siddiqi*.

—What's *siddiqi*?

—It means *my friend*. That's what you've been drinking.

—I deny it.

—Alan, I'm not the muttawa. And you're not the first businessman I've driven around. Wait a second.

Ahead there was a checkpoint. A pair of young soldiers stood in the median, stopping cars. On the side of the road, three more uniformed men sat in a police car. Yousef rolled down his window. The soldier mumbled a question to Yousef, Yousef answered, and the soldier waved him through. And that was that. Yousef drove on.

—That's it? He didn't want to actually see anything?

—Sometimes they do.

—They looking for someone in particular?

—Maybe. It's all for show. No one wants to be a soldier here. They'd give the jobs to foreign workers if they could.

They left the city and were soon on the same desolate highway. A truck carrying palm trees passed them, spraying dust.

—You hungry or not? Yousef asked.

—I'm not sure.

—Better to be very late than just a little late. I drove a guy from Texas around for a few weeks last year. He told me that. If you're half an hour late, it looks like a mistake. If you're two hours late, it looks intentional.

Yousef chose a roadside place a few miles up the road. They pulled over. The restaurant was open-air, a series of low-walled rooms. They walked inside the main building, and the smell of fish overwhelmed. Seafood was not what Alan had had in mind when imagining his first meal after the moonshine bender. He wanted bread and bacon.

Yousef led him to a wide display case, hundreds of fish on ice.

Alan almost retched.

—You have a preference? Yousef asked.

Alan wanted anything but this. He wanted to leave and get something dry. Crackers, chips. But he had grown used to eating whatever was put in front of him. —Up to you, he said.

—Let's get a couple of these, Yousef said, nodding at a pair of foot-long fish, silver and pink. We call it *najel*. Not sure what you would call it in English. Yousef ordered for them both.

They were seated outside, though there were no seats. The custom was to recline on the floor, each with a stiff cushion to lean against.

Flies alighted on their knees and arms. Alan waved them away, but they were not long deterred. The thought of eating fish outdoors like this, in this heat, chased away his appetite. An animal sound turned his head. Atop their low wall, a cat, looking a thousand years old, had taken up residence. Its left eye was cloudy and a lower tooth protruded upward from his mouth, an inverted fang. It seemed impossible that such a creature could survive one more day. Yousef barked to the maitre d', who came over with a small broom and shooed the cat over another wall and into the alleyway.

Yousef's phone vibrated. His thumbs went to work.

—My girlfriend, he said.

Alan could not keep Yousef's women straight and said so.

—I'll explain, Yousef said.

He had been engaged to a girl, Amina, who he'd known as a teenager. When they had presented their intentions to her parents, her father had refused to grant his permission to marry. The case against Yousef was tough: his family was Bedouin, and to some upper-class Saudis this was unacceptable. They think we're savages, Yousef explained. His father was a shopkeeper, a villager, an uneducated man. That he had done well — he had earned millions of dinar, Yousef noted, and had erected a massive compound in his home village, had leveled a mountaintop to build it — mattered not.

—And so that was that?

The possibilities flooded Alan's mind: couldn't they have just left the country? Eloped?

—There was nothing to be done. But it's fine. I don't think about her so much any more. Anyway, my parents found someone else for me.

The woman they'd chosen, Jameelah, was gorgeous, Yousef explained, the most beautiful woman he'd ever seen, and suddenly she was his. They were married a few months later, but though he loved to look at her, to watch her walk across the room, they're weren't in any way compatible.

—Dumb as a goat.

They were divorced a year later, and he was single again.

—I always have drama with women. But not with Noor.

Noor was his girlfriend, inasmuch as such a thing was permissable. She was a bit younger, twenty-three, a graduate student. They'd met online.

—She is so brilliant, he said. She kicks my ass every day. And she's descended from the Prophet Mohammed. I swear this is true.

Things were progressing with Noor, he said, and the two of them were trying to plot a way to tell their parents about their intentions, when he started getting texts from his ex-wife Jameelah. She was now married to a wealthy man in his forties, who Yousef suspected of being an extreme kind of international swinger.

—He goes to Europe and has sex with boys.

—He's gay? Alan asked.

—Gay? No. You think that means he's gay?

Alan wasn't awake enough to follow that tributary, so he let it go.

The food arrived. Plates filled with chopped lettuce and cucumbers and tomatoes, brown rice, *khobez* — a bread like naan — and then the fish. Yousef lassoed the meal with his finger. —*Syadya*, he said. The fish had been deep-fried, but otherwise was the same fish they'd seen under glass, eyes and bones and all. Alan ripped some bread and grabbed at the flesh of the fish. He took a bite.

—Good? Yousef asked.

—Perfect. Thanks.

—You fry anything, it tastes right.

The cat reappeared. Yousef threw his foot toward the blind, ancient animal and it meowed, outraged. It scurried off.

—Meanwhile she sends me ten texts a day. Some of the texts are just bored, like, 'What are you doing,' blah blah. And some are, like, really sexy. I wish I could show you some.

Yousef scrolled through the messages on his phone, and Alan found himself wanting to see the sexy texts from the bored Saudi housewife.

—But I have to delete them the second I get them.

Jameelah could prove her whereabouts for more or less every minute of their marriage, and the husband had not read the texts themselves, but his suspicions were nonetheless unbridled.

—If he had read them, Yousef said, I'd be dead. She'd definitely be dead. She deleted them in time. He called the phone company trying to get them. It was ridiculous.

Alan was aghast. His understanding of the judicial system in Saudi might have been incomplete, but still, this seemed to be extraordinary risk for little possible gain.

—She's actually jeopardizing her life for these texts, right? Wouldn't she be stoned by the government or something?

Yousef gave him a look. —We don't stone people here, Alan.

—Sorry, Alan said.

—We behead them, Yousef said, and then laughed, his mouth full of rice. But not so often. Anyway. She has a different phone now. She has two — one for regular calls, which he can monitor, and one she uses for me.

—All the married women, Yousef explained, have a second phone. It's a big business in Saudi Arabia.

The whole country seemed to operate on two levels, the official and the actual.

—She has a lot of free time. She's got Indonesians to do the housework, so all she can do is shop and watch TV. She's wasting herself. 'You're the love of my life,' she wrote to me last week. I don't know where she got that expression. So the husband wants me dead, and I live with that. I can't tell how serious it is, though. Some days I wake up in the night thinking he'll really kill me, you know, like any time. And other days I laugh about it. Not such a good situation.

And suddenly Alan felt paternal toward Yousef. He couldn't help it. This whole issue with the husband seemed simple enough. A simple problem with a simple solution.

—You need to sit down with him.

—What? No. Yousef shook his head and stuffed another piece of fish into his mouth.

—Sit down with him, Alan continued, and look him in the eye and tell him you've never done anything with his wife. Because you haven't, right?

—No. Nothing. Not even when we were dating.

—So you tell him this, and that's how he knows you're telling the truth. Because you look him in the eye. Otherwise you wouldn't be willing to meet him face to face, right? If you were actually screwing his wife, you'd never face him.

Now Yousef began nodding. —That's not bad. That's... That's an idea. I like the idea. But I don't know if he's reasonable. He might have gone nuts by now. These messages he's been leaving on my phone, they're not from a reasonable person.

—This is the way to do it, Alan said. I've been around a while, and I've got some experience in these matters. This will put it all to rest.

Yousef looked at Alan as if what he was saying was true and sensible. As if Alan was someone who had actually acquired wisdom in his many years. Alan was not sure what he had was wisdom. What he had was a sense that few things mattered much. That few people are to be feared.

And so he now faced all such situations with a sense of exhausted resolve, and he dealt with everything head-on. Except with Ruby, who he avoided more or less always. Alan chose not to tell Yousef that he had been generally unskilled in matters of love, and was now celibate and alone. That he had not touched a woman in any meaningful way for years now, too many years. He chose to allow Yousef to believe that he was now and always a successful man reveling in the sex-drenched cities of America. A triumphant man with a powerful appetite and unlimited options.

XVII.

BY THE TIME THEY got to the site it was noon. Yousef dropped him off at the cul-de-sac near the tent.

—I'm thinking I'll see you again, Yousef said.

—It seems likely.

Alan turned, and Yousef let out a gasp.

—Alan. Your neck.

Alan reached back, momentarily forgetting his self-surgery. His fingers met a wet smudge of blood.

Yousef got closer. —What is that?

Alan didn't know where to start. —I peeled a scab. Is it bad?

—It's going down your back. Did you have that yesterday?

—Sort of. It was different yesterday.

—We have to get a doctor.

Alan knew nothing about how the medical system worked in the Kingdom of Saudi Arabia, but he figured, yes, he should get it looked at. So he and Yousef agreed that they would go the next morning. Yousef would set it up.

—You keep thinking of reasons to see me, Yousef said. It's sweet. And he left.

Inside the tent, all three young people were now on the far side, away from the water, in the darkness, looking into their screens.

—Hello! Alan bellowed. He was feeling strangely upbeat.

He strode over to them and sat on one of the rugs. Looking around, everything seemed exactly as it had been the day before.

—Get a late start again? Brad said.

There was no acceptable excuse. Alan offered none.

—Still waiting on the wi-fi, Rachel said.

—I'll make some more inquiries, Alan said. I have an appointment at 2:40.

He had no such thing. Now he was making up phantom appointments. At least it would give him an excuse to leave the tent, and soon.

—Good news, though, he said. The King is in Yemen. So we won't have to worry about any sudden arrival.

The young people seemed pleased, then deflated. With the King in another country, there was no reason to do anything, and even if there was, without wi-fi they couldn't test their hologram anyway.

—Play cards? Rachel asked.

What Alan wanted to do was to be on the beach, with his feet in the water. —Sure, he said, and sat down.

They played poker. Alan had been taught a dozen variations by his father, and he could play well. But he did not want to play with these young people. He did, though, and listened to their conversation, and learned that last night Rachel and Cayley had stayed in Rachel's room talking until very late. Brad had been having trouble reaching his wife, and when he did he found out that his niece had whooping cough and who gets whooping cough any more? They talked about that, and other resurgent diseases from centuries past. Rickets and shingles were back, and perhaps polio was coming back, too. That began a line of discussion engineered by Rachel to reveal that she'd had friends who'd had horrific childbirth experiences — deformities caused by babies pulled too quickly by impatient doctors, a stillbirth, a mishap involving a suction. All of it seemed from another time.

They sat in silence. A gust of wind rippled the wall of the tent, and all four of them watched, as if hoping the wind would grow and knock it all down. Then they could do something. Or go home.

When Alan had been at Schwinn, and would find himself in a hotel anywhere, Kansas City, with a half dozen young sales reps, he knew he had an audience that wanted to hear about what had worked and had not for a Christmastime rollout, why the Sting-Ray had hit while the Typhoon hadn't, what things were like at the plant, what was in the works in R&D. They'd laugh at his jokes, they'd hang on his every word. They respected him and needed him.

Now, though, he had nothing to teach these people. They could set up a hologram in a tent in the desert, while he'd arrived three hours late and wouldn't know where to plug the thing in. They had no interest in manufacturing or the type of person-to-person sales he'd spent his life perfecting. None of them had been even vaguely involved in such things. None of them started, as he had, selling actual objects to actual people. Alan looked at their faces. Cayley and her upturned nose. Brad and his caveman brow. Rachel and her tiny lipless mouth.

Then again, was there ever a time when a young American wanted to learn from an older American, or anyone at all? Probably not. Americans are born knowing everything and nothing. Born moving forward, quickly, or thinking they are.

—The Statue of Liberty is moving, man!

That was something the man on the plane had said — maybe the only thing that had struck Alan as relevant or revelatory. The guy had just been in New York, had visited Ellis Island.

—Everyone thinks that statue is standing still, but she's in midstride!

The man was spitting. He didn't know or didn't care.

—When I saw her in person, it blew my mind. Check it out next time you're in town. I shit you not, she's walking forward, the gown swishing along, her sandals all bent and everything, like she's about to cross the ocean, go back to France. Blew my mind.

After a few hands of poker, Alan wanted badly to leave. He was in the tent, dark and smelling increasingly of people and their things, while outside, no more than fifty yards away, there was the Red Sea.

—Well, I better head out, he said.

They offered no argument. He stood and made his way to the tent door.

—I'm heading this way, he said, indicating north, so if you see the King, look for me up here. He smiled, and the young people smiled, and he knew they saw him as useless, and he left.

Outside the tent, he looked up to the pink condominium and saw a silhouette in the window. He did not believe it at first. But the shape was human and was moving in a fourth-story window. Then another shape. Then they were gone.

He had a thought that he might go to the building, find a way in, and listen for voices. He had not thought it through any further than that. He walked around the building and almost fell in a pit. It was as big as a quarry — an acre, surely. They had dug a foundation, apparently, for a structure to stand next to the Florida condominium. It was about fifty feet deep, and it had nearly become his grave.

There were wire frames for columns, giant ducts and pipes that would eventually carry water and heat. There was a makeshift stairway made of wood and mud. For no good reason, he decided to walk down. As he descended, the air cooled. It was wonderful. Every ten feet, each ostensible floor, the temperature dropped ten degrees. He continued down until he reached the bottom, where the air was positively civilized. The floor was cement, though there were patches of sand and piles of dirt. In one corner of the foundation, he found a simple plastic chair. It seemed made for him, for him at this moment, so he sat in it. He was sitting on a plastic chair on the floor of a foundation in the city by the Red Sea, and the air was cool, and the color of everything was grey, and he was deeply content.

He sat and stared at the concrete wall.

He listened to his own breathing.

He tried not to think of anything.

—I forgive you, Charlie Fallon said.

He said it many times. He was forgiving Alan for helping Annette move out. They'd fought too many times, and Charlie had made threats, Annette said. Alan had to hear about it every day, from both sides. He couldn't sort it out. But when Annette decided to leave, one weekend when Charlie was out of town, she asked Alan for help, and he provided it. He helped her empty most of the house.

The next day Charlie called. —That loony took all our stuff.

Alan went over, walked through the house. It looked like high winds had swept the contents away, leaving only papers, rolls of tape, some pillows.

—Got to hand it to her, Charlie said. I didn't see this coming. Can you believe how efficient she was? I'm gone one day and the house gets emptied. She is a fucking smart gal, always was.

Charlie didn't know Alan had helped and Alan couldn't find a good way to tell him. So for a while he didn't. What good would it do?

Eventually he found out. Annette probably told him. Charlie was angry for a while. But then he said he understood, and that he had forgiven Alan.

—She has a power over weak men like you and me, Charlie said.

Alan got up from his chair. He paced around the perimeter, counting his steps. The building would be huge. Two hundred feet on one side, a hundred and twenty on another. Alan felt good about being there. About being part of the project. There was nothing as good as this, being there at the beginning of something. When the city was another Dubai, another Abu Dhabi or Nairobi, he could say he'd walked the foundation of the buildings, he'd laid the groundwork for all the IT in the whole damned place. But he couldn't get ahead of himself.

He sat down again on his white plastic chair.

Terry Wren had gotten ahead of himself.

—Jesus, Al, it feels good.

Alan had seen Terry a few years ago, while passing through Pittsburgh. Alan had known Terry for twenty years, since the Olney, Illinois days. Terry had gone from bikes to steel to glass, and was working for PPG Industries, a large glass manufacturer outside of Pittsburgh. It seemed a brilliant move. What business could be more recession-proof than glass? Housing starts could go up and down, but there will always be broken windows.

They'd eaten dinner by Heinz Field, and Terry was crowing. PPG had gotten the contract to provide the glass for the first twenty floors of the new World Trade Center building. Twenty floors of blast-resistant glass, the technology painstakingly developed right there in Pennsylvania.

—It's like we were made for this one job, Terry said, his mouth full of ribeye, the fork in his hand like a sword raised in victory.

Terry had worked his ass off to get the contract, and now he couldn't wait to begin. The guys on the factory floor couldn't wait to begin. To be involved in Freedom Tower! It was the reason you go to work in the morning.

—Biggest thing we've ever done, he said. The work would be done with care, with urgency. Terry was wearing an American flag pin on his lapel. It all meant something. Until it didn't.

The next time Alan saw him it was over. They were both in New York, and PPG had just been pushed out. Terry was falling apart. They met for drinks. Alan thought Terry would cry.

Untangling it all was near impossible. Apparently, the Port Authority of New York had accepted a bid from another company, Solera Construction. That seemed fair enough. Their bid was lower, and they were a New York firm. It seemed simple to Terry — until he dug deeper.

—Oh, God, it's so fucking sick, Alan!

Terry grabbed him by the arm.

Turns out Solera was contracting the glass out to a Las Vegas firm. Terry was annoyed, but he still felt that they'd been plain old beat. He didn't know the Vegas people, but he assumed they were operating on some cheap real estate in the Nevada desert, probably employing some undocumented workers, keeping their costs low.

—Fair enough, right? Terry said, spilling his drink on his shirt.

But it turns out the Vegas people weren't manufacturing the glass. They were a front. The glass was being made in China. Sixty vertical feet of blast-resistant glass in the new World Trade Center was being made in China.

We accepted the lowest responsible bidder. That was the public statement from the Port Authority spokesperson.

—Goddamn, Alan said.

—Can you fucking believe it? Terry said.

But then there was a kicker, a big one: the Chinese glass maker was using a PPG patent. PPG had developed the glass, applied for and gotten a patent, and shortly before the bidding began, they'd licensed the patent to firms around the world. And one of those firms was Sanxin

Façade, based on the South China Sea. And Sanxin Façade, it turned out, would be the firm building the glass in Freedom Tower. So PPG had invented a new type of blast-resistant glass, only to have a Chinese company use that technology to build the glass, cheaper, and sell it back to the Port Authority, which was attempting, at least, to resurrect something like pride and resilience in the center of the white-hot center of everything American.

Alan was pacing now. He was walking around the floor of the new building, working up a sweat, wanting to punch the walls.

Maybe Terry would have retired either way. He was sixty-two. But the WTC deal did him in. It wasn't fun anymore.

—Call me a fool, Terry said, but I cared about that Freedom glass. I fucking cared about us being part of that building.

When Terry quit, that was the end of Alan's patience. The dishonor of it all. Not just the business aspect, the fact that the Port Authority had dragged PPG along, had indicated a dozen times that of course PPG, the originator of the technology, would be the supplier. It was the fact that they would go abroad for such a thing, would knowingly lead PPG on — millions in equipment upgrades and retooling to enable them to build the glass — my God, the whole thing was underhanded and it was cowardly and lacking in all principle. It was dishonor. And at Ground Zero. Alan was pacing, his hands in fists. The dishonor! At Ground Zero! Amid the ashes! The dishonor! Amid the ashes! The dishonor! The dishonor! The dishonor!

—Man!

Alan looked around. He stopped pacing. Who was talking to him?

—Man! You!

He looked up. There were a pair of workers in blue jumpsuits, looking down at him. Mister Man! No! No! they said, disapproving. They were gesturing, making big scooping motions, as if conjuring him from the underworld by urging him up, up, up. Their faces said, You are not supposed to be there, fifty feet under the earth, walking like that, pacing, angry, recounting unchangeable events from not just your own past but that of the country as a whole.

But Alan knew this. He started up the steps to the surface. He was well aware of everything he was not supposed to be doing.

XVIII.

THE DAY WAS OVER, and Alan rode back to Jeddah in the van with the young people, all of whom slept on the way home, or pretended to sleep. It was a quiet ride. At the hotel, they disembarked, more or less wordlessly, and Alan was back in his room, alone, by seven. He ordered a steak, ate it, and walked to the balcony. He could see a few figures, a few hundred feet below, trying to cross the highway and get to the shore. They made attempts, retreated. The traffic was moving too fast. Finally they made it, rushing and weaving, and Alan had learned nothing.

He leafed through the hotel guide and saw pictures of the fitness center Rachel had mentioned. Having no interest in exercising, he took the elevator to the basement, where he was greeted by a fitness person behind a crescent-shaped desk, a fluffy white towel around his neck. Alan told him he was just looking around, *to plan his regimen*, he said earnestly, and so was allowed to walk in wearing his business attire.

There were five people exercising, all men, running on treadmills and wrestling with Nautilus machines. The smell was a chemical clean and the TV, showing CNN, was loud. The fitness person glanced Alan's way, and Alan nodded seriously while looking at one of the machines, as if to say Yes, I will do some of this tomorrow in my fitness clothes.

Then he left. He wandered the lobby for a while, and decided to sit and observe. He ordered an iced tea and watched as Saudis and Westerners glided across the reflective surface of the floor. He listened to the fountains, the occasional raised voice echoing a hundred feet up into the atrium. The hotel was really without any character whatsoever. He loved it. But it was also a hotel without a bar and so there was very little to do down there. Upstairs, the bottle was waiting. So he stepped back into the glass elevator and floated back up to his floor.

Inside, he poured a few fingers in and began.

'Dear Kit, Something is different about me. Either this thing on my neck is causing me to lose my mind, or I've already lost it.'

No, he told himself. Stop the blubbering. Do something useful. He took a sip. It burned his tongue, strained his gums. His eyes watered. He took another long pull.

'Dear Kit, I have made some mistakes. That's why you won't be in school this fall. It's simple, true. I fucked up. But they do not make it easy on guys like me.'

He started again.

'First of all, let me tell you the good news. It looks like this Saudi deal is going through. You can sign up for classes in the fall. I'll have the money. I'll have enough to pay full-freight. The whole year up-front, if those bastards want it that way.'

Now he was lying. She didn't deserve that. She'd done nothing wrong. And yes, the economy was this, the world was that, these schools were overpriced, ridiculously overpriced — my God, did they simply pull that tuition number out of the wind and then add ten percent? — but still. Had he planned better, had he not been so incompetent, he would have whatever she needed. He had twenty years to save $200k. How hard was that? It was ten thousand a year. Much less assuming any kind of interest on the money. All he had to do was save $60k and leave it alone. But he didn't leave it alone. He played with it. He invested it, invested it in himself and others. He thought he could make the $200k at will, in any given year. How could he have predicted the world losing interest in people like him?

A year ago, he'd had the idea that he'd pioneer a new line of bikes — classic, durable, for the collectors and the tinkerers and the families who just wanted something indestructible. And so he went looking for a loan. He figured half a million would allow him to rent a small warehouse, some machinery, hire some engineers and designers, get a few prototypes made, buy a few trucks. He knew what he wanted — strong simple bikes with clean lines, tons of chrome, everything built to last a thousand years and never look weary.

He came up with a viable business plan, but the banks laughed him out the door. You want to make what? Where? I want to make bikes, he said. In Massachusetts. That amused everyone. Lots of amusement from the people holding the cash. One venture capital guy had actually laughed, a big and genuine laugh, on the phone — laughed a good long time. Alan, if I gave you five grand, let alone five hundred, that would be the end of us both! They'd have us committed!

This was not a good time to be asking banks for money for what they deemed a project of quixotic dimensions. The kindest among the loan officers referred him to the government. Have you heard of the Small Business Adminstration? they asked. Check out their website. It's very informative and easy to use.

So Alan went to smaller and smaller banks, whose officers were more and more quizzical about just what the hell Alan was talking about. They'd never heard of anything like it. Some of the bank people were so young they'd never seen a business proposal suggesting manufacturing things in the state of Massachusetts. They thought they'd unearthed some ancient shaman, full of clues to a forgotten world.

Now he wants to be the union man! Ron chuckled. Alan had made the mistake of telling his father about his plans. He thought he'd be impressed. Maybe it was a shot at redemption? Ron was not supportive.

—Too late, Sonny.

When he said *Sonny*, he meant *Pissant*.

—I don't think so.

—You helped all that move to China. You can't put that genie back in the bottle. But why listen to me? Why not get some consultants to tell you what to do?

Ron had always been dismissive of consultants. —What can they tell me about my own business? They're paid obscenely to misread spreadsheets.

Alan stopped asking advice from his father.

On the few occasions when Alan had been invited to start filling out the loan paperwork, it went from hopeful to tragic with alarming speed. And the factor that seemed to move his proposal from risky to toxic was not American infrastructure, or the market for American-made goods, or the competition from China. It was Banana Republic. Banana Republic was killing the ability of entrepreneurs like himself to move this country forward. Banana Republic killed his credit, and that had killed America.

Alan had never checked or known his credit score but was told, by every bank and even a few venture capital firms, that his score made him untouchable. His score, 698, was 50 or so points below what would qualify him as trustworthy or even human.

After days of digging he realized that the defining moment of his current financial life, and the barrier to his being considered for any and all loans, was a certain purchase at Banana Republic six years earlier.

He needed a new jacket, and the salesperson told him that if he signed up for a Banana Republic store card, that he'd get fifteen percent off that day, and he could cancel the card shortly thereafter. But somehow, after he'd canceled the card, it had not been canceled, and bills continued to be sent, but because he'd canceled the card, he hadn't opened the envelopes, figuring they were junk mail.

So he went to 30 and finally 90 days overdue, and then 120, and collection agencies were called, and at that point he paid the $32.00 due, some kind of finance fee, and he killed the card dead, again.

But all that had pushed his credit score below 700, and any kind of loan, let alone a third mortgage — he'd taken out a second before the Banana Republic debacle — was out of reach.

The bank people would point to the score and throw up their hands. When he would explain that he had paid his mortgages, all of his actual credit cards, dutifully for thirty years, they seemed to care, and value this, but then not so much. There was the score.

Alan tried to reason with them.

—You're seeing my actual credit report.

—Yes sir.

—And you see that the only blemish is this Banana Republic card.

—Yup. That's the main one, I'm pretty sure.

—And you recognize that a $72 charge on a Banana Republic card six years ago is not a very significant indicator next to thirty years of perfect performance with bills and mortgage payments?

—Yes, I agree.

Alan thought he'd broken through.

—So we can get around this?

The man laughed. —Oh, no. I'm sorry, sir. The score is below our threshold. We can't grant loans if the applicant's score is below 700.

—Mine is 698.

—Yes. But even below 740 prompts a review at the highest levels.

—But you don't even compile these scores yourself.

—Right.

—Some outside agency does. Experian.

—Right.

—Do you know how they assess what cards or payments trigger what kinds of deduction to your credit score?

—No, no. That's proprietary information. The man chuckled, as if the two of them were considering the motivations of God himself. They protect that very closely, the man said.

Alan tried to call Banana Republic. They had no idea. —We don't deal with the credit cards on that level, a rep said. She referred him to a company in Arizona. The number in Arizona repeatedly hung up on him, as if by design.

The age of machines holding dominion over man had come. This was the downfall of a nation and the triumph of systems designed to thwart all human contact, human reason, personal discretion and decision making. Most people did not want to make decisions. And too many of the people who *could* make decisions had decided to cede them to machines.

Alan stood. The lines of the room went everywhere, like a game of pick-up sticks. He found the bed, and allowed it to swallow him. It spun like a pinwheel. —Maybe I drank too much, he said, chuckling. He put his hand flat to the wall and the spinning slowed and stopped.

Not bad, he said, thinking he was very funny and capable. He wanted to stop the spinning and did. —Congratulations, young man! he said, aloud, to the ceiling.

There was a sound like a phone. It seemed very hard to believe, that this phone in this hotel could be ringing. Alan looked at it as it rang twice, three times. He watched it as he would watch an animal in a zoo that had done something extraordinary and might do it again.

Again it rang. He picked it up.

—Hello?

—It's Hanne.

—Good. This is incredible. How are you?

She laughed. —I didn't ask you how you are.

—I guess I just felt you should know.

She laughed again, her low strum of a laugh. —Are you already in bed?

—No, he lied. Why?

—There's a party at the embassy tonight.

—The Danish embassy?

—Yes, and it will be bacchanalian.

—I'm already drunk. That moonshine.

—That's good. You'll fit in. Will you come?

XIX.

HE TOOK A CAB to the embassy, and within twenty minutes witnessed two women licking a man's pierced nipples, bestride him like barbarian consorts. There were people in their underwear and so many pills. Barrels of moonshine. It was desperate and deranged and even intermittently enjoyable.

There was a fat man dancing by the pool, dancing well. Such tight pants for a bigger man. Hanne was gone, to the bar.

Alan was alone and wandered. He did not need a drink.

The fat man's pants glittered like the scales of a fish. Alan had doubted the man, had wondered why there were women so close to him, intrigued by him, but then the fat man had started dancing, and all was justified. He was fantastic. And Canadian. A fat Canadian dance phenom.

There was a game being played in the pool. People diving for pills.

There was no pot at the party — that might have been too easy to detect by neighbors, the smell on the wind — so instead there were pills. There were so many pills, and wine and liquor in unmarked bottles. It was a bootlegger's paradise.

There was the tall man, built like a Viking, straw hair in a ponytail, throwing the pills in the deep end, hundreds of them. He threw them in and people dove. You must eat them so I can see, he said to the party-goers, in their underwear, diving in. You could only play the game if you waited till you resurfaced and swallowed the pill in front of him. And so people jumped, in their underwear, into the pool, diving for the drugs — white and blue pills that were very difficult to see in the pool floor at night. What were they?

Someone said Viagra, someone said Ambien, but that couldn't be right. Soon someone emerged from the pool naked, and that created a stir. In the pool, there were men and women entwined, flesh refracted and moving rhythmically, and there were the pills, the moonshine, but the man who emerged from the pool naked apparently crossed a line. He was quickly covered in a towel and ushered inside.

Where was Hanne?

The people were older than he had ever seen behaving this way. Old people, people his own age, in their underwear. Old people with the pills, throwing the pills into their mouths and washing them down with giant bottles of homemade liquor. Something pent up had been un-leashed. What about the woman with the cleavage? She carried it like a tray in front of her. Just walking around the party, around and around, with no other plan or purpose, it seemed. Never seemed to talk to any-one. As if she'd been hired to do what she did, walk around, be admired.

Such things were done in New York and Vegas, but here?

Alan drank out of a dozen clear bottles, the contents always looking like water and tasting like broken machinery.

Alan ran into an American architect. He said he'd designed part of KAEC, the financial center. He had designed at least a few of the tallest buildings in the world. He was from somewhere very surprising, very flat. Iowa? He had been warm, humble, maybe a bit haggard. They compared notes about lack of sleep. The architect had just come from Shanghai, where he was building a new tower, taller than anything else he'd done. He'd been working for ten years in Dubai, Singapore, Abu Dhabi, all over China.

—I haven't worked in the States in, wow, I can't think of when I last did, he said.

Alan asked why, though he knew the answer. It was about money, sure, but also vision, courage, even a bit of competitive ego.

—Not that it's about the biggest or tallest, but you know, in the U.S. now there's not that kind of dreaming happening. It's on hold. The dreaming's being done elsewhere for now, the architect said. Then he left the party.

—Come talk to me.

It was Hanne.

—Where have you been? she asked.

Alan didn't know.

She pulled Alan's hand. He followed.

—Let's make a mistake, she said.

They went to the garage. Three refrigerators still in their boxes.

And her face in his chest, then those small eyes looking up to him, trying to be sultry but achieving something more like searching. He felt found, and looked away.

But they kissed for a moment, and then he stopped. He pretended it was an issue of chivalry. A matter of dignity.

—This feels silly, rushing like this, doesn't it? he said.

She stepped back, looking at him like he'd revealed a terrible secret, that he'd been a member of the SS in his youth. Then she laughed. Admirable caution at your age, Alan!

He brought her close to him, and held her for a long time. He kissed the top of her head. That was too far, and he knew it. Now he was her father. Her priest? He was an idiot.

She pulled away. —Don't patronize me.

He apologized, and told her how much he liked her, because he did.

—You can't hurt me, you know, she said. I'm indestructible.

This was the go-ahead, one person telling another that her eyes were open, and he needn't worry about her falling in love with him or even remembering him.

Was she being cruel? People don't like to be kept from what they want. Especially when it appears within their reach. It makes one doubly angry. Clearly Hanne felt she was doing Alan a favor. And then he had tasted her and said no. She didn't talk to him the rest of the night.

But by then the party was almost over anyway. This happened at the end, near the end, at least near the end of his time there. The spaceman!

A man in a spacesuit. It was a costume, but it was very good, very realistic. Something like a cross between the Apollo suit and Kubrick's *2001*, angular like that, the ribbed arms and legs. He just walked around in that suit, feigning weightlessness, and then he went back inside. He emerged later without the helmet and he turned out to be in his mid-sixties. What had he been drinking or taking? A man in his sixties walking in slow motion around the party, pantomiming with people, pretending to grab the breasts of the cleavage woman.

There was music in the basement, a kind of dance floor, a disco ball crafted with tin foil. Motown was the only thing, Diana Ross and the Shirelles. The Jackson 5. Men and women in their forties grinding, ass to crotch. It was unsettling, how they were doing it. Alan had had to leave the basement.

There were bright young people. Out by the pool.

They had their moonshine in hand, in red cups, and they made their way to the dance floor for a song or two, and Alan found himself next to them, on deck chairs, watching the pill-diving. There were three of them. One, a young woman, from Ethiopia but speaking like an American. Born in Miami, now working for the Ethiopian embassy. Her hair leapt out of her head in all directions, with her thin straight nose, her enormous eyes, eyelids painted as if with blue smoke. With her were two earnest young men. They looked sixteen, faces like ripe fruit, eyes small and alight. One was Dutch, the other Mexican. They were interested in Alan, in KAEC, in everything.

—This place is about to pop, the Ethiopian woman said.

—This place is about to pop? Alan thought she meant some kind of war. Some kind of terror. Something like the 1979 massacre at Mecca, all those pilgrims dead.

—No, no, she said. The women. The Saudi women have had it. They're done with all this shit. Abdullah's trying to open doors, hoping the women plow through, take it from there. He thinks he's Gorbachev. He's setting up the dominoes. The co-ed college was the first. KAEC is the next.

Alan turned to the other two. —You agree with this?

The other two nodded. They probably knew more than he did.

There was foosball. Some kind of tournament, very serious, with names on a chalkboard, single-elimination. A big flatscreen TV playing the films of Russ Meyer. The astronaut was watching, leaning forward, his helmet in his lap.

XX.

JUMBLED MEMORIES AND REVELATIONS assaulted Alan throughout the next morning as he showered and dressed and read his copy of *Arab News*. What was that by the sink? Another bottle of illicit alcohol. Hanne had sent him home with one. Hanne cared about him, the fool. He thought of the kiss on her head. A terrible thing to do. Underslept and with a foot still in the nocturnal world of the Danish embassy, he knew he would be brittle this day. He drank his coffee and flipped through the newspaper, seeing a small photo of King Abdullah and caption noting that he was back in the Kingdom.

This was the first day, then, that the King might actually visit KAEC. However unlikely he'd arrive at the city, and even though Alan felt like he'd spent the night in the trunk of a car, he and the Reliant team had to be on time, ready and presentable.

—Yousef?

—I can't believe you're awake. It's not even ten yet. Wait. It's only seven!

—You want to drive to KAEC?

—When? Now?

—I'd like to be there by eight thirty.

—Make it nine thirty. No one will be there before nine. That way I can take you to a doctor to look at that thing on your neck.

Alan met Yousef in the hotel turnabout and got in the Caprice.

—Your sleep schedule worries me.

—I had a weird night.

Alan knew he shouldn't mention the party at the embassy, but he wanted badly to tell Yousef. Yousef would find it funny, and would either be amazed that it happened at all or would say, *Oh, those happen all the time.* Either would be satisfying. But he had promised all those people, including the man in the space suit, and he had never in all his years broken such a promise, no matter how small.

They passed the man on the tank with the beach umbrella, and this time Yousef took a right, not a left.

—Where's the doctor?

—Couple miles. Noor knows the woman who works in reception.

—Thanks for doing this, Alan said.

—It's easy, Yousef said, and lit a cigarette.

—So I heard a good joke last night.

—I'm glad.

—You know what the foreign legion is?

—Sure. Like the French Foreign Legion?

—Right. So there's a captain in the foreign legion, and he's transferred to a desert outpost. On his orientation tour he sees this very tired, filthy camel tied out back of the enlisted men's barracks. He asks the sergeant leading the tour, 'Hey, what's the camel for?' The sergeant says, 'Well, sir, we're out here in the middle of nowhere, and the men have natural sexual urges, so when they do, we have the camel.' The captain is taken aback, but he's new there, and he doesn't want to rock the boat. So he says, 'Well if it's good for morale, then I guess it's all right with me.' He goes about his business, and after he's been at the fort for about six months the captain can't stand it anymore, so he tells the sergeant, 'Bring in the camel!' The sergeant shrugs his shoulders and leads the camel into the captain's quarters. The captain gets a footstool and steps up, drops his pants, and has vigorous sex with the camel. He finishes, and steps down from the stool. He's buttoning his pants and he asks the sergeant, 'Is that how the enlisted men do it?' The sergeant looks at his shoes. He can't figure out what to say. Finally he says, 'Well sir, they usually just use the camel to ride into town to find the women.'

—Oh God! Yousef was laughing, banging the steering wheel. For a while I was worried — I thought it was going to be some anti-Arab thing. You know, the camel-fucking and all that. But that is *good*. That's my favorite one yet. Noor will love that one.

Yousef pulled up to a large hospital, ringed by high walls. He stopped at the gate.

—The gate's only a problem for me, not you.

Yousef greeted the guard, and as usual made head nods toward Alan, using the word *Amreeka* a few times until he was waved through.

They parked and walked into the hospital, and soon Alan was seated in a room painted avocado. The magazines were a mix of American and Saudi. A nurse soon entered, alone, and took his pulse and other vitals.

She left, indicating the doctor would arrive shortly.

Alan stared at the floor, wondering how he might explain his decision to attempt surgery on himself with a steak knife. He saw no point in lying. Only an animal could have caused that wound.

A shadow darkened the floor beneath him and he looked up to see a short woman in a white coat.

—Mr. Clay?

—Yes.

—I am Doctor Hakem.

She extended her hand. He shook it. She couldn't have been much more than five feet tall. Her hijab was worn tight, obscuring her hair but for one strand that had escaped and was flowing recklessly down her cheek. Her eyes seemed to take up most of her face and filled the room. Again his guidebook had been incorrect. He had been told unequivocally that though there were plenty of women doctors in the Kingdom, they wore abayas, and rarely if ever treated men. Only in circumstances of emergency, life and death, when no male doctors were near. Maybe, he thought, her presence proved he was dying.

—You have a growth of some kind on your back?

—It's on my neck, really. I'm not sure if...

As he spoke she drew close, swept behind him, and her hands were upon him before he finished his sentence. She encircled his wound with her fingers. His composure fell off a cliff.

—Ouch, she said. Did you do something to it?

Her accent was not exactly Saudi. It seemed to intermingle a half dozen others, from French to Russian.

He chose not to lie. —I did a bit of investigating.

—With what?

—A knife.

—Was this an attempt on your life?

Alan laughed. He couldn't tell if she was kidding him.

—No, he said.

—Are you taking any medications? Prozac or—

—I'm not depressed. I was curious. I was just trying to see if—

—It looks like it was a serrated blade.

—It was.

—Did you sterilize it?

—I tried to.

—Hm. You have a minor infection.

She backed up to look him in the eyes. Her face was heart shaped, her chin small, her lips luxurious and pink. He felt wrong looking at her. He wanted too much from her.

—Well, it's just a lipoma, probably.

—And that's not bad?

He stared at her name tag: Dr. Zahra Hakem.

—No, it's just a growth. Like a cyst.

—And it's…

—Benign.

—You're sure?

Now looking at her hands, small and with short, bitten fingernails, he asked about its proximity to his spine, the likelihood that it had caused his clumsiness, his slowness, his lack of energy, every other malady and weakness he'd felt.

—No. I see no connection to any of those things.

—I just want to be sure. It would explain some things.

He listed his ailments, his many scattered worries.

—And your feeling is that this bump is the cause of it all?

She was looking at him, studying, smiling warmly.

—Is that unlikely?

—I would say it's unlikely.

—I just need someone to say there's nothing wrong with me.

—There's nothing wrong with you.

—But you haven't been in there yet.

—No, but I know what it is.

As if to honor his concern, she took another look at the bump, prodding it, seeming to measure it with her fingers.

—It really couldn't be anything but a lipoma.

—Okay, he said.

She came around in front of him and sat down. She looked at him directly, her eyes open and studying him.

—This really has you worried, huh?

He cleared his throat. There was suddenly something stuck.

—I'm worried about a lot of things, he said.

She stood and wrote a few notes in her chart.

Alan had the sudden thought, which hadn't surfaced before but which must have been there all along: if the bump was cancer, and he was dying, he would not have to worry anymore. Bankruptcy would not be a concern. Kit's tuition and future would not be a concern. Surely they waive the tuition when fathers die.

Dr. Hakem retrieved some supplies from a drawer and returned to his neck. She was behind him, and he inhaled deeply. He hoped for an airy, sunny scent, but hers was something else. He couldn't place it. He thought of trees, earth. It was musky, rich. He thought of a forest after rain, a hint of wildflowers.

—I had the same thing a few years ago, she said. A tightening in my chest. Like a panic, a heart attack kind of sensation. And I was sure when I got an EKG and all that I would find out that I had a murmur, or an irregular rhythm, something that would explain my fatigue and everything.

She put some ointment on a bandage, taped it to his neck, and returned to her stool in front of him.

—And? he asked.

—And it was nothing.

—That's too bad, Alan said, and they both laughed.

—We're stuck with our stupid good health, she said, and he laughed harder. But really, I can see why it would worry you. The placement of it would cause anyone some concern. So we'll remove it, and then we can be sure. How's that?

He was still looking at the wall. He didn't know if he should turn to face her. He glanced her way and found she was looking directly at him, her eyes steady, huge. They were brown, with spokes of green and grey and gold. Her age was hard to place. She could be anywhere between forty and fifty, maybe a bit older. Unable to sustain her gaze, he looked down. Her shoes were stylish, low-heeled and strapped. He turned again, focusing now on the wall, on a bundle of wires there, entwined like arteries, leaving the room and heading down the hall.

—I can do the surgery in about a week. Does that work?

Alan had hoped with great fervor to be gone from this country in a week, but he found himself agreeing. They made the appointment and she stood.

—I'll see you soon, Alan.

—Thank you.

—Don't worry.

—Okay.

—Nice to meet you.

—Nice to meet you, too.

Back in the lobby, Yousef paced like an expectant father. When he saw Alan, his eyes went wide.

—So what is it?

—Benign. It's nothing. Lipoma.

—It's not cancer.

—She doesn't think so.

Yousef shook Alan's hand. —I'm very glad.

—Me too.

—Abdullah's in Riyadh. Heard it on the radio.

Alan didn't know if he was relieved or not.

They left the building.

—And you had a woman doctor? Where was she from?

—I don't know.

—Saudi?

—I didn't ask.

—An Arab?

—I think so. I can't be sure.

—But probably an Arab?

—My guess would be yes.

Yousef thought this was fascinating. There were plenty of women doctors, he explained, but still, odds were against Alan running into one at first opportunity.

—Was she veiled?

—Just a hijab.

—She saw you alone?

—Yes, she did.

They reached the car, Yousef twirling his keys. He seemed pleased.

—Interesting. Interesting.

XXI.

INSIDE THE TENT, it looked like the young people had been gassed. They were splayed out in the middle of the tent, legs overlapping, arms drifting outward. It looked like Jonestown.

Alan rushed to them.

—Cayley? Rachel? Brad?

They slowly opened their eyes. They were alive.

—Air-conditioning stopped working, Rachel managed.

They rose slowly, groaning.

Brad checked his watch. —Been asleep about an hour. Sorry.

Cayley looked up, eyes glassy. —Wait. What happened to your neck?

Alan explained his trip to the hospital. He showed them the bandage, discussed the prognosis, and they seemed as hopeful as he was — that there might be some medical explanation for whatever was afflicting him.

—So you think after you get it removed, you'll be better? Cayley asked.

There was an uncomfortable pause.

—Signal was strong today, Rachel said, rescuing her. She opened her laptop but soon issued a disgusted scoff. Now there's nothing.

—Any chance of the King showing up today? Brad asked.

—Afraid not. He's in Riyadh, Alan said.

Brad fell back to the rugs. Rachel and Cayley followed. Alan stood over them for a few moments, as they all thought of things they could say to each other, and, mutually failing, said nothing.

Alan decided to let them sleep the day away. He stepped outside and looked around, having no particular notion of what he should do.

He walked down the promenade until it ended and met a dune. He turned to the water. He wanted badly to step onto the sand, but worried about the staff seeing him. There were those gauzy windows in the tent.

Farther down the beach, Alan saw a high mound of sand with an unmanned tractor, a bucket loader, next to it. If he could get past the mound, and disappear behind it, he could touch the water undetected.

He hustled down the shore, around the mound, and sat down in its shade. Once there, Alan peeked over the pile, confirming that he could not be seen by the white tent, by the Black Box, by anyone in the pink condominium. He was invisible to all but the fish in the sea.

Alan wondered, continually, about his own behavior. No sooner had he done something, something like hiding behind a hill of dirt by the Red Sea, when he would wonder, Who is this man who leaves the presentation tent to hide behind a hill of dirt?

He took off his shoes and scooted closer to the water. A light wind kicked up hairline ripples in the sea. The sand, just a shade from white, was messy with fragments of shells, as though someone had been dropping dishes for a hundred years.

The beach was narrow, and soon he could feel the light spray of the tiny waves on his instep. Alan rolled up his pant legs and dipped his feet into the water. It was as warm as the air above, but it cooled as it deepened. He stood now, careful not to show himself too much. Again he stepped outside his skin and doubted his sanity. It was one thing to wander the site. Another to make his way to the beach. But to take off his shoes, roll up his pants and wade in?

The sea ahead of him was unbroken by the mast of any sailboat, any vessel of any kind. This seemed a remarkably underused body of water, at least what he'd seen of it. In the eighty or so miles they'd driven to get here Alan hadn't seen much in the way of development. How could so much coastline go so little exploited? He thought about buying one of the properties here. He could buy one or even two, rent them out half the year and still come out ahead. He was in the middle of the calculations when he realized he was not the man who could do such things. He had nothing to spend.

He reached down into the water to examine a shell that appeared unbroken. It was whole, pristine, something like a scallop. He put it in his pocket. He found another, this one a cowrie, glassine, tan-colored and leopard-like, with dozens of white spots. He'd owned cowries before, and probably still had five or six in a box somewhere. But he'd never found one in the water like this. It was perfect, too — he turned it over and over and found it flawless, unscratched. Its teeth were smooth, variegated. There was no reason for it to be this beautiful.

When he was young he'd been a shell collector. Nothing serious, but he knew the names of some of the basic varieties. He'd had a book, the look and heft of which he could still recall, that listed all the world's most prized and valuable shells. There had been one shell, *Conus gloriamaris*, The Glory of the Sea, said to be worth thousands. He could picture it today, a long cone decorated with thousands of small half loops, obsessive and seeming hand-drawn. The shell had been incredibly rare. Legend had it that in 1792 a collector, owning one of the world's few specimens, bought another at auction, only to destroy it, making his first specimen more valuable. Alan used to pore over that book, and his mother, thinking the collecting, the memorization of figures, the obsession with risings and fallings of the market, was giving him a sharp mind for business, bought him other books, other shells, and he memorized the names, the seas where they were found.

He rolled his pants up to his knees, and, while bending over, he brought some water to his face. He licked his lips, tasted the salt.

When Kit was very young, they would sit on the beach, on the Cape, on the Maine shoreline, sometimes Newport. She in his lap, they would rake their hands through the rocks and sand, looking for sea glass and notable shells and sand dollars. They compared their findings, dropping the best into a jar they'd emptied of pennies and nickels. He missed her at that age. The size of her then, the weight of her when she sat in his lap. She was three and four years old then, when he could lift her, he could envelop her. He could hold her close, cover her completely when she cried, smell her matted hair, nuzzle her behind the ear. He nuzzled too much, he knew. He didn't stop when she was seven, when she was ten. Ruby would give him disapproving looks, but he couldn't stop. When she was fourteen he still wanted to bury his nose in her neck, smell her skin.

He thought of a letter he could write to Kit. He would tell her that her expectations for her mother were unfair. He wondered if Kit knew Ruby had given birth to her naturally, with no drugs, no epidural. Would that impress Kit? Probably not until she tried it herself.

'Kit, you say your mother hasn't changed, but she has. A hundred times she's changed. It's important to know that with adults, though there is continual development, there is not always improvement. There is change, but not necessarily growth.'

This was not likely to be helpful. Maybe he was wrong. Ruby had not changed much at all. She had always been impossible. Too strong and too smart and too cruel and, all the while, too restless to be satisfied with a man who sold bicycles. And everything after their first meeting was a disappointment.

He had been in São Paulo for business. This was with Schwinn. The idea was to open a factory there, roll out a half dozen models, sell them to South America, avoid the tariffs. But the trip had been a bust. The local contact was a lunatic, a thief. He'd thought they would pay him up front some astronomical fee, and Alan was sure he'd disappear the second he cashed the check. So he called Chicago, told them they were starting from scratch down there. They shrugged and shelved the whole thing. But Alan's flight home wasn't for another eight days.

He could have just left. But Alan hadn't had a vacation in two years, and Schwinn had counted on him being gone a week or more anyway, so he went back to the hotel, saw a sign in the lobby for a riverboat trip down the Rio Negro, and signed up. He went up to his room and spent the rest of the night on the balcony, watching the traffic on the road and the sidewalks, the children in their school uniforms out on the streets until eleven o'clock. For an hour he had watched one girl, no more than eight and lean as a country cat, wandering safe and alone with a stroller full of white roses. She sold not one.

In the morning, he took a quick flight to Manaus, the mouth of the river, and his first glimpse of it didn't distinguish it much from the lower Mississippi, or really any river. It was wide, it was brown. He had signed up for the trip expecting dense and canopied jungle, and a narrow river winding through, monkeys visible from the water, crocodiles and piranhas snapping, pink dolphins leaping. But instead he arrived on the riverside, walked across acres of mud on a makeshift bridgeway built from pallets, and was soon on an old wooden paddleboat, three stories, looking as likely to float as an old clapboard church.

The days were simple and glorious for their simplicity. The passengers woke with the sun, dozed for an hour, and then spent another puttering however they liked, on the decks, looking dully at the passing scenery, chatting idly, playing cards, writing in journals, reading about the topiary. At eight or so, breakfast was served, always something fresh — eggs, plantains, melon, fresh breads, juice from oranges and mangos. After breakfast was another free block of time, and at ten or eleven, the boat would have reached a port of interest. One day it was an ancient village of thatched huts elevated above the floodplain, another day it was a hike through the forest, looking for snakes and lizards and spiders.

On the boat Alan slept more than he thought possible. The higher oxygen content to the air, the crew members said. Northerners slept a lot the first few days, they said. He found himself asleep everywhere — in his cabin, on the second deck, in his chair, everywhere. And always the sleep felt as good as any he'd ever known.

There were twelve herpetologists aboard, most of them over sixty, and Alan, and a young woman his age. This was Ruby. She was tall and lean, tightly coiled, short dark hair. The crew were all in love with her, and though they were all married, they made overtures toward her, and she carved them up. —Your poor wife, she said to the one of them, a married Peruvian, when he took her hand during dinner. You don't deserve her, Ruby continued, whoever she is, *wherever* she is.

Alan had stayed close to her after that, just to listen to her talk.

After the day's excursion, the boat would take off again, slowly down the river, and the afternoon would stretch out without a plan or obligation. Dinner was always spectacular, washed down with beer. After dinner, they sat on the deck playing cards or dominoes and hearing stories from Randy, the captain with two wives, and Ricardo, the assistant captain with many wives more. Later, the group would disperse to their cabins and Alan would sit on the top deck, almost invariably alone. From there he could see the broad unimaginable dome of the sky, the treetops passing left and right, the click and whir of birds and hidden monkeys.

Alan had not counted on any kind of romance on that boat, but he found himself sitting near Ruby at meals, and then walking with her during the hikes, and soon they were friends, some kind of pair. It might have been as simple as the two of them being the same age on a boat full of older people. And was he the only one willing to listen to her talk for hours a day? Something about the river air, the wide open sky, had her pontificating, she laughed. —Are you okay with listening to me babble? she asked, and he said he was, he was.

They walked through the jungle and she talked about the work she wanted to do, which sounded like saving the world.

—No, no! she said. That's the opposite of what I mean. That's what the flakes do and say. I'm talking about something far more serious.

She raged about people of great skill and empathy wasting their time on sideshows, on minor issues, trivial matters. She had a thing about animal rights. It wasn't so much the pandas and whales that bothered her, but the cat-spaying people, the hamster-saving people.

—Fine, fine, treat them well, she fumed, meaning the animals. But all the money, all the lawyers and ad campaigns and protests for bunnies and rats in laboratories! If you could channel all that energy toward saving the lives of the world's underfed!

Alan would nod. He didn't know that there was a zero-sum equation at play. But this was exactly her point. The energy expended on nonessential issues was what was holding back any progress on the most pressing problems. Alan was in awe of her brilliance and energy, if not her anger. She was exasperated by the persistence of global crises that seemed to her imminently solvable. She wrote letters to senators, to governors, to people of influence at the IMF. She insisted he read each one, while she sat across the room, her look positively postcoital. She thought, each time, that she'd written the Magna Carta. Afterward, his job was to tell her that Senator Y or Z would be insane not to see the logic in her reasoning, all while trying to temper her expectations.

But this was impossible. There was no middle ground in what she wanted for the world, for herself, for a husband.

A machine roared alive. Alan turned to see a man in a small bulldozer. There were two other men nearby. They were about to start work on the nearby portion of the promenade.

Alan imagined some future legend among the workers at KAEC, the strange story of the American man, dressed for business but wandering aimlessly around the beach, hiding behind mounds of dirt and in the empty foundations of buildings. This had happened to him before — in an effort to disappear, he had made himself more conspicuous.

He walked back to the tent and found the young people sleeping in the plastic darkness. He rolled one of the rugs up and rested his head.

He was alone atop the riverboat. It was just before midnight, under the most star-choked of skies, as the boat pushed quietly through a narrow tributary, the wind hot and the fires far off. Ruby was standing at the railing in a threadbare yellow shirt, and Alan walked up behind her. Before he even reached her, though, she leaned back into him. He wrapped his arms across her chest and she turned quickly to him, and he fell into her, her mouth tasting of beer. They found their way to her cabin and spent much of the remaining days there.

They were married in a breathless hurry, but Alan felt early on that she was looking through him. Who was he? He sold bicycles. They were mismatched. He was limited. He tried to rise to her level, to broaden his mind and see things as she did, but he was working with crude tools. The saving element of his work was the travel, the various trips for Schwinn to new markets, and Ruby valued these greatly. In those early trips to Taiwan, to Japan, to China and Hungary, Ruby came along, and she was wonderful. She was charming as hell, radiant. She saw everything, met everyone. She was a dazzling guest, the most headstrong and intellectually curious and vivacious American any of them had ever known.

But she was embarrassed about Alan. He didn't know half the people she talked about — dissidents and philosophers and leaders-in-exile. He would try to find an industrialist at the table, one of the husbands who knew unit costs and ship dates and not much about the potential for civil society in Sri Lanka. Sometimes he was lucky and they would hide together from the light of the idealists at war over the details of unworkable plans and unfundable mandates.

Her ideal mate, Alan knew then, would have been a Kennedy, a Rockefeller. Maybe Aristotle Onassis or George Soros. She needed a wealthy patron who had political influence, who could pull back the curtain of power and show her the levers and knobs. Who could fund her plans. When she was frustrated, when she saw him as sand in her gears, she got mean.

—There's no such thing as "The One," she once said. They were at dinner in Taipei, with a supplier and his wife. The couple had been married forty years. The idea that there's just one person in the world you're meant to be with, it's illogical, she said. She'd had a few drinks and was enjoying her own loud thoughts. The math just doesn't work! Who you end up with, it's really just an accident of proximity.

Alan opened his eyes in the tent by the sea. The young people were asleep. They thought he was a nothing, an irrelevant man. Did they know he had swum in the Rio Negro with crocodiles? That he had almost been torn asunder one morning, with his constantly cruel ex-wife the only person who fought for him then or any other day?

Alan had seen some of the crew members jump into the river occasionally, and that had prompted some discussion about crocodiles, and there had been lectures then and after about how rare attacks were, how they had no interest in human flesh unless the water was very low, unless there were extraordinary conditions and their usual food sources were scarce or gone.

So while the boat was docked at the village, a handful of the passengers were lured in, and swam without worry. It's fine, they said. They stood in the shallows, and village children splashed nearby, everyone in the river and no one being devoured by giant reptiles. There didn't seem to even be any in that part of the river, until a few minutes later, when there was a commotion from the other side of the boat. A crew member had been fishing, and had just caught a baby crocodile, the size of a shoe.

Alan and Ruby rushed over to look at it, and indeed it looked every bit like the ones he'd seen in books. It had an unbelievable underbite and looked apoplectic.

He had no intention of swimming. But to see it there, flopping on the deck, knowing that it had coexisted so closely to the passengers and children in the shallows, proved to Ruby that there was no danger, so she jumped in, splashed about, and tried to entice Alan in, too. He declined, and afterward, she stood with him on the deck, a towel around her shoulders, leaning into him.

—You should do it, she said.

And that's all he needed. He decided to go further, though, and found a rowboat on the boat, and put it on the river and himself in it. He figured he would row deeper into the river, and jump from the boat into the deep.

The rowboat was very small, more like a kayak in how low to the surface it was. He was rowing, his feet straight in front, and this seemed normal enough. But there was soon a crowd, the entire crew, watching him from the deck below Ruby's, and they seemed very amused by his progress. So Ruby began watching with interest, and soon saw what was amusing them. The boat Alan had chosen wasn't seaworthy, was full of holes, and it was sinking. The crew's laughter increased as they watched him slowly sinking into the river, and once Alan noticed he was sinking, they laughed even louder watching how quickly he began trying to turn the boat around, to row back to the main boat before he sunk completely.

Alan had been told of the utter lack of danger from the crocodiles, that they would only strike something human if they were starving and the water level was very low, but still, there were anomalies to any animal-human détente — every week some zookeeper's assistant lost an arm in the jaws of a tiger, elephants crushed their trainers underfoot — and here was Alan, sinking into the Rio Negro, about thirty yards from the boat, far enough away to ensure that if something went wrong, if the crocodiles deemed him food, no one from the boat would reach him in time.

Alan was trying not to seem panicked, trying to remember how unlikely, impossible really, any attack would be, but then again: What if? When he was about twenty yards away, the water crested the rowboat and swept in with alarming speed. His forward motion ceased, most of the boat quickly disappeared into the rusty water, and soon he was sinking in place, into the river, overrun as it was by crocodiles and whatever else.

He wanted badly to swim back to the boat, and quickly, but feared that the splashing would attract teeth to his flailing limbs. At the same time, he wanted to bring the canoe back to the boat, for it had been his idea to go for a row-around, a wonderfully stupid idea, he now knew. He didn't want to let the rowboat, which he was holding between his legs now, sink to the bottom. And meanwhile he knew the dangling of his legs was probably being observed with great interest by the river's flesh-eaters. And still the faces were laughing. There were even those among the faces that had become bored. They turned away from him.

Alan had a moment where he looked at the riverboat, thinking, Well, this really might be it. This could be the last thing I ever see. It's a pretty boat, and on top of it, lovely Ruby, leaning over and now suddenly screaming.

—HELP HIM!

She was practically jumping in. She was bent over the top rail, trying to get the attention of the crew on the deck below.

—FUCKING HELP HIM YOU FUCKING ASSHOLES! Ruby yelled again, and repeated this and other versions of the directive until, a minute later, three of the crewmembers were in a rowboat and were upon Alan and towed him in.

XXII.

WHEN ALAN REACHED his room at the Hilton, his phone's red light was blinking. There was a message from Hanne.

—Call me, she said.

He did, and she picked up on the first ring.

—What are you doing tonight? she asked.

Alan thought of his room, the desperate adventures to be had here. The bed, the mirror, the moonshine.

—Nothing, he said.

—Come over to my house. I'll make something.

—Can I do that?

—Where I live, they don't care.

—You don't have to cook. I can take you out for dinner.

—No, no. It's more fun to eat at my house. Easier, too.

He called Yousef. He got his voicemail.

—Call me. I'm heading to the home of a ladyfriend and need a ride.

Yousef would love that. Alan expected a return call any second, but after thirty minutes, nothing. Yousef had never been unavailable before. A dull worry rose up in Alan. Alan texted him and got nothing in return.

Alan had the concierge arrange a different driver, bought some flowers in the hotel lobby, and in an hour he was outside Hanne's gate.

He rang the bell. He saw a shadow moving through an upper floor.

The door opened and there she was. She wore a sleeveless silk blouse and black pants. She was sleek, composed, her face aglow.

—Some flowers, he said.

—I see, she said.

The house was not unlike her office — it looked as if she'd moved in hours before. There couldn't have been more than five pieces of furniture. A couch, a table, a few stiff wooden chairs. They walked past the kitchen, where a pot was simmering.

—I made a stew, she said.

Alan told her it smelled good, though he couldn't smell much of anything beyond new paint.

—I have some wine. You'll partake?

Hanne was holding a thermos and a child's water glass bearing the image of a pair of cartoon fish. Alan smiled and she poured a pinkish liquid until the glass was half full.

—A friend here in the compound started making it recently. He's South African. They're the wine specialists.

Alan tasted it and winced. It was somehow both weak and bitter.

—That good, eh?

—No, it is. Thank you, he said, and drank a third of it in one pull.

—I got you more siddiqi, she said, and pushed another olive oil bottle across the counter.

—I can't tell you how grateful I am, he said.

She laughed. —People drink more here than Finland.

She walked to the living room.

—Come and sit. It's been a while since anyone's visited this place.

They sat on the couch, occupying the ends.

—It must be strange here, he said.

—It is *so* strange. But it's so quiet that most of the time I love it. The utter lack of social responsibility. You have no familial responsibilities, no real friend responsibilities. I'm lucky to have one guest a month. It's monastic, which is a relief.

Alan nodded. He knew. —And then there are the embassy parties, he said.

She lit a cigarette. —There are those. Did I embarrass myself?

—Not at all, he said. Everyone was doing crazy stuff.

Maybe that would do it, he thought, put her attempt somewhere in the realm of loony, something that no sane person would believe.

At that, a light in her eyes seemed to go out.

But just as soon, she recovered, forcing a smile.

—So I have news about the King for you. He'll be in Bahrain next week. So you're free.

—Oh, he said, unable to hide his disappointment. This wasn't the kind of freedom Alan sought. He wanted to be free to give his presentation, to get confirmation of the deal, to pack and go home. He wanted to be free to leave the Kingdom of Saudi Arabia.

Hanne set the food out on plastic placemats, and soon she knew all the salient facts about him and he her. He had guessed she was divorced, and she was, but he had been wrong about her having kids. She had none, and that had been the agreement between her and her ex when they'd married. Hanne wanted none, and he wanted none. But then, five years in, he did. So they argued and drifted and soon he impregnated another. They were still married at the time.

The whole thing was very simple from then on, she said. She let McKinsey know she was up for far-flung assignments, and a few months later, she was in Seoul. Then Arusha. Then Jeddah and KAEC.

Soon dinner was done and the plates cleared and when Alan expected her to invite him back to the couch, or to lead him to the door with a yawn, she said, —You want to take a bath?

—A what?

—A bath. Just a thought I had.

—Both of us, you mean.

She laughed, dismissing it. —Just something that popped into my mind.

But then she wasn't ready to abandon the thought.

—We can pretend it's a hot tub.

He thought about this, but not soundly. He thought only that he would rather extend the night with her, however bizarrely, than be alone.

—Why not, he said.

—Good! she said brightly, and took a few quick steps to the bathroom. The thunder of water into tub began. As it filled, she returned to the couch, picked up her drink and finished it.

—You plan to do any snorkeling, scuba, anything like that?

He said he hadn't thought about it.

—It's very good here. Very few people do it, so it's unspoiled. I went a few weeks ago just off the KAEC beach. I wore a bikini, actually, but I shouldn't have. After an hour a coast guard boat arrived. It was *haram* to be out there with so little on.

—So you were arrested, or...?

—No, they just told me that I needed to give them some warning next time. They're very accommodating around Jeddah, you know, to Westerners. They look the other way in most cases, but they want to know where you're doing whatever you're doing. Mostly so they can be assured that other people don't *see* you doing whatever you're doing. Want more?

She poured more wine and then went to check the state of the tub.

—Looks ready.

And so they were naked, facing each other, neither of them with any idea of what to do next. She had undressed first, stepping gingerly into the bath, seeming not at all familiar with it. He watched her, thinking she was lovely, her shape generous, her skin pale, freckled, her back sunburned. He waited until she was occupied with some candles behind her head, and then rushed in before she could see the whole of him.

Soon they were sitting, their knees up, their wine in hand. Now he wanted much more than he had in his cup.

—Do you take a lot of baths? Alan managed.

—Not really, she said.

Hanne had tried to use dishwasher soap to create some bubbles, but the result was anemic and soon disappeared.

—Too hot? she asked.

—It's good, he said, and meant it. He appreciated her, and admired her courage, and was fine with this whole situation, sitting in a comfortable tub with a new friend. But then again, he thought, What the fuck was he doing in this woman's bathtub?

The problem was one of giving offense. He didn't want to give offense, so he too often said yes to invitations like this. He had found himself at weddings, at christenings, with women who considered him more than a friend while insisting otherwise. He was an idiot.

There really must be something in that growth on his neck, he thought. The growth was too close to his spinal cord, and had altered the passage of signals from his brain to the rest of him. It would explain his inability to read all human signals.

She was now soaping his knee, softly, as if polishing a banister. He smiled at her. She frowned.

—I excite you that much, she said.

He wasn't aroused, and he knew it was a matter of time before she felt insulted. If he hadn't gotten into the tub in the first place he'd have been far better off. Then there would be no question of erections, how they reflected on this naked, affable Danish woman opposite him.

—No, no, he said. You're gorgeous.

—Would you take offense if I tried?

She reached for his penis.

—I wouldn't take offense, but I'd prefer if you didn't.

She dropped her hands and collapsed on her side of the tub.

He tried to explain it to her, the ease of his life without, about the simple purity he felt, how life was altogether more streamlined now. Her face was twisted into a mask of horror.

—Why would you want that kind of simplicity?

—So says the woman who left Europe altogether.

—I didn't leave all of hu*man*ity.

—I haven't, either. I'm in a tub with you.

—But you live with these barriers. So many rules.

—One rule.

They sat in the quiet water for a moment.

—This is very frustrating to me, she said. I can't place why.

Alan knew why. She'd thought she was doing him a favor tonight. And the other night. He wasn't the most handsome man in the world, and she'd figured he was an easy catch. But now that he was not within reach, she was annoyed. He did not say any of this.

All he said was, —This has happened to me before.

She sat silent for a few seconds, then let out a short scream. It was more comic than primal, and seemed to bring her back to good humor.

—Then why come to dinner? she asked.

—Because I like you. Because we're in the middle of nowhere.

—Because you're lonely.

—That too.

—I think you're absolutely hollow.

—I told you that myself.

—Maybe not hollow. More like defeated.

Alan shrugged.

—What made you that way? There's no light in there. She leaned over to tap his temple with her finger. Her breasts rested, briefly, on his knee, and he felt a stir within.

Alan had been pondering the same question for the better part of a decade. After the divorce he'd been angry for years, but at the same time he was alive. He'd laughed, he'd dated, he'd enjoyed the things he was expected to enjoy. But now he was something else. He stood in the same spot where he once would have taken great pleasure with something — a cousin singing an Irish folksong at a bar, a friend's young daughter demonstrating some trick on her scooter — and he smiled in a way that he hoped would be seen as warm. But he felt no warmth. He wanted only to go home. He wanted to be alone. He wanted to watch his Red Sox DVDs while drinking Hanne's moonshine.

—There are those who would theorize that you haven't gotten past your ex-wife. That you're frozen in stasis.

Alan was uninterested in theories, and he told Hanne so.

—Will you touch me at least? she asked.

Alan looked at Hanne, whose eyes were steady.

—Sure, he said.

She stood up in the tub, turned around, and sat down again, her back to his front. She leaned into him, her weight feeling not unlike a dentist's lead bib. His hand dropped between her wet legs, her fingers guiding his.

—Can you reach? she asked.

—Not quite, he said.

She inched up.

—That better?

—Yup.

She leaned back again.

He pinched her clitoris. A quick intake of breath. Then a moan. He had just begun but her noise grew louder. Her sounds were beautiful and guttural and strange, and again he felt stirred. He wondered if he would find arousal. He felt a twinge, but the moment passed.

She directed his fingers in a circle. Then in a figure eight. Her eyes closed, and he knew she was far away, in a teenage bedroom or a beach, and in her mind he was someone else — a stronger, younger man. A vital man, an available man. He continued to circle and pinch and oscillate. Her breath grew erratic and loud and her body grew heavier against him.

He had just read some magazine full of futurists' predictions, which had included the certainty that soon we would have computers in our contact lenses and would be able to access all the world's information with our eyes alone. That we would engineer better organs, that nanotechnology would allow us to create cancer-killing agents within our bodies, that we would live to two hundred. People worried about our passing over into some robotic state, but we were so much like robots already, programmed and easy to manipulate. We had buttons, we had circuits, and it could all be mapped and explained, reprogrammed and calibrated. The utter mechanical simplicity of being able to move this oddity, the clitoris, up and down and around, to provoke the greatest pleasure, seemed laughably easy. And so we did it, because it created happiness of some kind. We push the buttons that provide the rewards.

Again the greatest use of a human was to be useful. Not to consume, not to watch, but to do something for someone else that improved their life, even for a few minutes.

—Now faster, she hissed, her accent suddenly more pronounced.

He moved faster. He strummed and circled, and her breathing grew more labored. Her hand gripped his, her other hand grabbed her nipples, one and then the other. His strokes grew longer and she nearly screamed. Years ago, he had had some skill in this. Ruby's mad orgasms, the way she shook her head back and forth, a blur of defiant *No*s, her hair flagellating him with each furious turn of her head.

Soon Hanne was bucking, a series of *Yes*es, *Faster*s. The water over-topped the tub. Her back arched and she was there and then was done.

She turned to him, touched his cheek, his lips. She looked in his eyes, feverishly, for some sign that she had broken through, that she had changed him. Not finding it, she turned back again, her face to the tiled wall. She pressed her back against him and laughed. There would be a time when the world created people stronger than them. When all of this got worked out. But until then there would be women and men like Hanne and Alan, who were imperfect and had no path toward perfection.

XXIII.

IT WAS THE SAUDI weekend and such an unstructured expanse was not good for Alan. There was too much time and nothing to do. He watched TV for most of the morning and then went to the gym. He sat on three machines, pushing and pulling, feeling numb, and was back in his room within thirty minutes. The afternoon arrived before he'd had a meal, so he ordered an omelet and grapefruit. He ate on the bright balcony, watching the tiny men fish at the pier far below.

Inside, Alan checked his voicemail, dropping another $100 to learn that Jim Wong, to whom he owed $45k, was consulting with a lawyer.

—Just a precaution, Jim said. I know you're good for it, but I just want to know my options.

That was the first message. The second was worse.

Kit had decided to spend the fall working at a food co-op in Jamaica Plain. She didn't even want to go back to school now, she said.

Like hell, Alan thought.

Annette, Charlie Fallon's widow, left a message, asking for copies of any letters Alan might have received from him. How could he tell her he'd thrown them away? *I thought the man was losing his mind,* Alan could tell her. No, he would not tell her that.

He checked his email and found that the young people from Reliant had gone to Riyadh. *Hope that's okay with you!!!* Rachel wrote in her message. *We wanted to take a look around this crazy place!!* Brad wrote in his.

Soon enough Alan looked at the clock and it gave him good news: it was six, and it was okay to open his siddiqi. Hanne had replenished his supply, and he thought fondly of her as he retrieved a new glass from the bathroom and poured the first inch.

He sipped, and the concoction went down easily. Days earlier it had tasted acrid, offensive, but now it was almost smooth, whispering kindly to him, *my friend, my friend,* as he finished the first dose.

He stood and found that already his head was lighter, his limbs heavier. This was stronger than the last batch. Hanne had warned him as they said goodbye, his hair still wet, on her porch.

—See you around campus, she'd said.

Alan poured another splash and took it to the bathroom. He downed half the glass and took off the bandage Dr. Hakem had applied. The wound felt raw, inflamed, and he had the sudden realization that the doctor was probably wrong. They were often wrong about such things, weren't they? A doctor would look at a freckle, a bump, and say it was nothing, but then it would fester and grow and darken, and death and lawsuits would ensue.

Alan finished the siddiqi and poured himself another. It was this second glass that always felt best. This was takeoff. This was weight-lessness. Now things were moving. Now things were happening. He went back to the balcony, feeling tipsy, feeling wonderful.

Charlie Fallon was cracking up, Alan had been sure of it. Putting transcendental pages in his mailbox? It was the work of a nut. All of it, the letters and clippings, the copies, were about God, oneness with nature. That was the stuff Charlie was moved by. Grandeur, grandeur — that was the word he liked. Grandeur and awe and holiness, communion, communion with the outside world. 'Alan, all the answers are in the air, the trees, the water!' he'd written in the margins of this or that Brook Farm manifesto. And then he'd walked into a freezing lake and let it kill him. Was that his idea of communion, his idea of oneness?

Charlie had two daughters, Fiona and the other one; Alan couldn't conjure the name. They were both older than Kit, too old to have played together. Their hair was straight, their eyes wide-set, and each held her head out in front, low, like a hat hung on a hook.

There had been that one time with Fiona, that strange fire in the tree. That afternoon was dark, a light rain accompanied by small but hysterical winds. Alan was driving home early when he saw Fiona standing on the street, looking up. She was about sixteen then. He stopped his car and rolled down the window.

—You're brave to be out here, he said. She had her cellphone in her hand, its face pointing skyward. You doing some kind of science experiment?

She smiled. —Hi Mr. Clay. That tree's on fire, she said, pointing to a tall oak across the street.

Alan got out of his car and saw a very small fire flickering in the nook of the tree, about twenty feet up. The fire was the size of a squirrel and was similarly situated.

—Electric pole went down, she said.

Beside the tree, the pole had been cracked in half. In the process a cable had been severed, left naked, and a spark had ignited a small pile of dead leaves.

She had already called the fire department, so the two of them just stood, watching the fire glow white with each small gust of wind.

A faint siren. Help was on its way.

—Well, that's that, she said. See you later, Mr. Clay.

They were both adults now, Fiona and the other one. Where were they? Alan had seen them at the funeral, looking much the same, looking too young. But they were old enough. They'd had a father, he'd held out long enough. *Fatherhood kills fathers.* Someone said it in jest once, during a round of golf. But he did enough, Charlie had. That's all that matters. They had a father, they'd grown up strong, and now he was gone. It all seemed fair enough. Or maybe not.

A nice man, a sweet man, a frozen man on the muddy banks of a lake, surrounded by people in uniforms attempting to revive him.

Alan went inside and got out a piece of paper.

'Kit, Live long enough and you'll disappoint everyone. People think you're able to help them and usually you can't. And so it becomes a process of choosing the one or two people you try hardest not to disappoint. The person in my life I am determined not to disappoint is you.'

No, no. Stupid. Shit. He downed another inch of moonshine and started again.

'Kit. When I traveled a lot, sometimes I would get home after you had gone to bed, and I knew I would be gone in the morning before you were awake. This was when you were about three. We were in Greenville, Mississippi. You loved it there for a while. We had a big spread. Ten acres. Your mother hated it. My God she hated Mississippi. But I would come home late. The factory was a mess. The workers had no idea what they were doing. We'd moved all of Schwinn down there and it was a disaster. You were still in diapers, though maybe you shouldn't have been. But there would be times when you'd wake up, wet, and I would get up to change you. I would make sure your mother allowed me to, and I would change you, and though I didn't want you to wake up, to startle, I hoped you would open your eyes long enough to know it was me. I wasn't around enough then, and I wanted you to see me. *Just open your eyes*, I would think. *Just enough to know it's me.* This is what I would think. *Just open your eyes long enough to know it's me.*

No, no. Probably unhelpful. All of it. But that's enough for tonight, Alan thought, and rewarded himself with a long pull.

Soon he was content, so content with siddiqi's glow. *Grandeur*, he thought. *This is grandeur.* He arranged himself on the bed, found an old Red Sox game on cable, and was out cold by nine.

In the morning, he finally got Yousef on the phone and asked if he wanted to come for a meal. No, can't, Yousef said. Not for a while. He was hiding in a cousin's house, afraid to leave. The texts from the husband and his henchmen had hit a new level of menace.

Alan ate his lunch in the hotel restaurant, reading the *Arab News* and watching a group of businessmen, European and Saudi, at the table across the way. He heard a loud trilling laugh and looked around. A pair of women, Western, were talking to the concierge. They were wearing scarves on their heads but the rest of their clothing was uncompromising — tight pants and high heels. Their voices were too loud, bursts of cackling laughter. They were asking about beaches.

In the afternoon he went to the gym and spent an hour there, pretending at various machines, and rewarded himself with a tri-tip and the rest of the moonshine.

When he was feeling good, free of self-censor, he tried for coherence with Kit. He tried to address her concerns, her complaints, one by one. He typed madly away.

'Kit, in your letter you mention the thing with the dog.'

Kit was six. The three of them had just left church, and the woman was walking by, led by her dog, a beagle. Ruby asked if the dog was friendly, and the woman said yes, and right then the dog went straight for Kit's face and bit her chin. What the hell! Alan had yelled, within earshot of the priest, the congregation. He'd shooed away the dog, who was cowering, whimpering, as if it knew both his crime and his fate.

'There was blood soaking your mouth and your blue dress and you were screaming in front of hundreds of people. Yes, your mother said

"That dog will be dead by Wednesday." I was there. I heard it, too. And the dog was indeed put down that week. I know you think it was some sign of her coldness or sadism, but...'

Alan paused. He had another long pull.

There was a terrible, clinical precision to how she said it, wasn't there? But a dog lashes out like that, bites a girl, they put it to sleep. What was Ruby's crime? Being correct?

Alan recalled the venom of those words. *That dog will be dead by Wednesday.* To have the presence of mind! In the seconds after the bite, Alan was panicking, scrambling, wondering if he should run Kit the twelve blocks to the hospital, or call 911, or put her in the car and drive her there. But Ruby was already sentencing the animal to death. That kind of calculation!

After the animal was dead, the owners sent a photo of the dog. Or dropped it off. An envelope in Alan and Ruby's mailbox, a photo of the dog inside, in happier times, wearing a bandanna around his neck.

But enough of the dog. He'd settled the matter of the dog. He poured some more, drank some more. Now there were just the matters of the DWI, the clearing of all of Kit's possessions while she was at school, the strange presence of Ruby's boyfriends at Kit's most delicate ceremonies, confirmation and graduation among them...

He was feeling good, despite the letters. He was feeling buoyant, flexible. He wanted to go jogging. He stood. He couldn't go jogging. He called room service and ordered a basket of breads and pastries. Wanting to be presentable for the waiter, he brushed his teeth and straightened his hair, and while in front of the mirror he had a notion. He would need a safety pin.

He looked through the room's drawers and found nothing. He looked in the closet and found a sewing kit. Even better.

The bread came and he signed for it, holding his breath. He did not want trouble with the muttawa. Alan had brushed his teeth, yes, but perhaps the waiter would know. Alan glanced at him as he set the tray on the bed, but the waiter's eyes seemed benign. He was not interested in Alan, and he left, and Alan closed the door behind him and felt spectacular. He lay on the bed and ate his pastries, looking at what he'd written thus far to Kit. It made no sense.

'I would not do what Charlie did, in case you're wondering,' he wrote, then crossed it out. Kit would not have thought such a thing in the first place. Stay focused, he thought.

'Oh God Kit I'm sorry for that time in Greenville. I was part of that stupid decision. We were getting squeezed by the unions in Chicago and we decided to move it all to Mississippi, where we wouldn't be bothered by any organizing. Oh hell what a mess. The bikes we made there were junk. We'd tossed out a hundred years of expertise. We thought it would be more efficient and it was the opposite. And I was gone all the time. I was already onto Taiwan and China. I missed a few years there. I didn't want to be in Taiwan, did I? But everyone else was. I missed a few of your important years there and I regret that. Goddamnit. More efficient without the unions, cut em out. More efficient without American workers, period, cut em out. Why didn't I see it coming? More efficient without me, too. Hell, Kit, we made it so efficient I became unnecessary. I made myself irrelevant.

'But your mother was there. Whatever she's done that has displeased you I want you to know that you are who you are because of your mother because of her strength. She knew when to be the tugboat. She coined that term, Kit. *The tugboat.* She was the steady, she navigated around the dangers lurking below. You think of me now as the steady, but did you know that all that time it was your mother?'

He knew as soon as he finished writing he wouldn't send any of this. He was a mess. But so why did he feel so strong?

He went to the mirror and found the needle. He had in mind the trick when baking cakes — insert the toothpick, see what sticks. If it comes out clean, the cake is ready.

He looked for a match. He had no matches. He was drunk and tired of looking for things. The needle seemed sterile enough. Turning back to the mirror, he held the lump between with his left hand and aimed the needle with his right. He knew what it would feel like; he'd punctured the skin before. But now he needed to go deeper, deep enough that whatever cancer was there would adhere to it. Of course it would. The foreign clings to the foreign.

It would be best to go fast, he thought to himself, and plunged the needle in. The pain was acute, white-hot. He felt like he would pass out. But he stood, and he pushed the needle further. He knew he needed an inch at least. He pushed and twisted and the pain, miraculously, diminished. It was dull now, throbbing everywhere, throbbing in his heart, his fingertips, and it all felt very good.

He removed the needle and stared at it, expecting something grey or green, the colors of debasement. But he only saw red, viscous red, as the blood poured down his back in tendrils as it had before.

He felt good, he felt satisfied, as he dabbed at the blood on his back and washed the needle clean. This is progress, he thought.

The next morning would be the start of the Saudi work week. He was still half-drunk but ready to get his act together. He called Jim Wong and told him to fuck off, that there was money coming imminently, and if he wanted it he needed to grow a pair and remember they were supposed to be friends. He did ten jumping jacks and called Eric Ingvall and told him that the King was coming next week and everything would be taken care of. Ingvall couldn't prove otherwise and Alan could always retract. And anyway, Ingvall could fuck himself with a fucking disease-ridden telephone pole. Alan was feeling strong. He did two push-ups and felt stronger still.

He re-applied the bandage, finished the moonshine and got into bed. *Grandeur*, he thought, and laughed to himself. He looked around the room, at the phone, the trays, the mirrors, the towels soaked in blood. This is grandeur, he said aloud, and felt very good about it all.

XXIV.

IN THE MORNING, feeling spry, Alan took the shuttle with the young people. The sun, hotter than any other day so far, screamed obscenities from above but Alan did not listen. He talked loudly to the young people and made plans. Today, he told them, he would get at least some semblance of a timeline. Some assurances, some respect. He would check about not just the wi-fi but the air-conditioning in the tent. He felt capable this day, and because he hadn't bothered anyone in the Black Box for a while, he could stride right in, make demands and ask questions, as many as he wished.

—Whoa Alan, where's all this bluster coming from? Rachel asked. Alan did not know.

He left the young people in the tent and strode to the Black Box.

—Hello, Maha said.
—Hello Maha. How are you? Is Karim al-Ahmad in today?

Alan heard himself speaking like a salesman from another era. His voice was loud, confident, almost overbearing.

Money! Romance! Self-Preservation! Recognition!

—No, I'm afraid not.

—And *will* he be in?

Maha seemed to look at him differently now. Now he was loud, vital, full of expectations. She appeared to cower before him.

—I don't think so, she said, meekly. He's in New York.

—He's in New York? Now Alan was almost yelling. Is Hanne in?

—Hanne?

Alan realized he didn't have her last name.

—Danish woman? Blond?

He meant it as a question but it came out like a command: *Blond!*

Maha lost her footing and said nothing.

Alan saw his opening.

—I'll just go upstairs to visit her.

What had just happened? The visit with Dr. Hakem had given him some strange power. He was a healthy man! He was a strong man! Soon he would have a simple operation and would then grow stronger still, and would conquer, conquer! Blond!

And so he walked into the building and toward the elevator. Maha did nothing to stop him. He felt like he could fly up to the third floor, but instead he took the elevator. Once inside, as if it were some kind of Kryptonite chamber, he returned to his previous self, the power draining from him.

When he arrived on Hanne's floor, he found her office and found it empty. He saw no sign of her having been there at all that day.

—Can I help you?

Alan spun, and found himself looking at a young man, no more than thirty, in a black suit and a violet tie.

—I was looking for Hanne.

He tried to sound like the man he'd been in the lobby, but couldn't find the register. —The Danish consultant!

There it was. Maybe it was just volume? One notch above civilized and you sounded like a president. Immediately the man's attitude changed. He straightened, adopted a more formal face. Volume was the difference between being treated like a nobody and being treated like a man who might be important.

—I'm afraid she's in Riyadh today. Can I help you?

—Alan extended his hand. Alan Clay. Reliant.

The man shook it. —Karim al-Ahmad.

The man he'd been chasing.

—You're not in New York, Alan said.

—No I am not, al-Ahmad said.

They stood for a moment. Al-Ahmad assessed him. Alan did not blink. Finally al-Ahmad's face softened into a glossy smile. —Should we have a chat, Mr. Clay?

The conference room had an unobstructed view of the entire development. The canal was visible, the welcome center and the water beyond. Al-Ahmad had apologized for the delay in their meeting and welcomed Alan to the conference room.

—Soda? Juice?

Alan accepted a glass of water, still trying to figure out why this unattainable man was in the building when the receptionist had claimed he was not. Your receptionist said you were out today.

—I'm sorry for that error. She's new.

—Were you here the last two days?

—I was not.

Alan stared at Karim al-Ahmad. He was young and handsome and overpolished, as if sculpted from chrome and glass. His teeth were blinding, his skin had no pores. To look as he did, so crisp and well-groomed, and to speak as he did, with that posh English accent, made it difficult to give him the benefit of the doubt. They modeled movie villains on men like this. As if knowing Alan's thoughts, al-Ahmad did something with his face just then, twisting it into an apologetic smile, making himself just a bit less handsome.

—It's not acceptable how you have been treated thus far.

Alan liked that. Not acceptable.

—I assure you no vendor is more important to us than Reliant.

Alan decided to take him at his word. —I'm glad to hear that. But we have some issues.

—I am here to solve them.

Al-Ahmad pulled out a leather-covered notebook and fountain pen, uncapped it, and readied himself. The theatricality of it was jarring, but Alan forged on.

—We can't set up our presentation out there.

—Why not?

—We need a hard line.

—I cannot do that.

—We need wi-fi at least.

—I will have it fixed. What else?

—The air-conditioning doesn't work. My staff is suffering.

—It will be addressed immediately. What else?

—How do we eat? We've been bringing food from the hotel.

—Starting tomorrow, you will have catered meals every day.

Alan was feeling immensely powerful. He had no clue if any of this would actually happen, but it was fun to pretend. He went for the most important question of all.

—How long will we wait for the King?

—I do not know that.

—Do you have a ballpark?

—A what?

—An estimate on the timeline?

—No, I don't.

Now al-Ahmad was putting away the notebook.

—Days?

—I do not know.

—Weeks?

—I do not know.

—Months?

—I hope not.

Alan had nowhere else to go. The man had given him what he asked for, and he hadn't expected him to know anything about the King anyway. He was resigned to the fact that no one here knew anything about King Abdullah's movements. Satisfied and eager to bring all this news back to the staff, he stood and extended his hand to al-Ahmad. As they shook hands, Alan saw a strange sight, far off in the canal below.

—Is that a yacht?

—It is. It arrived yesterday. Are you a sailor?

In minutes Alan and Karim al-Ahmad had been driven out to the canal and were being shown the workings of the vessel, a thirty-foot sport-fishing yacht, white and untouched. It had three miles on it. It was brand new.

—You've driven something like this? al-Ahmad asked.

The closest thing Alan had piloted was thirty years old and worth a few million less, but he wanted to try this thing out.

—Pretty much, he said.

—Excellent, al-Ahmad said.

The man taking care of the yacht, a wisp of a man named Mahmoud, had a brief Arabic conversation with al-Ahmad, during which, Alan surmised, al-Ahmad was convincing Mahmoud to allow Alan to pilot the yacht down the canal. It was the kind of privilege Alan was used to as an executive — or had become accustomed to back in the day. There were Aston Martins to test, there were prop planes to briefly take command of. But more than anything there was fishing. The Schwinn guys fostered a culture of fishing, on Lake Michigan and anywhere else. There were weekends up on Lake Geneva with the VPs, with a chosen few of the best retailers. Alan missed all that.

Al-Ahmad handed him the keys.

—I'm trusting you to captain us.

Alan put the key in the ignition and turned. The engine rumbled awake. Alan wondered what kind of speed or course would be prudent here, in a canal of unknown length. Did it extend to the sea at a depth where he could leave the city and motor onto the open water?

—As long as there are no hidden sandbars, we're fine, Alan said, and they both laughed, because the canal was as flat and clear as a swimming pool.

Alan pulled back on the throttle. They left the berth and were soon cruising down the turquoise waterway. There were no blemishes to any of it — not a dot of debris in the water, not a scratch on the floor.

The air, which had been stifling moments before, was now blessed by a wonderful wind, blowing back their hair. Alan turned to al-Ahmad, who was smiling widely, raising his eyebrows as if to say, *Did I set us up or what?* Alan loved the man, and loved the boat, and the canal, and this nascent city.

They passed the beginnings of more buildings on their right, and saw an overhead pedestrian bridge ahead. Al-Ahmad explained the plan for this part of the development.

—You lived in Chicago, right? he said.

It was to be a bit like that, he explained, a bit like Venice. Promenades on each side of the water, frequent berths, step-down restaurants, water taxis. It was an aesthetic thing, but an environmental choice, too. The air around Jeddah had a tendency toward smog, and there would be discharge from the plastics factories, so they were trying to reduce any and all emissions. People can kayak to work.

—Take a water-bike, hire a gondolier, anything, al-Ahmad said. Turn here.

The canal split off into a smaller tributary, Alan followed it, and soon saw the makings of the financial center, the place the American architect had been talking about at the embassy party. There wasn't much of anything there now, just an enormous disc of land in the middle of the water, but it was stunning nevertheless. Those glass towers, rising from and reflecting in this crystalline water.

Alan wanted to stay here. He wanted to watch the city grow, and he wanted to be a charter owner. Maybe in Marina Del Sol. What had they wanted for condos there? After this deal, he could afford it. And the deal, now, seemed well in hand. It was just a waiting game. Al-Ahmad liked him, and trusted him enough to allow him to pilot a gleaming white yacht through the pristine canals of the city. Alan was already part of the early history of this place. He circled the financial island twice, three times.

They were both happy men, men of vision. Alan felt, for the first time since he'd arrived, that he belonged.

Back at the tent, Alan burst through the door, finding two of the three young people awake and working on their laptops. Cayley was asleep in a corner. When he woke her and gathered them and gave them the news, they became, more or less instantly, the motivated and capable people Reliant had hired them to be.

Within the hour, the wi-fi was strong enough to work with. Al-Ahmad had kept his promise and proved to be, much to Alan's relief, a man who could get things done. Soon after, technicians were inside the tent, fixing the air-conditioning. By early afternoon, it was a cool sixty-eight degrees and the young people had set up all the equipment — the screens, the projectors, the speakers. They'd taped down the marks on the stage, had done a brief rehearsal.

By four o'clock they were ready to test the hologram. They got in touch with the London office, the closest Reliant outpost that had the capability to do it, and by five o'clock, just as the shuttle arrived, they had completed two full run-throughs of the twenty-minute holographic presentation. It worked fluidly. It was astounding. One of their colleagues in London appeared to be walking around the stage in their Red Sea tent, could react to live questions, could interact with Rachel or Cayley on the stage. It was the kind of technology that only Reliant had, only Reliant could deliver for a price. Making the prototype in the U.S. had been catastrophically expensive, but they'd found a supplier in Korea who could build the lenses to their specs, at about a fifth of the cost in America, even cheaper if they shopped it out to a Chinese factory. Reliant would make a robust profit on any unit, but more than that, the telepresence technology was part of an overall Reliant juggernaut of baseline telecom abilities, the ability to wire an entire city, and on the higher end, this kind of astonishment. Alan was utterly confident that the presentation, when Abdullah arrived, would seal the deal quickly.

When the second demo was finished, Alan instigated high-fives all around, and the young people laughed at his enthusiasm. But they laughed with a newfound respect for him. He was a new man, a vital man. They knew he had gotten the job done. He'd fixed what needed to be fixed, he'd paved the way for their success, he was again captain of the ship.

XXV.

THE NEXT FEW DAYS passed like clouds. But on Wednesday, when they arrived at the turnoff to KAEC, it was bedlam. For the first time since Alan had been passing through the gates, there was traffic. There were ten vehicles in front of the shuttle — SUVs and trucks carrying palm trees, and a cement mixer, and a string of taxis and vans. Everyone was honking.

In the tent, young people darted around, arranging chairs, taping down speakers, testing the microphones.

Rachel saw him first. —Is this really happening today?

Alan had no idea. —Looks like it, he said.

Brad looked up from the projector. —We'll be ready.

Along one side of the tent, a vast table had been erected, easily forty feet long, covered in a white tablecloth and bearing dozens of silver heating trays. The catering had already arrived, a mix of hot and cold foods, Saudi and Western, everything from fava beans to risotto to shawarma.

There was an array of white couches, a team of Pakistani workers arranging them in rows facing the stage.

Alan left the tent, running to the Black Box to see if he could get any clarity about the timing of the visit. He heard a helicopter, and looked up to see two of them, flying low, landing somewhere near the welcome center. He jogged to the front door.

Maha at the reception desk, who had been so unhelpful before, was now eager to talk. *Blond!* She told Alan that the King's people, if the King were to arrive that day, would send word twenty minutes beforehand. Otherwise Reliant should be ready immediately and all day.

Alan returned to the tent. Brad was on the stage, sitting cross-legged, typing furiously into his laptop. Rachel and Cayley were standing below, talking on their cellphones. Alan approached Brad.

—We ready?

—Two minutes.

In two minutes, just after Brad announced that they were ready to test the holographic presentation with their team in London, a man they hadn't seen before entered the tent. He was Saudi, tall and wearing a white thobe, carrying a leather attaché. He stood in the doorway, as if reluctant to invade their personal space, and raised his hands to get the attention of all those rushing around inside.

—Ladies and gentlemen, I am sorry to say that the King will not be here today. You have been misled. He informed them that there had been some miscommunication somewhere along the line. Someone in the King's communications department had given unauthorized and incorrect information to someone at Emaar, and the news had been wrongly and widely disseminated. The King's schedule for KAEC was still up in the air but for now he was, in fact, in Jordan, and would be for the next three days.

The mood among the young people, at least for a moment or two, was something like despair. Alan had the feeling, looking at Brad's deflation, that this was among the bigger disappointments of his life. Rachel and Cayley, after a short period of mourning, went back to their laptops, and seemed happy enough now that there were couches in the tent, and food, and a strong wi-fi signal, so they sat eating contentedly while Brad lay on the stage, between the various projectors, his legs akimbo, like a toy bear.

Alan went outside, where he saw the same sort of activity as earlier, only in reverse. The delivery trucks were leaving, the taxis and vans were gone, the place was shutting down.

He wandered around the grounds of the development, noticing various improvements they'd made that morning. There was suddenly a wide moat of flowers around the Black Box. The promenade now was crowded with palm trees — maybe a hundred more had been installed that day. Far off he could see the fountains around the welcome center, now shooting bright plumes of water high into the air.

Standing at the bottom of the steps to the Black Box, he spotted a black SUV emerging from the underground garage. It stopped next to him and the rear window dropped, revealing a blond head, a smiling face. It was Hanne.

—Thrills galore, she said.

—I guess so.

—Sorry for the false alarm.

—No need. Probably good that we practice.

—I'm going back to Jeddah. You need a ride?

Alan thought about it. There was no need for him to be on the site.
But he did not want to be alone with Hanne.

—I should stay with the team, he said.

—You okay?

—I am, he said.

She raised her eyebrows, some indication that she would pry if he
had given her reason to think it would be welcome. He said nothing
more, and with a wave she was gone.

Before he could move, he heard his name.

—Alan!

He looked up to to the Black Box. A familiar man was racing down
the steps. Alan couldn't immediately place him. The face came into
focus just in time. The man was upon him, extending his hand.

—Mujaddid. From the tour. Remember?

—Of course. Good to see you again, Mujaddid.

—A lot of excitement today, huh?

Alan agreed that it had been exciting.

—I've been looking for you, Mujaddid said. I happened to talk to
Karim al-Ahmad, and he let me know about your trip down the canals,
and how enthused you were about the development.

—I was very impressed. I *am* very impressed.

—Excellent. Well, as you know, I am in charge of private home sales,
and I hope it's not presumptuous of me to think you might be in the

market for a home here in the King Abdullah Economic City.

Before Alan could protest, Mujaddid had explained the various advantages of having a second home — he used the phrase *pied-à-terre* — here at KAEC, especially for a man like himself, who was likely to be spending some time here implementing the IT plan. Hearing what seemed to be the near certainty in Mujaddid's statement, the strong implication that Reliant's grip on the IT sale was unshakeable, gave Alan a burst of confidence. He agreed to a tour of the condominium.

—Were you aware that some of our people are already living here? Mujaddid wanted to know.

Alan had not been aware, but it explained the faces he had seen, occasionally, in the high windows.

They entered the building and Mujaddid stopped them in the vast foyer. The ceiling was thirty feet, a glass rotunda above.

—It is both grand and welcoming, don't you think? It was garish and daunting, but Alan nodded cheerfully.

—Now, as you may know, one floor of the building has been finished, and a number of the staff members are currently occupying the units. I'd like to show you their homes, so you can see the level of luxury and convenience available, even at this early stage of the dev—

Mujaddid paused, retrieved his phone and looked at its screen. Something alarmed him, so he answered it. A brief conversation in Arabic ensued, and when he was finished, he smiled apologetically.

—Would you excuse me for a moment? I have received some urgent news from the office, and they'd like me to run over there for a meeting. It's unavoidable, I'm afraid.

—No problem.

—I will return shortly.

Alan must have looked put out, and maybe he was, because he didn't want to be alone. Mujaddid conjured a new plan.

—Why don't you go up to the fifth floor yourself? Ring the doorbell at number 501. I will let the owner know you're coming, and he will show you the unit. Actually, that's best. He has lived here from the beginning and gives a better testimonial than I can. His name is Hasan.

Mujaddid apologized again and left.

Alan wandered the first floor, through the sites of the future Wolfgang Puck, the future Pizzeria Uno. The floor was covered in dust and sand. The only piece of furniture on the entire level was an enormous steel cooling rack, standing alone in the middle of the floor like the framing of a mobile and lonely skyscraper. He felt silly wandering around the empty building, but he couldn't be rude. He had to take the tour. It might be some kind of quid pro quo situation. He buys a condo, they give him the IT. At the very least, it was the friendly thing to do.

He walked to the end of the building, and there he found another stairway, dark and made of concrete. When he got to the third floor, he heard voices, close, just on the other side of the fire door. Had Mujaddid said the fifth floor when he meant the third?

Alan opened the fire door and a roar of echoes flooded through. He was in a large raw space full of men, some in their underclothes, some in red jumpsuits, all yelling. It looked like pictures he'd seen of prison gyms converted to dormitories. There were fifty bunks, clothes hanging on lines between them. The beds were empty, though — all the men were gathered in the center of the room, barking, pushing. Alan had interrupted some kind of fight. These were the workers Alan had seen around the site; Yousef had said they were Malaysian, Pakistani, Filipino.

Alan wanted to leave, and quickly, but couldn't tear himself away. What was happening? He needed to at least see what they were fighting over. There was a pair of men in the middle, their arms entangled. One of them held something. Alan couldn't see it — it fit into the man's hand. Money? Something very small. Keys?

A man at the periphery saw Alan and got the attention of the man next to him. They both stared, dumbfounded. One of the two men gestured for Alan to come to them, presumably to break up the fight that they couldn't. Alan took a step toward them, but the second man flicked his hand at Alan, shooing him away. He stopped.

Now a few other men saw Alan, and within seconds they had announced his presence to the room. It grew quiet, and the fighting stopped. All the men, all two dozen or so of them, stood still, as if Alan had come to inspect them. The man who had originally urged him forward did so again. Alan took another step toward them, but didn't see a deep groove in the floor. His shoe caught and he found himself flailing backward. He regained his balance momentarily, but then slipped on the sandy floor, causing him to teeter quickly to the left. He almost imploded completely but found a wall in time and steadied himself. The twenty-five men saw it all.

Alan had two options now. He could simply retreat, having made an ass of himself before opening his mouth. Or he could press on, given they had not laughed and still seemed to see some aura around him. Something about his strangeness, his clothes, said he belonged here more than they did.

Alan raised his hand. —Hello.

A few men nodded.

Stepping toward them, Alan took in the smell of working men, of sweat and cigarettes and stale laundry.

—Now what's happening here? Alan said. What's this all about? He heard in his own voice some hint of a British accent. Where had that come from? No one said anything, but he had their attention.

Alan stepped between them, bolstered by their apparent faith in him as mediator, and demanded that the two men open their palms. One man's were empty. In the right hand of the other man, a cellphone. It was an older model, a flip-phone with a cracked screen. It looked like someone had thrown it out. Then, with a shudder of recognition, Alan realized someone had. It must be Cayley's. It was the phone she'd tossed the first day.

—Where did you find this? he asked the man who held it.

The man said nothing. He had no idea what Alan had said.

—Does anyone here speak English? Alan asked.

A few of the men recognized this query, but shook their heads. No one spoke a word of Alan's language. This would be difficult. He couldn't find out how they'd gotten the phone, or who had a right to it. He couldn't get at any of the reasons why they were fighting, or who

was right, or the history between the two men, or the men they represented. Maybe this was some rivalry, some feud going back months or
centuries? He had no way to know.

He hoped he had a quarter. He reached in his pocket and found one.
A coinflip seemed as fair as any other way to settle it.

—Okay, he said, whoever guesses right, which side is up, he'll get
the phone. Okay?

He showed the men the two sides of the coin. They seemed to understand. He flipped it in the air, caught it, covered it and pointed to
the man who had last held the phone.

—You call it, Alan said.

The man said nothing. They hadn't played this game. As Alan was
trying to decide how to explain heads and tails, the other man grabbed
the phone and left the room, bounding down the stairwell. For a few
long moments, the second man didn't know what to do. He seemed to
expect that Alan would have a solution. But Alan did not have a solution, and once this had been established, the man ran out, following the
first man into the stairway and down.

The mood of the room quickly darkened. The rest of the workers
surrounded Alan, yelling in his face. His sleeve was being pulled. Someone pushed his back. They wanted him to leave. He backed away, apologizing, not sure if he should turn his back and run. Finally he did, and
fled the same way the two men had, but knew he couldn't go straight
down — he might encounter the second man, the losing man, coming

back. He ran up, hearing footsteps in the stairwell. At least a few men were chasing him.

He got off on the fourth floor. He swung the door wide and ran across the empty floor. There was nothing there but columns — no walls, no framing, nothing. The door didn't close behind him. He heard a thump as the men passed through. They were still after him. Would they actually harm him? *He was in a white shirt and khakis!* He didn't turn around. He made it to the other end of the floor and to another stairwell. He thrust open the door and scrambled up.

He needed to find room 501. Now footsteps below him, following him up. His breath was labored, heaving. At the fifth floor, he pushed open the fire door, leaned against it, to rest and to block their entry. When he looked up, he found that he had leaped forward in time. It seemed to be an entirely different building. The fifth floor was finished, modern, no detail forgotten.

He waited for the men following him to burst through, but there was no sound on the other side of the door. Had they been scared off by this, the finished floor? Did their run of the building end here? It seemed to make a certain sense.

He jogged down the long hallway, illuminated brightly by a colonnade of chandeliers. The ceiling was the deep blue of a summer storm, the wallpaper a symphony of stripes in cornflower and ochre. The carpet was lush, cream colored and undulating as if swept by tiny winds. There were fixtures, outlets, polished teak tables, fire extinguishers, every last sign of civilized living.

Dazed and disbelieving, he found room 501 and knocked on the door. It opened immediately, as if the man, wearing a suit and what appeared to be an ascot, had had his hand on the knob all day.

—Mr. Clay, I presume. He was a man of about Alan's age, clean shaven, wearing glasses and a sly smile.

—Hasan?

—So good to meet you.

They shook hands.

—I worried you'd gotten lost.

—I think I did.

—Come in.

His home was vast and open and bathed in amber light. It occupied the full width of the building, panoramic window to panoramic window. The decor was sophisticated, with gleaming hardwood floors, custom rugs, a mix of low-slung midcentury couches and tables, the occasional antique flourish — a huge mirror with gold leaf and a lightning-shaped crack through the middle. Over the mantle, a quartet of drawings by someone who was either Degas or drew dancers precisely as he did. Classical music spiraled from every corner.

—Are you okay? Hasan said. You look like you just ran a few miles.

Alan heard no sounds from the hallway, and was sure that whoever was pursuing him would not come here. He was away, he was safe. This was somewhere else entirely.

—I'm fine, he said. Just the stairs. I'm out of shape.

Alan moved toward the window facing the sea, and soon found himself standing there, looking out. He could see the tent, just below, looking far smaller than seemed possible from only five floors up. Beyond it was the beach, and quickly he could see where he had spent his days at the water.

—Tea?

Alan turned, about to answer.

Hasan raised an eyebrow. —Or something more compelling?

Alan smiled, thinking he was kidding, but Hasan was standing before a fully stocked bar cart of glass and gold, his hand on a crystal decanter.

—Yes, please.

Alan understood nothing in this country. He had not seen even one rule observed consistently. He had, moments before, been among an army of impoverished Malaysian laborers seeming to be squatting in an unfinished building and now he was two floors up and in the most sophisticated dwelling possible. And drinking with a man he had to assume was a Muslim of some influence.

Hasan handed him what seemed to be Scotch, and gestured to the couch. They sat on opposite sides of a U-shaped configuration of immaculate white leather.

—Soooo, Hasan said, stretching the word until it implied any number of things, all unsavory. He folded his left leg over the right with something just short of elegance. There was something slightly unnerving about Hasan, and Alan figured out what it was — a facial tic, or a pair of them, working in concert. His left eye would wince, and his mouth frown, as if repeatedly disapproving of the distraction caused by the tic of the eye. It happened again: blink, frown.

—Have you seen much of the building?

Alan told him of coming upon the men on the third floor. He said nothing of the fight, given the possibility that the workers, as disposable as they were no doubt considered, might be fired en masse and quickly replaced.

—I'm so sorry. How did you get to that part of the building?

—Just found myself there, I guess.

—What did you see among the workers?

—I saw them just there, you know, milling around.

—Were you shocked to find them here?

—Not really. Nothing here surprises me.

Hasan chuckled. —Good. That's really good. We house the rest of them offsite. You might have seen some of the trailers. More?

He topped off Alan's Scotch. The first pour had disappeared quicker than it should have.

—How's business? Alan asked, considering the question rhetorical. The man was trying to sell the condos at KAEC. His answer would be effusive.

—Honestly? Quite trying.

Hasan explained that he had had trouble getting firm commitments from anyone, and the few chains that had bought in originally, years ago, when the city was announced and groundbreaking began, had since backed out. There was fear about the viability of Emaar, the development company. There was concern about having the bin Laden family contracting company involved. There was, above all, the concern that the city would die with King Abdullah. That without his reformist spirit, his tolerance of small acts of progress, things would regress, and all the liberties promised at KAEC would be ground into the sand.

—But on the ground floor, you have some restaurants just about open, Alan noted.

—That's a bluff, I'm afraid. We have not sold those spots. Another drink? Alan had finished his second.

Hasan went back to the bar and made his preparations.

—Alan, there are deals to be had here. If you were to come in for one of these units, you'd pay a fraction of what people will pay a year or two from now. You could flip it and make a tenfold profit.

Now Alan heard Yousef's predictions ricocheting back to him. That the city was broke, that Emaar was broke, that it would never happen. That the whole idea would die with Abdullah.

Hasan brought the drink to Alan.

—Thank you my friend, Alan said.

Hasan smiled. —I'm very glad to have a drinking partner.

Alan asked about the King, why he didn't simply spend the money to build the city, to see it finished, or at least functional, during his life-time?

—We have an expression in Arabic: 'You cannot clap with one hand.' We can't make this city alone. We need partners.

—Come on, Alan said. Abdullah could build this city in five years if he wanted to. Why drag it out over twenty?

Hasan sat with that question for a long moment.

—I have no idea, he said.

And so they shared their frustrations of being at the mercy of factors out of their control, too many to count. Hasan had been living at KAEC for a year, had committed to being a pioneer here, and had hosted dozens of men like Alan, trying to help them envision themselves there, too.

—It could be a good life someday, Hasan said. But I fear the will is not here to finish the job.

And lacking the will to leave or do anything else, Alan stayed with Hasan, playing chess and drinking Scotch, for the next many hours. When he left, Alan was approaching drunkenness and felt wonderful. He stepped into the stairway, intending to go down, but instead he went up. He passed a closed floor, but the stairs kept going up until he found himself opening a door to the roof. The view was startling, beach and buildings and canals and desert all dusted with a murmuring golden light. He needed to leave but could not bring himself to move.

XXVI.

ALAN SLEPT WELL, not knowing why, and when he woke, the hotel phone was again blinking red. Alan listened to the message, from Yousef. He was leaving for a while, he said, and wanted to come by and say goodbye. He'd be there that morning unless he heard otherwise. Alan's relief was great. A feeling of dread had crept up on him overnight, a sense that something had happened to his friend. This is the peculiar problem of constant connectivity: any silence of more than a few hours provokes apocalyptic thoughts.

Alan dressed and dropped through the atrium to the lobby.

—You're here.

—I am. Yousef looked unwell.

—You okay?

—I don't know. I'm a little freaked out.

—The husband?

—And his henchmen, yeah. They showed up at my house.

—I thought you were at your cousin's.

—I was, but he got nervous. He lives with his grandmother and he didn't want trouble around her, so I went home. I get there and an hour later, they show up.

—What did they do?

—Should we sit for a second?

The waiter came, and Yousef ordered an espresso. Last night I was sitting there, watching Barcelona against Madrid — did you see that game?

—Yousef!

—Right. So I heard some noises outside. I stood up and saw three men at the window. I almost crapped in my pants.

—And what did they do?

—Just stood there. That was it. That was enough. It means they know where I live and they're not afraid to come there, to stand a few inches from my window and watch me. I have to leave.

—I'm so sorry.

—Yeah, well.

—Where are you going?

—Up to my father's place in the mountains. They won't go there. And the other guys in the village will look out for me. We have guns and all that.

Alan pictured some kind of Wild West standoff. It intrigued him more than he could explain.

—No, no, he said. Stay here. I'll get you a room. They have security. You'd be safe. Invisible.

As Alan described it, it began to seem like a very viable idea. Yousef waved it off.

—No, no. I want to be home. It's the weekend. Good time to go.

—How long will you be gone?

Alan had the sudden fear he wouldn't see Yousef again.

—I don't know. I have to feel safe for a few days. I just need to get to a place where I can see everything around me from a clean vantage point. Then I'll, you know, assess. That's why I wanted to come to see you. I might be there for a while, and wanted to say goodbye, in case this is the last time I see you.

Yousef's face betrayed no particular emotion. He was not that kind of man. But Alan felt that he needed to be around Yousef, that Yousef was the only sane man for a thousand miles.

Ten minutes later Alan was in Yousef's car, his duffel bag tossed in the trunk and together they were on their way to the mountains. They were on the highway for a few minutes, Alan feeling euphoric, before Yousef pulled off.

—We have to stop at my dad's shop. I have to get keys to the house, permission to stay there, all that.

—You don't have your own key? Alan asked.

—That's what I mean. He treats me like a teenager.

They spiraled up a six-floor parking garage in the middle of the city.

—This is the Old City?

It all looked very new.

—The Old City is about three square blocks at this point, Yousef said. They knocked down the rest of it in the seventies.

The garage was attached to a shopping mall. Alan and Yousef took a series of escalators down, past a half dozen luggage and jewelry shops, past groups of young women in abayas, glittering handbags on their forearms, groups of young men hungrily inspecting them.

When they got to the first floor, Yousef led Alan out of the mall and into an alleyway, dropping a century or two along the way. This part of the Old City was a series of interconnected alleys where merchants had set up small shops. They sold nuts, candy, electronics, soccer jerseys, but the most popular category for sale was women's lingerie, displayed prominently in the windows. Alan raised an eyebrow to Yousef and Yousef shrugged, as if to say, What, you've just discovered the contradictions of the Kingdom?

—Here it is, Yousef said, and stopped about twenty feet in front of a corner store, all glass, a thousand sandals visible within. There were two men standing behind the counter. One was about Alan's age, and seemed the likely father. There was another, much older man beside him, hunched over, leaning heavily against the counter, as if it were holding him up. He was at least eighty.

—Which one is…? Alan began.

—Surprise, the old one, Yousef said sullenly. I'll introduce you.

As they approached, the old man looked Yousef up and down. His eyes narrowed, his lips pursed. Yousef coughed into his shoulder, the word *asshole* disguised within. They stepped inside.

—Salaam, Yousef said brightly. Handshakes were exchanged between father and son and employee, some words in Arabic, and after what Alan guessed was his introduction, the father glanced briefly at him. Alan extended his hand, and the man patted it, as you would the paw of a begging dog. Yousef and his father spoke for less than a minute, then the father turned and went into the back of the shop. His assistant followed.

—Well, you met him. What a great man, Yousef said.

Alan didn't know what to say.

—I told him I was heading to the mountains. He said he'd let the caretaker know. I don't need a key, I guess. So we can go.

They turned to leave. Yousef stopped at the doorway.

—Wait, you want a pair of sandals? You should have one.

—No, no.

—Yes, Alan. What size are you?

Sandals filled every available space, floor to ceiling. They were all made of leather, elaborately decorated and stitched. They were hand-made, rough-hewn. And so they chose a pair, Yousef left some money on the counter, and they were back in the alley again.

—So that's dear old Dad, Yousef said, lighting a cigarette. He's not a very friendly guy in general. And he really doesn't like my work. And when I'm driving around Americans? Not his favorite.

They walked back to the parking garage.

—But you're in school. What does he want you to do?

—He wants me in the shop, if you can believe it. I worked there for a while but it was terrible. We lost all respect for each other. He is a horrible guy to work for. So abusive. And he thought I was lazy. So I quit. I should learn not to bring guests to the store.

—I have to say, Alan began, and caught himself. He was about to buttress Yousef's claims against his father, but realized he couldn't do that. Now that he was Ruby's defender, he had become the mediator between all children and their mystifying parents — was that it?

Alan worried about Yousef. He worried for his life, and he worried about his father. Both seemed trivial to Yousef, because all problems, at his age, seem solvable or not worth solving.

—I have to say, Alan started again, I respect what he's done. Your father makes shoes and sells them. It's clean and it's honest.

Yousef scoffed. —My father doesn't make these shoes. He buys them. Other people make them. He just marks them up.

—But still. It's an art.

Joe Trivole called it a dance, Alan thought.

—I'm sure he could make them if he wanted to.

—No, no, Yousef said. He just buys them wholesale. They're made in Yemen. He's never made a shoe in his life.

A few minutes on the road and Yousef was cheerful again. He seemed to be looking forward to showing Alan this fortress, the vast compound that his father had built. He leveled the top of the mountain, he said. Alan could not remember how many times Yousef had said that. It was a central point of pride for Yousef, the fact that his father, as much as he battled him, was strong enough, powerful or wealthy or visionary enough to level a mountain.

They were traveling south through the city as it unspooled itself from its modern center to the sprawl of sand-colored apartment buildings and Somali and Nigerian automotive shops, when Yousef got a phone call. He laughed and exchanged a few words in Arabic before doing a sudden U-turn.

—Salem's coming, he said, his eyebrows leaping.

Yousef explained that Salem, one of his oldest friends, worked in marketing at an American-owned diaper factory. —But he's a hippie, not some kind of hardcore salesman type, he said, then appeared worried he'd offended Alan. Sorry, he said, but Alan was anything but offended. There was no context in which the word *salesman* could offend him.

They parked in an alleyway between a half dozen small apartment buildings. Yousef honked, and a man of about twenty-five bounded down the steps carrying an acoustic guitar case. He got into the backseat, shook Alan's hand, and they were off.

Salem looked like someone who wouldn't be out of place in Venice Beach or Amsterdam. His hair was long, streaked with grey, a salt-and-pepper goatee covering his chin, stylish eyeglasses over his large eyes. He was wearing a paisley shirt and jeans. His English was even more American than Yousef's, though Alan had not thought that possible here.

Salem spent the first ten minutes of the drive with his hands on the front seats, his face between Alan and Yousef, talking about the strangest experience he'd recently had — he'd encountered a slave in his apartment building.

—Tell him about how you saw him crying there, Yousef said.

Salem told the story of finding, a few days before, a middle-aged man sitting on the steps inside the building. Salem stepped around him, and then noticed the man was distraught, weeping inconsolably.

—I asked what was wrong. He said that he was a slave, and that his owners had just freed him. But he didn't know what to do with himself. Those people were his family.

—These are people in your building?

—In the apartment below.

Salem had been living there for a year, and had seen this family of five come and go, and had occasionally seen the middle-aged man, too. But not until then did he realize that the man was not some friend or uncle, but a slave brought with them from Malawi.

—I have to find a new place, Salem said.

—That makes two of us, Yousef said. They discussed moving in together, in some other part of town, or some other country. Salem was finished with the KSA for the moment. It had nothing left to offer him.

—The boredom is infinite, Salem said.

Alan was recovering from the slave story when Yousef and Salem began talking about depression and suicide in the Kingdom.

—It's probably not as bad as it is where you are, Salem said to Alan. But you'd be surprised. Half the women are on Prozac. And the men, like us, the energy leaks out in dangerous places.

He talked about a certain recklessness in the face of a grinding lack of opportunity, about how death was not much feared. About the drag races held deep in the desert, where young wealthy men raced their BMWs and Ferraris and some of them would be hurt or killed and none of it would be widely reported or known. Yousef and Salem began speaking quickly in Arabic, debating, Alan soon learned, whether or not they could bring him to see a race.

—Maybe on the way back, we'll take you, Salem said.

—Maybe a concert, too, he added.

These, too, were held in the desert. Salem was a musician, and a filmmaker, and a poet, but mostly a singer-songwriter, though he couldn't practice his music in the open, couldn't play live unless at underground concerts or in the desert. It was far worse in Riyadh, but even in Jeddah the life of a music-maker was a constant struggle. That life, which had originally held some romantic appeal, had lost its luster. Salem was now thinking of moving to some Caribbean island to play in a bar band.

They left the city behind and soon the road was cutting through desert, flat and red, the occasional rest stop or rock outcropping. The highway was wide and fast, the sun hanging lifeless above, and Alan was tired. He dozed off, his head cradled by the seat belt, the chatter of Yousef and Salem, in Arabic and very earnest, lulling him off and away.

He woke to the sound of a door thumping closed. The car was stopped. They were in a vast parking lot ringed by stores and restaurants. Yousef was gone, and Salem was fiddling with his phone. Alan squinted, seeing Yousef jogging into a grocery store.

Alan sat up and wiped the drool from his cheek.

—How long was I out? he asked.

Salem didn't look up from his phone. —Maybe an hour. You were snoring. Very cute.

A girl of about seven, wearing a burqa, came to Salem's window. Immediately he pushed a button to lock the doors. She stayed before his window, tapping it, rubbing her fingers together.

Now Alan noticed there were dozens of women and young girls, all in black burqas, floating from car to car, approaching windows, floating away.

Alan began rolling down his window. Seeing a more sympathetic face, the girl hurried to his side, her hands outstretched.

—Don't, don't! Salem said. Roll it up.

Alan obeyed, and the rising glass almost caught the girl's tiny fingers. Now she tapped on the glass with increased urgency, her head tilted in inquiry, her mouth moving feverishly. Alan smiled and showed his empty palms. She didn't seem to understand or care. She continued her tapping.

Salem got her attention and extended his index finger upward. Like that, she turned and left. It was like some kind of magic trick.

—What does that mean, Alan asked, when you point upward like that? He mimicked the gesture.

Salem's attention had returned to his phone.

—It means *God will provide*.

—And that works?

—It does. It ends the discussion.

When the next child approached their window, her eyes glazed and yellow, Alan pointed to the sky. She disappeared.

—Don't feel bad, Salem said. They do fine.

Alan looked around the parking lot, finally seeing what should have been obvious: that there were an unusually large number of disparate peoples all driving in the same direction at the same time. And now he saw it clearly. A man in the Mercedes just ahead, wearing only a few white sheets and sandals. Families together, stocking up for the trip.

—Is this the pilgrimage? Alan asked.

Salem was scrolling through his phone again, the sound like the clicks of a Geiger counter.

—Not the official Hajj. That's in November this year. This is the

Umrah, like the lesser pilgrimage, for people who can't come during the big one.

Yousef emerged from the market pushing a cart full of provisions. Salem unlocked the doors and Yousef loaded the trunk. In seconds they were on the road again, and Alan was again dozing off. The black highway, so smooth, and the sun so small, it lulled him to sleep. He was woken by a heated discussion between Yousef and Salem.

—What's going on? Alan asked.

Yousef turned to him and pointed to a sign over the road up ahead. The highway was about to split, the main three lanes open to Muslims only. A sign in red marked the exit leading to the detour around Mecca, for non-Muslims passing through. Yousef was entertaining the idea of trying to drive Alan through the main route.

—We can put you in a thobe. You'd pass.

—It's not worth it, Salem said. He wasn't happy. The detour around is only twenty minutes longer. Please.

Yousef turned back to Alan. —You want to get smuggled?

Alan did not. He did not want to break any such rule. But they were still in the leftmost lane, and the exit for non-Muslims, three lanes to the right, was fast approaching.

A stream of Arabic from Salem. Yousef didn't respond. Suddenly all was chaos. Salem's torso was in the front seat, and he was lunging for the wheel. Alan was pushed against the door. Yousef batted Salem's hands away and slapped him in the face. Hearing the sound, a loud whap, he laughed with delight. Salem retreated to his seat, deflated.

Then, in one fluid motion, Yousef slid laterally across the expressway and was soon on the highway for non-Muslims.

Through the rearview mirror, Yousef leveled a disappointed look at

Salem. —Dude. I was kidding. *Kidding*. Relax.

Salem was still seething. —*You* relax.

Yousef grinned. —No, *you* relax.

The night dropped quickly as they rose through the mountains.

—The Sarawat range, Salem explained. Wait till we get to the top. You'll see the baboons. You like baboons?

And then there they were. At the top of the range, Yousef pulled over along a lookout, about five thousand feet up, the desert visible below for a hundred miles. And everywhere in that lookout parking lot, baboons sat, ate, walked around, tame as house cats.

They flew through Taif, a mountaintop city of bright colors and cool winds, and then dropped into the rough terrain beyond. The road grew more desolate as they got closer to the village of Yousef's birth, and by the time they arrived, Salem was sound asleep and Alan was nodding off.

Yousef stopped the car suddenly. —Wake up, useless people!

Salem moaned and punched the back of Yousef's seat.

Ahead, a sawtoothed ridge ringed a small cluster of lights tucked into a small valley. The settlement couldn't have been more than a few dozen buildings, a few hundred people.

—That's the whole town, Yousef said. We'll see it tomorrow.

They turned into a driveway and climbed up the mountainside a few hundred feet, doubling back twice, until they arrived at an enormous structure. It looked nothing like a house.

—This is it? Alan asked.

—Yes, Yousef said. The house that sandals built.

It looked more like a hotel, some kind of municipal building. It was a three-story structure of adobe and glass. They had parked in a vast lot, big enough to accommodate twenty vehicles. There was even a small mosque on the property, just down the slope.

—I didn't realize... Salem said. He hadn't been there, either.

As he and Alan were marveling at it all, a man came out of the house and rushed toward them. He was short, smaller than Yousef and more portly. His face was round, his smile wide and toothless. He took Yousef's hand and pumped it. He was introduced to Salem and shook his hand, too. When Alan extended his hand, though, it was as if the man had to relearn the gesture. He took it and shook it, and then retrieved his hand, slowly, as if from the mouth of an animal he did not want to provoke.

—This is Hamza. The caretaker, Yousef explained. He's been working for my father for twenty years. But I didn't tell my dad you were coming.

—Why not? Alan asked.

—No offense, but this is my father's pride. He wouldn't want it sullied by, you know, you. Just kidding.

But he was not kidding.

Hamza turned, led them to the door and opened it.

Yousef stepped in and turned around in the doorway.

—Ready? This is it, Yousef said, his posture quickly changing from that of scorned teenager to proud son.

Inside, the house looked very much like a series of empty, carpeted ballrooms, each big enough to fit a hundred people or more. In each room, a few enormous chandeliers illuminated vast spaces without any furniture but the benches along the walls. The whole house, it seemed, was meant for entertaining only.

—The entire village fits in here. He made sure of it. Every wedding in the village happens here. I have to bring you to one of them, he said to Alan. You'd love it. You could wear one of the outfits, get a special knife, everything.

Alan tried to square the builder of this home with the brusque and bitter man he'd met. It seemed impossible that *that* man had built *this*. This was an act of great vision and generosity, and Yousef's father had seemed to possess neither. They walked to the third floor. The stairs, of poured concrete, were uneven, as if the mason hadn't been quite paying attention this far up.

—They finished this floor a bit quicker, Yousef said, smiling. But the view is worth it.

They stepped onto a wide balcony. The air was clear and cool, the view magnificent. Alan and Yousef and Salem and Hamza stood, looking out over the valley.

—Oh, I have to show you. Yousef said, bounding down the stairs.

He led Alan and Salem into a smaller room, empty but for a giant safe on one wall, and a stack of thin mattresses on the other.

—Somewhere in here, he said, grabbing at the mattresses, dropping them to the floor. Alan had the feeling he'd had when his friends' kids brought him to their rooms, to show him every toy they owned, growing more passionate with every word of awe he uttered. Yousef toppled seven or eight before he found what he was looking for: a cache of rifles. There were at least a dozen, some new, some old and handmade, with wooden handles and carefully carved details.

—This one was my grandfather's, he said, holding an ancient-looking rifle in two hands. He handed it to Alan as if he were handing over a newborn. It was heavy, made of solid hardwood.

—This one's newer. Yousef took the first rifle away, handing it to Salem. He replaced it with the new model, which looked like a standard Winchester .44. Alan checked and it was just that. Salem politely admired the rifles, but his disinterest was hard to mask. Alan, though, was fascinated. He'd been a decent marksman in his youth, and maintained an affection for old rifles like this. He wanted badly to aim one, to shoot one, but wasn't sure of the protocol. He settled for praising them all, and when Yousef began packing them back into the mattresses, he assumed he wouldn't see them again.

He half hoped Yousef was serious about needing them to repel those aligned with his ex-wife's husband. The idea of them coming here, and staging a raid on this fortress, was preposterous, but at the same time it gave Alan a surge of hope, of possibility. He pictured himself perched on the balcony, sighting invaders. He wanted to do something dramatic to protect his friend.

—What are the chances those guys will actually come here? Alan asked.

—What guys?

—The husband, his men?

—You're serious? They have no idea this place exists. You think they'd drive four hours through the desert to follow me here?

Alan shook his head, tossing the notion away, but something passed between them. Yousef got his meaning: that Alan, far from being scared of their attack, was open to it, was welcoming of it. He put his hand on Alan's shoulder, turned him, gently pushed him out of the rifle room and turned out the light.

They settled on the second-floor deck. Hamza brought rugs and cushions out and arranged them in clean lines. He hurried inside and returned with a full tea set, which he served with great solemnity.

Alan drank his tea, sweet and minty, as Salem did some perfunctory tuning of his guitar. Alan didn't know what to expect, but when Salem started strumming, slapping the wood for percussion, it sounded like a Western pop song, something you'd hear while shopping.

The night cooled, and a gentle wind came up the valley and swept through the fortress. As if carried by the breeze, a light appeared below. Then two more. It was a motorcycle, followed by a small truck, both making their way up the driveway.

Yousef nodded at the guitar and Salem took the cue. He packed it up, quickly retreated inside, and came back without it.

Soon three young men appeared on the deck. All were wearing white They were somewhere between thirteen and sixteen and all built like Yousef, short and full in the middle. All were wearing white thobes, red gutras — miniature businessmen with wide bright smiles. They rushed up to Yousef and hugged him.

—These are my cousins, Yousef said to Alan. Two of them, anyway. This third one is their friend.

Alan shook their hands, and Yousef and the cousins spoke for a time in Arabic. Salem stayed on the balcony, as if knowing that these village men were a different species. Yousef was the bridge between the urbanity of Salem, of Alan, and these young men, who Alan guessed were being raised more conservatively, far from things like pop music and American guests. The night wore on, and more tea was served, and there seemed to be a lot of catching up to do, stories being told, and Alan felt in the way. When Salem went inside, citing exhaustion, Alan took it as his cue, too. Yousef bid good night to them both, and instructed Hamza to see them to their accommodations.

In Alan's room, as big as a formal dining room, one of the thin, pliable mattresses that had been hiding the rifles was now set up on the floor, covered neatly with a sheet and wool blanket. His duffel bag had been brought from the car and set upon a wooden chair near the bed. Hamza showed them the bathroom, gave them towels, washcloths, even sandals of soft leather.

Alan arranged himself on the mattress and pulled the heavy wool blanket over himself. The house was cooling quickly.

Salem passed by the doorway.

—Night, he said.

—Night, Alan said.

It must have been close to midnight. Out the window, he could see the near face of the mountain, no more than ten yards away, and above it, a gunmetal sky and pinprick stars. Now that he was lying down, and warm, what he wanted to do was wander among the mountains that night, with Yousef or Salem or alone. He was not tired. He stared up through the window above him, the mountainside so blue in the clean moonlight. He was growing more awake every minute.

He thought of a letter but he had no paper. He found a large envelope by the door and began: 'Dear Kit, I'm writing to you from a castle. I am not kidding. I'm in some kind of modern fortress, on a hill in the mountains of Saudi Arabia. The man who built this place sells shoes. He is not some kind of major manufacturer of shoes. He is a man who owns a 400-square-foot shop in Jeddah and sells simple shoes, mostly sandals, to regular people. And with the money he's made and saved selling shoes, he went back to his village, leveled a mountaintop and built a castle.'

He put down his pen. He moved slowly to the door, sure not to wake Salem. The house was silent, but most of the lights in the house were still on. He stepped lightly to the stairway, and made his way up the uneven steps and to the roof. There he walked from corner to corner, taking in the view from all sides. He decided he could live here. He decided he could be content this way, if he'd built a home like this. All he needed was some space, somewhere removed from anywhere, where the land was cheap and building was easy. He shared the dreams of Yousef's father, the need to return to one's origins, build something lasting, something open and strange like this fortress, something that could be shared by family and friends, everyone who had helped nurture him. But what were Alan's origins? He had no ancestral village. He had Dedham. Was Dedham an ancestral village? No one there had any idea who he was. Was he from Duxbury? Was he attached at all to that town, or anyone to him?

In Duxbury, Alan couldn't even build a wall.

Alan did not want to think about the planning-board guy, but there he was, his smarmy face. All Alan had wanted was to build a garden, cordoned off with a small stone wall. The soil was rocky in the part of the backyard he'd chosen, so he figured he'd build the garden above the yard, elevated a foot or so. He'd seen one in a book and it seemed to make sense, and looked good, too. The one in the book had been enclosed in wood, like a sandbox, but Alan wanted to match the old stone walls that bordered some of the properties around town — walls built, some of them at least, hundreds of years ago. Some of those old walls had no mortar at all, were just rocks stacked carefully, but Alan figured he'd use cement to keep it all together. So after flipping through a library book about masonry, he went to the hardware store and bought two sacks of ready-mix cement.

Then he went to a place off the highway that sold rocks. This was the best part, something he hadn't known anything about. He walked around the lot, where they had great mounds of rocks in small enclosures, a zoo of rocks. Finally he found a grey and pink kind, tending toward the rounded, that seemed to match those in front of his house.

—How's it work? he asked one of the men working there. The man was tall, thin, too slight to be working at a place filled with rocks. It didn't look like he could have lifted his pants around his waist, let alone the stones he was selling.

—You hauling your own stones?

Alan didn't know. —Should I?

—Might as well, the man said, unless you're building a castle.

Alan snorted. The joke seemed very funny at the moment.

—Nah, just a wall.

—That your wagon? he asked, nodding toward the station wagon.

—It is. Will it work?

—Sure, but we gotta weigh it first, the man said. Scale's over there.

Soon Alan was back in his car, driving it onto two tracks that rose up onto a platform. The platform was next to the lot's office, and once on top of the scale, Alan could see inside, where another man was giving him the thumbs-up.

Alan drove down the tracks, and back to the area where he'd chosen his stones, and started loading them up. He had no idea how many to buy, and there wasn't any sign to indicate how much they cost. But he was having so much fun with the whole process — the scale, the tossing of stones into his car, each giving the shocks a bounce, the car weighing down a bit more every time. He decided to fill it until the rear bumper sank enough to warn him off more loading. So he did, closed the back hatch, and then drove back to the scale.

Again, the man through the window gave him a thumbs-up, and Alan drove down, and parked next to the office. He walked in and the man behind the counter gave him a friendly wink.

—Four hundred and sixteen pounds.

If the price per pound was anything more than a dollar, Alan thought, he was screwed. He'd budgeted a few hundred dollars for the whole garden project.

The man was working the numbers on a calculator and looked up.

—Any cement?

Alan shook his head.

—Okay. So that's a hundred and seventy dollars, sixty-eight cents.

Alan almost laughed, and he smiled all the way home. It was so simple, a transaction like that. It was simple and it was good. He saw some rocks. Threw them in the back of his wagon and weighed the car, the guy had calculated the difference, determined the weight of the rocks, and charged him about forty cents a pound. It was beautiful.

Building the wall gave Alan as much pleasure as he'd known in years, even though he had virtually no idea what he was doing. He'd forgotten to buy any masonry tools, so he used a wheelbarrow to mix the cement and a spade to apply it. He tried to fit the stones in some sensible way, spreading the cement on top and between. He had no sense of how long it would take to dry, or how sturdy it would be when finished. He should have waited, laid down one row of stones before stacking upward, but he was enjoying it far too much to slow down. As with many of his projects around the house and yard, he wanted to finish it in one session, and, four hours later, he did.

He stepped back and saw that it was more or less square. The walls rose about three feet and were utterly medieval in their homeliness. But when he put his foot on the first section of wall he'd completed, it was already solid. He pushed on it, and it did not budge. He stood on it, and it was as sturdy as any floor in his home. He was deeply moved by this. Cement! It was no wonder architects loved it. In a few hours he'd made a wall that would take a jackhammer to dismantle. In a few days, he figured, he could probably build a home of some kind this way. He could build anything. He was elated.

But then came a visit from the zoning department. He woke up the next day to find a red piece of paper stuck to his front door. The notice told him to come to city hall, to submit building plans, to apply for a permit. All for a three-foot wall. And then there were the arguments with that bastard at the planning board, all of which were futile. Alan hadn't built the wall to the town's specifications, hadn't worked with a licensed contractor, and so the wall had to be destroyed. They made him pay a pair of men to jackhammer his wall, his garden, until it was rubble. They trampled his vegetables, everything ground into the soil. The plants were dead. The mess was hard to look at. And then he had to pay another pair of men to haul it away.

XXVII.

WHEN ALAN WOKE the sky was a sickly grey. He walked downstairs. He heard no voices and saw no movement, no evidence of sunrise. The banquet rooms were empty, the kitchen vacant. Someone had finally turned out the lights. He thought about going back to bed but was sure that would come to nothing.

He opened the front door and saw the valley below, blue and brown in the low light. He sat on the railing and noted for the first time that on the property, on another level area fifty feet down, there was a flock of sheep. They were penned in, and the ground beneath them was all dust and rock but for a few stray patches of green. A plume of smoke unzipped the blue sky beyond the mountains. Alan went inside and got his camera.

He walked over to the driveway and took pictures there, of the drive down the hill, of the hills backing up against the property behind the house. He walked down the drive, met up with the main road, and started toward town.

The valley was silent. He stopped to take a picture of a spiked tree, a cluster of white flowers, an old Pakistani bus, painted brightly, out of commission and pushed to the side of the road. He took a picture of a stray goat.

A burst of dust arose over a nearby hill. It was a truck, a small white pickup. It continued toward him, and stopped alongside him. A window came down. A man of about forty was driving, wearing a clean grey thobe. He looked a bit like Yousef, though taller and thinner.

—Salaam, he said.

—Salaam, Alan said.

—You need a ride?

—No thanks. Just taking a walk.

—Taking some pictures?

—Yeah, I guess. Beautiful morning.

—I was watching you from above, he said.

Alan looked around, trying to assess from what overhead perch the man could have been observing. The man smiled grimly.

—You're taking a lot of pictures.

—I guess so, Alan said.

Something was happening but he couldn't touch it. Then he knew.

—American? the man asked.

Ah. As always, Alan had the momentary inclination to lie.

—Yes, he said.

—All these pictures. You work for the CIA or something?

The man's smile seemed more genuine now, and it must have loosened something within Alan.

—Just some freelance work, Alan joked. Nothing full-time.

The man's head snapped back an inch, as if he's smelled something disagreeable, something unnatural. Then he put the truck in gear and was off.

When Alan got back to the house, Yousef and Salem were awake and dressed, and Hamza had set out the tea set. Salem was on the deck, as he had been the night before, playing the guitar. Yousef saw Alan approach.

—Alan! We thought you'd been kidnapped.

Yousef and Salem were grinning.

—Just went for a walk. I woke up early. Beautiful here at dawn.

—It is, it is. We'll have some breakfast outside. You approve?

Hamza set a wide white tablecloth on the deck and they sat down. He brought more tea and bread and dates. The air was cool but the sun was rising and Alan could taste the coming heat, the warmth of the rocks all around them. They stayed in the shade. Alan wanted to tell them about his encounter with the man in the pickup, because he knew he had botched it, and knew that trouble might soon arrive, even if just in the form of a phone call. But he held out hope that the man would forget it, that it had been inconsequential, that his terrible joke would be seen as that and nothing more.

When breakfast was finished Yousef jogged inside, inspired. He returned with a pair of the rifles he'd shown them the night before. Alan expected this to be another show-and-tell session until he saw Yousef shaking a box of bullets onto the tablecloth. They were .22s, and Yousef loaded one into the rifle's chamber.

Among strangers or new friends, the loading of a gun always brings a moment of assessment. Alan had been around guns for many years, and he had a comfort level with them, and he had a comfort level with Yousef, and yet he had to pause, briefly, and think about his friend, and the gun, and their position, and any possible motives and outcomes. They were far from anyone who would care about Alan's life. He trusted Yousef, considered him his friend, something of a son, but then there was a small part of him that said, *You do not know any of these people very well.*

Yousef left the gun on the tablecloth and went to the other side of the balcony, where the property backed up against the mountainside. He retrieved a can from the shrubbery and placed it atop the low wall. Then he jogged back.

—Let's see if I'm still any good, he said.

Alan expected Yousef to lie on his stomach, or to stand, but instead he sat, with his knees out in front of him. He rested his elbows on his knees, the rifle nestled in his shoulder. Alan had never seen someone shoot this way, but it made a certain amount of sense.

Yousef aimed at the can — it was about twenty yards away — and shot. The sound wasn't very loud, not as loud as a .45. These .22s were quiet, elegant, almost polite in their noises and demands.

The bullet disappeared into the thicket. He'd missed. He muttered in Arabic, emptied the chamber and loaded a new bullet. He aimed, fired, and this time, after a second of teetering, the can fell forward from the ledge to the driveway, like a movie cowboy falling off a roof.

—Very good, Alan said.

Hamza ran to set up the can again.

—Now you? Yousef handed him the gun.

Alan took the gun and loaded one of the small, gold-cased .22 bullets. The rifle was very light. He wanted to stand, or lie on his stomach, but felt that custom dictated that he follow Yousef's way.

It was comfortable enough, mimicking the shape of a tripod. Alan found the can in the sights, exhaled, and squeezed the trigger. A small fist of dust rose just left of the can. Yousef and Hamza seemed mildly impressed, but also appeared satisfied that Alan was an inferior shot. What would it look like to them if Alan, middle-aged, heavy and wearing khaki pants, could sit down, pick up a gun and outdo them?

This was what Alan was determined to do.

—Can I have another? he asked.

Yousef shrugged and nodded toward the box of bullets. Alan loaded another into the chamber, and again took aim. He sighted, he breathed, he squeezed. This time the can took a bullet to its gut and fell from the wall.

Everyone, even Salem, murmured their approval. Alan handed the gun to Yousef, who was smiling broadly.

They continued this way, trading turns, replacing the can, filling it with holes, for about twenty minutes, until a truck barreled up the driveway. It was the white pickup that Alan had encountered earlier. As soon as the man emerged, looking agitated, Alan knew that he would soon be explaining himself. It did not help that when the man pulled up, Alan was holding a gun. As the man strode toward them, Alan placed it on the tablecloth, as close to Yousef as he could, but within his own reach. How could he know what was about to happen? He needed options.

First the man threw a barrage of Arabic at Yousef, pointing at Alan all the while. Then Yousef was standing, and Salem was standing, and all three men were yelling, and Hamza was unsure what to do. The man from the white pickup was surely someone whom Hamza saw every day, a man living in the town, and he couldn't openly defy him, no more than he could blindly side with Yousef. Alan sat, trying to appear as harmless as possible.

Finally Yousef came to Alan.

—Did you tell this guy you were from the CIA?

Alan rolled his eyes. —He asked me if I was from the CIA, and I joked that I did some freelance work for them.

Yousef squinted at Alan. —Why did you say that?

—I was joking. It was a joke. He asked me. It was a ludicrous question.

—It's not ludicrous to *him*. Now I have to convince him that you're not from the CIA. How do I do this?

Alan wanted to be gone, up on the roof, anywhere. But an idea came to him. Tell him that if I was from the CIA, I wouldn't go telling the first guy who asked me about it.

At this, Yousef laughed. Thank God, Alan thought. There had been a moment when the whole thing was getting away from him, from them all, and there would be all kinds of trouble for Yousef, for Yousef's father, for Alan. By lunch he'd be in the next cab back to Jeddah. But Alan's explanation had broken through, had reminded Yousef who he was, and who they both were. They were friends and there was trust.

Yousef turned to the man, put his arm around him, and walked him back to his truck. The man got in, sat behind the wheel for the next five minutes as Yousef talked to him through the window, calmly and with occasional emphatic gestures Alan's way. Yousef tamped down the remaining embers of the man's fury, and was soon finished.

—When the pickup was gone, Yousef returned, sat down, and exhaled theatrically. You shouldn't have said that.

—I know.

—People don't like jokes like that.

—I knew it as soon as I said it.

—It's like joking about having a bomb when you're in airport security.

—That was the analogy I had in mind, too.

—So we agree.

—We always do.

—Most of the time.

—I'm sorry.

—Okay. Let's shoot some more.

And they did, until Salem said he wanted to at least see some of the town or land. So they got in one of Yousef's father's trucks, Hamza driving, and descended into the flats of the valley and through the village. The truck ambled over the rough road so slowly that there seemed to be no point in all of them riding in a vehicle at all. Walking would have been faster and less ridiculous. They passed by the humblest dwellings and an array of well-made adobe homes and apartment buildings. The whole village couldn't have been more than two hundred people, but there was a tidy school, a clinic, a mosque, even what Alan took to be a hotel.

After the main cluster of buildings, they drove up the dusty road to the other end of the valley, and after passing through a narrow passageway between two enormous stones, they were in another, smaller valley. They descended briefly, the next village in view, and Yousef stopped the truck.

—This is my grandparents' home, Yousef said, indicating a small and ancient dwelling. It had been constructed of a few thousand flat stones, without mortar. It was probably no more than eighty years old, but would not have been out of place in an entirely different epoch.

They got out, and Alan followed Yousef through a window and into the shelter. The home was one small room. The roof was gone, but the round beams remained. Yousef took off his sunglasses and hung them on his thobe. He took a pull of water from his plastic bottle.

—I would have no idea how to live that way, he said. Can you imagine?

They got back into the truck.

They spent the next few hours driving lazily through the valleys, up and down the terrible roads. Along the way they passed a succession of improbable rock formations. Two-story stones that had been half hollowed, sitting like empty helmets. They drove to the upper ridge of the valley of Yousef's father and looked down on the village. From their vantage point, it looked impossibly small and fragile, the kind of settlement that would be swept away in seconds by a flash flood, buried utterly by any kind of minor avalanche. It seemed a ludicrous place to live for a day or two, let alone for centuries. The people here would have been acutely vulnerable to drought, to the one road out being made even temporarily impassable by mud or falling rock. Looking over the valley, the work of humans so small next to the work of wind and water, Alan had the reaction he had had so often, which was *People shouldn't live here.* People should not settle in a rocky terrain devoid of water or rain. But then where should they live? Nature tells man that she will kill him anywhere. In flat land, she will kill him with tornadoes. Live near a coast and she will send tsunamis to erase centuries of work. Earthquakes mock all engineering, all notions of permanence. Nature wants to kill, kill, kill, laugh at our work, wipe itself clean. But people lived wherever they wanted, and they lived here, too, in this impossible valley, and they thrived. Thrived? They lived. They survived, reproduced, sent their children to the cities to make money. Their children made money and came back to level hilltops and build castles in the same impossible valley. The work of man is done behind the back of the natural world. When nature notices, and can muster the energy, it wipes the slate clean again.

On the way back to the fortress, they passed a pair of men erecting a stone wall. The setup looked remarkably like the one Alan had used — a stack of rocks, a wheelbarrow full of mortar.

—Can we stop? Alan asked, before he had fully formed the reason why.

Hamza stopped. The two men looked up from their work and waved. Yousef greeted them from his window, making some joke in Arabic. The men laughed and came over.

—Ask them if they need help, Alan said.

—I'm not helping them! Yousef was momentarily puzzled. You mean you? You want to help?

—I do. I really do.

And after a few minutes of Yousef and Salem trying to reason with Alan, Yousef made the offer to the men, and the men accepted. They put Alan to work, and Hamza and Yousef and Salem drove off.

Alan's job was to keep the mortar from hardening, stirring it, adding water periodically, and when that was taken care of, to help find the appropriate stones to place next on the wall. The work was slow, and the language barrier made it frustrating for both sides, but Alan felt good being outside, using his arms and legs, sweating through his shirt and khakis, and by the end of the day, they'd completed about eighteen feet of the wall. It was three feet high, it was solid, it was far better than the one he'd built in his own yard. They nodded to him, shook his hand, and he was done.

The sun was setting as he walked back to the castle. Getting lost was not a possibility: the fortress could be seen from every corner of the valley. In twenty minutes Alan reached it and Yousef and Salem were, as always, perched on the wall of the balcony, Salem strumming his guitar.

—Have fun? Yousef said.

—For a while I did. Then it was a fucking pain in the ass, he said.

Yousef and Salem both laughed. They were looking at a fool.

Yousef had a light in his eyes. —After dinner, I have a treat for you. You'll love this.

Salem, in the know, raised his eyebrows, agreeing that Alan was about to be made very happy.

—What is it?

—You want to hunt some wolves?

—Why? Where?

—There are apparently some wolves killing sheep lately. They're organizing a hunt. They need anyone who can shoot.

Alan hadn't heard a more intriguing invitation in years.

—I do want that, he said.

—Told you, Yousef said to Salem.

—I didn't deny it, Salem said. He picked up his guitar and composed a song, on the spot, about Alan and the hunt.

It was not half bad.

XXVIII.

AFTER DINNER, TWO PICKUP trucks pulled up to the house. Again Salem hurried to hide his guitar. Both trucks were white, but neither was driven by the man who suspected Alan of being a CIA operative. There were about four men in each, as old as Alan or older, with a few teenagers mixed in.

Alan was offered the front seat in the first pickup, but he wanted to be in the open air. It was a crisp and clear night and he wanted to see everything. Voices were raised among the men, but finally Yousef intervened and assured them that this was indeed what Alan wanted, that their hospitality was best expressed by granting him this wish. Normally he wouldn't have forced the issue, but tonight he did, because after weeks of life in that sterile hotel, he wanted the night air, and the stars, and the bouncing around in the truck bed.

And so he crawled into the back with the two youngest cousins and an older man. All three had rifles. Yousef sat in the passenger seat.

—You coming? Alan asked Salem.

—You kidding? Salem said, see you later.

The pickup sputtered to life and began a slow rumble down the driveway. The man across from Alan, about his own age and build, was smiling at him. Alan extended his hand. —Alan, he said.

The man shook it. —Atif.

A pothole sent them all into the air. When they landed, they all laughed. Atif, Alan hoped, had not been apprised of the possibility that Alan was CIA. He wanted the simplicity of being who he was: no one.

Atif raised his chin to Alan. —Did you hunt a wolf before, Mr. Alan?

Alan shook his head.

—But you have...

The man couldn't find the word for shot so instead pretended to shoot his own gun. —You do this?

—Yes, many times, Alan said.

The man tilted his head, not quite adding it up.

—But no kill the *animal*?

—No, Alan said.

The man smiled. He was missing most of his teeth.

—Kill the *man*?

Alan laughed. —No.

—*Eat* the animal? the man asked.

—Yes, Alan answered.

The man seemed satisfied for a moment, then a shard of mischief appeared in his eyes. —Eat the *man*?

Alan chose to laugh. —No.

The man smiled. —Never *once* eat the man?

Alan chose to laugh again.

The man reached out and took Alan's hand, shook it again.

—Good, he said.

The roads were a mess and got worse as they rose higher through the mountains. The truck whinnied and grunted, and Alan wondered aloud if any wolves would remain within miles of their loud convoy.

Finally, high atop the ridge, they stopped, and the cousins got out, helping Alan down. Yousef appeared from the other truck. He was loading his rifle.

—The farm below is where the sheep were taken last.

Alan sighted the pen, and guessed they were about seventy yards away.

—So the plan?

—Just to wait here, I guess.

—But won't they smell us? Alan asked. No one answered, and he assumed the question was irrelevant.

—You and I will go over here, Yousef said.

They walked a hundred yards to a cluster of boulders, low and smooth, and Yousef draped himself over one. Alan followed suit, and they both pointed their rifles at the pen below. They had a clear shot. The owner had left a floodlight on — this had not deterred the wolves before, the men had said — and there was little wind, so it was a shot he could make if the wolf was moving slowly and predictably. Alan didn't have much experience leading a target, but without any obstacles, in a spotlit open pen, he thought he could at least get a piece of the animal.

He watched as the rest of the hunting party spread itself out around the perimeter of the pen. He counted nine shooters, including the young cousins. Should a wolf penetrate the perimeter, there would be plenty of guns ready to put it down.

Alan did not want to kill any animal. He dreaded the moment when the wolf, hit by a bullet, would jerk, stagger about, and, immobilized, be filled with lead. He dreaded hearing its labored breathing as they stood around it, waiting for it to die. But it seemed unlikely that any animal, however stupid or desperate, would enter the pen under these circumstances, with so many people nearby, such bright light. Then again, Alan knew nothing about hunting, about wolf hunting, about wolf hunting in the mountains of central Saudi Arabia.

Alan's father had taught him to shoot, or at least had brought him along hunting a few times. He didn't teach him much. When Alan was ten, he handed him an antique Winchester .22 rifle and had said, Do as I do. Ron was using a .45 semiautomatic rifle, and Alan had followed behind him. When Ron lifted his rifle Alan had lifted his, too. Eventually Ron taught him to breathe into the shot, to keep the rifle as close to the body, to the cheek, as possible. But Alan didn't take to it the way Ron had hoped, and after those first few times, that was that.

Across the valley, another pair of headlights appeared as a blue sunrise beyond the ridge's ragged silhouette. Alan looked to Yousef. Yousef shrugged. —This is a big event here. Everyone wants to be part of it. This is like Christmas. Yousef considered this for a second. Maybe not like Christmas.

Alan looked into the pen and saw nothing. The sheep were safe under their corrugated roof, and the wolf still hadn't dared to cross the stage. Yousef lowered his rifle and rubbed his shoulder and neck.

He looked to Alan. —Hey, how's your neck?

—Fine. Sore.

Alan watched as Yousef, smiling, took in the sight of Alan draped over the rock, poised to shoot.

—Were you ever in the army? he asked.

—No, I told you.

—You said you weren't in the CIA.

—I wasn't in the army, either. My dad was.

—And he fought?

—He did. In World War II.

Yousef made an impressed sound. —Where?

The mythology of the World War II vet dictates that they don't like to talk about the war, but Ron never hesitated. Anything could get him going. An Italian accent in any TV show started him in about the two Mussolini soldiers — he didn't call them Italian, for, he said, true Italians didn't follow or fight for that maniac — he'd killed, or helped kill. The sight of a nurse triggered stories of the German nurses he'd known, the British ones aboard his ship home, the Polish one he'd known quite intimately. That story he began telling after Alan's mother died. Ron had really become a strong dose in his old age, hadn't he? But there were these stories, better stories than Alan had or would ever have, stories that began with any injury, stories prompted by hearing Schubert, Wagner, by documentaries on the History Channel.

Alan told Yousef the best part, that his father had been captured by the Nazis, imprisoned at Muhlberg, and when the Soviets overran the region, they expected to be freed, but were not. They had a feeling that

Stalin was bargaining for the prisoners somehow, that he was holding them while he weighed his options. Ron and his bunkmate knew something was amiss, and though their orders were to stay put, to be patient and respect the process, they wanted out of there. They wanted to be home. So one night they stole a pair of Soviet bicycles, sped to the fences, found a hole, snuck through, and rode off through the German countryside.

Yousef was loving all this.

—Ah, that's why you went into bicycles, he said.

—How do you mean?

—Because your father escaped on a bike.

Alan spent a moment with that. —Huh, he said, finally. I'd never made that connection.

Yousef didn't believe him. To have never drawn the line from his father's escape aboard a bicycle, the only vehicle that would have taken him so quietly and so quickly? *Was* there a connection? Alan didn't attempt to parse it all.

—But you didn't want to join the army?

—No.

—Why? No good wars?

—Exactly.

—But you would have fought in World War II?

—I wouldn't have had a choice.

—What if you had?

—A choice?

—Yes.

—I would have gone. I would have tried to avoid the Pacific.

—And if you were young now?

—Would I join? No.

—Why? Still no good wars?

—Why all these questions, Yousef? You thinking of joining the army?

—Maybe. I'd like to be a pilot.

—Well, don't.

—Why not?

—Because you should just get back to college and finish. You have a great brain. Stay safe, go to college, give yourself options.

—But there's no options here. I told you that.

—So leave.

—I could leave.

—Then leave.

—But it would be better to stay here, and have things be different.

They lay in silence for a while. Yousef turned to him.

—Alan, would you fight for us?

—Who?

—People like me, in Saudi.

—Fight for you how?

—Like you guys fought for the Iraqis. Or what you said you were fighting for. To give them *opportunities*.

—You mean would I fight personally?

—Yes.

—Maybe. As a young man, I would have.

—Would anyone else?

—Yousef, this is nuts. No one's invading Saudi Arabia.

—I know. I'm just curious. Just about individuals.

—You want to know if individual Americans would come here to fight alongside you?

—Exactly.

—I don't know. Probably. I think we have a lot of people willing to fight to support the people who are trying to be free. Americans like a cause. And they don't think too much about it.

Alan laughed at his joke. Yousef did not.

—So if I start a democratic revolution here, you would support me?

—Is this your plan?

—No. I'm just asking. Would you?

—Of course.

—How?

—I don't know.

—You would send troops?

—Me personally?

—You know what I mean. The U.S.

—Send troops? No chance.

—Air support?

—No, no.

—Shock and awe.

—Here? No way.

—Advisors of some kind, maybe. Spies?

—Here in Saudi? There are plenty already.

—What about personally? Would you personally come to support me?

—Yes, Alan said.

—That was quick.

—Well, I'm sure.

—With your twenty-two-caliber rifle.

—Exactly.

Yousef smiled. —Good, good. When I start the revolution, I'll at least have you on my side.

—You would.

—You're crazy. Yousef shook his head, grinning, and went back to his rifle, positioning himself again to be ready. Then he turned again to Alan.

—You know I was kidding, right?

—About what?

—About wanting the U.S. to invade our country.

Alan didn't know what to say. Yousef was still grinning.

—You're so ready to believe it! It's kind of funny, don't you think?

—I don't know if it's funny, Alan said. I'm sorry. I didn't know you were kidding.

—It's okay. I'm still happy you'd bring your twenty-two to fight with me. Even if I'm not about to start a revolution.

They went back to watching the valley below, but Alan was shaken. Yousef had been lighthearted during his questions, but there was something very serious and very sad under his smile, and Alan knew what it was. It was the knowledge that there would be no fighting, and there would be no struggle, no stand taken, and that the two of them, because they were not lacking materially, because despite injustices in their countries they were the recipients of preposterous bounty, would likely do nothing. They were content, they had won. The fighting would be done by others, elsewhere.

Down below, movement. Alan lifted his rifle and pressed his cheek to the smooth wood. But it was one of the sheep. Somehow it had gotten loose, and now wanted to rejoin its brethren in the shelter. Alan had it in his sights, and a good part of him wanted to shoot that sheep. He harbored no ill will toward the animal, and he'd get in trouble for shooting it, but then again, he had a gun and had been waiting for forty minutes. Just waiting, watching. If he shot it, it would be something that had happened. The gun wants to be fired. The waiting must end.

A wind swept through the valley and up toward the ridge where they all gathered. A fine dust swirled about, making it difficult to see, but Alan felt that with the wind came the strange but absolute certainty that he would kill the wolf.

He was not one for premonitions, and had never felt any sense of destiny about himself, but now, with his cheek pressed against the cold wood of the rifle, he was sure he would pull the trigger that would send the bullet through the heart of the wolf. He was so sure that he felt a wonderful calm, a calm that allowed a smile to overtake his face.

This will be good, he thought. It will be good to be the one to see and shoot the wolf. To shoot a wolf in the mountains of Saudi Arabia will be something. The man who pulls the trigger will have done something.

He waited this way, content and certain, for some time, even as voices approached from behind him. He didn't look back, but it seemed that some of the other hunters had given up their posts and were either settling in here to wait for the animal or had come to collect Yousef and Alan. But as if intuiting that Alan was locked in, that he knew something they did not, they kept their distance. Amid the steady wind their voices were distant and, to Alan, irrelevant.

What would they do when he shot the animal? They would shake his hand, pound his chest with their palms. They would all say that they knew it would be him. The second they saw him, they knew he would be the one to get it done.

Suddenly, movement below. A figure swept into his sights. It was large, dark, quick. Alan's finger touched his trigger. His barrel was steady. The figure emerged, and Alan saw the head of a wolf.

It was time.

He breathed out and squeezed the trigger. The rifle sent the bullet into the night with a low pop and Alan knew that he would be the shooter. He would be the killer.

Then he saw a head. A mess of black hair. It was not the wolf. It was a boy. The shepherd. He'd emerged from the shelter to lead the sheep inside. There was a fraction of a second wherein Alan knew that the bullet might hit the boy, might kill the boy.

He waited. The boy was looking up to them, following the sound of the gun, and Alan waited to see him jerk back or fall.

But the boy did not fall. He was not hit. He waved.

As Alan's heart hammered, he lifted the rifle from his cheek and set it down on the rock beside him. He didn't want to see the boy anymore, and didn't want the boy to see him, so he turned away, his back to the valley. And then he saw the men.

Yousef was there, and the young cousins, and the man who asked him if he ate the animal or ate the man, and the man who he had told he was with the CIA. They were all standing, their guns at their side. They had all seen Alan shoot his rifle at the shepherd boy, and no one seemed surprised.

Yousef sat with Alan on the ride home, in the cab of the truck. They said nothing until they reached the fortress and went inside.

—You should sleep for a while, Yousef said.

He led Alan to his room.

—I'm sorry, Alan said.

—I'll have a car drive you back in the morning.

—Fine.

—Good night, Yousef said, and closed the door.

Alan did not sleep. He tried to calm his thoughts, but everything came back to what he'd almost done. Because he hadn't done anything, for years or ever, he had almost done this. Because he had no stories of valor, he had almost done this. Because the efforts he'd made toward creating something like a legacy had failed, he had almost done this.

Somewhere near dawn, a car arrived.

Alan walked to the driveway, where Yousef was waiting.

—This is Adnan. He'll take you to Jeddah.

Adnan stayed in the car, looking tired and unhappy. Yousef opened the back door and Alan got in.

—I'm so sorry, he said.

—I know, Yousef said.

—It's important to me that you're my friend.

—Give me some time. I have to remember what I like about you.

Alan tried to sleep on the drive back but couldn't. He closed his eyes under the white sun and saw only the face of the boy, the face of the men, Yousef's placid expression when Alan turned away from the valley and saw them all. An expression that spoke of suspicions confirmed.

When he returned to Jeddah, though, he would see Dr. Hakem and she would open him up. Then he would know what was wrong with him, and she could rip it out.

XXIX.

ALAN WAS NAKED beneath a wispy blue smock, in a waiting room in a Saudi hospital about which he knew nothing. He was about to have a growth removed from his neck, one that he still suspected was attached to his spine, sucking away some significant part of his spirit, his will and his judgment.

As he lay on a mechanical bed in a white room, Alan felt glad to be away from the fortress in the mountains. Since leaving, he'd spent a day and night asking himself, What have I done?

The answer was Nothing. He had done nothing. But this brought little relief. Relief would be the task of Dr. Hakem.

He was at the King Faisal Specialist Hospital and Research Center, where he had been admitted and asked to strip and stuff his belongings into a plastic bag. Now he was sitting on the bed, feeling cold in the papery smock, looking at his possessions, reading the plastic bracelet he'd been given, looking out the window, wondering if this was the turning point, after which he would be a sick man, a dying man.

He waited for twenty minutes in the empty room. Then forty.

—Hello!

Alan looked up. A man had entered, pushing a gurney. He arranged it next to Alan's bed.

—Yes now, the man said, and indicated that Alan should move himself onto it.

Alan did, and the orderly, perhaps Filipino, covered him carefully with a blanket.

—Ready now, he said, and they left the room. They traveled a dozen grey hallways before finally reaching a humble room of track lighting and cinderblocks painted powder blue. He had not expected an operating table, but there it was, and he was asked to move himself from the gurney and onto it. He had foreseen something like a dentist's office — small, private, a step removed from the consulting room where Dr. Hakem had seen him. Now he worried that everything had become more grave. Again he had the feeling his concerns were warranted: this proved that lump on his back was very serious, the results of the operation more pivotal.

But where was she? There was only one person in the room: a man in scrubs, perhaps a Saudi, standing in the corner. He had looked to Alan with what seemed like hope, as if he thought the man being wheeled in was a personal friend. Seeing it was only Alan, his face fell and turned into a sneer. He removed his gloves, deposited them in a bin, and left. Alan was alone.

Moments later, the door opened and a young Asian man walked in, pushing a machine on wheels. He nodded and grinned at Alan.

— Hello sir, he said.

Alan smiled and the man began an elaborate process of preparing his machine.

—Are you the anesthesia man? Alan asked.

The man smiled, his eyes bright and happy. But instead of answering, he began to hum, loudly and almost deliriously.

Alan leaned back and looked at the ceiling, which told him nothing. He closed his eyes, and within seconds found himself close to sleep. If not for the crazed humming of the Asian gas-man, he would have nodded off immediately. People died during surgery, he thought. He was fifty-four, old enough to die without causing too much consternation. His mother had died of a stroke at sixty. She'd been driving through Acton, on her way to visit a cousin, when it happened. Skidding off the road, her car collided with a telephone pole, causing no real damage to herself or her car — she'd almost missed it. But she wasn't found until the morning, and by then she was gone. To die alone, somewhere in the middle of the night, on the side of the road. Alan saw it as a message: in death, you can hope for dignity but should expect disarray.

—Hello Alan. How are you feeling today?

He knew the voice. He opened his eyes. Dr. Hakem's head blocked out the light. He saw only a smudge of her face.

—Good, he said, looking around. Somehow the room was now full of people. He counted six or seven, all wearing masks.

—I'm glad to see you, she said, her voice like cool water. We have quite an international group here to help with this procedure. This is Dr. Wei from China, she said, indicating the gas-man. He'll be our anesthesiologist. Dr. Fenton here is from England. He'll be observing.

She introduced the rest of the members, from Germany, Italy, Russia. They were nodding, only their eyes visible, and it was all too quick for Alan to keep track of exactly who was who. Lying on his back, naked but for a blue cape worn backwards, Alan did his best to smile and nod.

—When you're ready, you can turn onto your stomach, Dr. Hakem said.

Alan turned, his face now in the starched pillow, smelling of bleach. He knew he was exposed, but immediately a nurse placed a sheet, then a blanket, on his legs and lower back.

—Is that warm enough? Dr. Hakem asked.

—Yes. Thank you, Alan said.

—Okay. Do you feel comfortable turning your head to one side?

He turned to his left and flattened his arms against the table.

—I'm going to prep the area around your growth, she said.

He felt her untie his gown at the top. Then a wetness on his skin. A sponge, dabbing. A rivulet of water speeding down his clavicle.

—Okay. Dr. Wei will now inject the area with a local anesthetic. There will be a few stings from the needle.

Alan felt the sharp entry of the needle just below his cyst. Then another entry to the left. And then another, another. Dr. Hakem had promised a few, but now Dr. Wei had stabbed him four, five, and finally six times. If he didn't know better, Alan would have thought the man was enjoying it.

—Can you feel this? she asked. I'm pressing on your cyst.

He felt something, but he said no. He didn't want to be oversedated. He wanted to feel a version of the pain, however muted.

—Good. You ready? she asked.
He said he was.
—I will now begin, she said.

He created mental pictures to correspond to the pressures he felt, the sounds and movement of shadows above him. There was a series of small cuts, it seemed. The movement of Dr. Hakem's arm told him this much. After each, with her other hand, she was dabbing the area with some kind of sponge. He felt it pushing against him. Cut, dab, cut, dab. In the background, the humming of the gas man, and from above, the music of what seemed to be Edith Piaf.

—Okay, I've made the incisions, Dr. Hakem said. Now you might feel some pulling as I extract the cyst. They can be sticky.

And like that, whatever tool she was holding grabbed at something within him and pulled. His chest tightened. The pressure was extreme. He pictured a hook of some kind entering his back, grabbing at taffy, trying to pull it, snap it loose. He had never had anything removed from his body, he realized. This was new and was not natural. My God, he thought. How strange to have hands inside me. Tools grabbing, scraping. My God. Alan was hollow, his body a cavity filled with wet things, a messy array of bags and tubes, everything soaked in blood. My God.

My God. The scraping continued. The pulling. He felt a cloth catching rivulets that had traveled down his neck, toward the bed.

If he got out of this alive and unharmed, Alan vowed to be better. He would have to be stronger. His mother had tried to rally his strength, inspire him. She would read him passages from the diary of some distant relative, a woman living in the woods of what was now western Massachusetts. She had watched her husband and two of her children murdered by Indians, and had herself been abducted. She lived with her captors for almost a year until being returned to her people. She was reunited with her daughter, the only survivor of the attack, and they commenced to build a thriving dairy farm over six hundred acres of Vermont. She survived a heavy winter where the snow collapsed her roof, a beam falling on her leg, which was soon amputated. She survived a smallpox plague that took her daughter, who had just gotten engaged. The fiancé moved onto the farm and ran it when she died, at ninety-one. *Would you rather be here, now*, Alan's mother liked to say, *or abducted and living in the woods with one leg?* She had no tolerance for whining, for any sort of malaise in the midst of the bounty of their suburban life. *Forty million dead during World War II*, she would say. *Fifteen million during the war before. What was it that you were complaining about?*

Alan could hear conversations in various languages. A bit of Italian murmuring to his right. Arabic chatter near his feet. And still the cheerful humming from the Chinese anesthesiologist. It was curious that they all put up with it, his demented, frenetic tune, but no one said a word to him. The anesthesiologist seemed to be in his own world, pleased with himself and only glancingly involved in the surgery at hand.

—I'll be going deeper now, Alan, Dr. Hakem said.

The motion was now that of an ice cream vendor digging, twisting round, pulling. Then more dabbing, wiping. Alan imagined his blood rising upward, spreading across his back, free at last.

He could hear Dr. Hakem breathing, laboring as she pulled and dabbed. There were a series of snapping sounds, as if the gummy substance inside him was resisting all but the most forceful extraction. Alan considered the possibility that her silence was evidence that she had found something. Underneath the benign mass of lipoma, she had found something. Something black and fate-changing.

Alan tried to send his mind elsewhere. He thought of the sea, the tent, what the young people were doing. He pictured them being told of his death here, on this table in this room of blue cinderblocks. What would they say? They would say he liked long walks on the beach. That he liked to sleep in.

He thought of Kit. Kit alone without him. This would be more troubling. Ruby needed a counterweight. He had taken Kit away a year ago, when she and her mother had been fighting. He took her out of school and they'd gone to Cape Canaveral to watch the Shuttle. There were only a few more flights.

The day before the launch, they got a tour of all the facilities. The mood among the NASA people was all over the place — somber, bitter, loose, defensive. A promotional video insisted that NASA was *not just putting billions of dollars into rockets and shooting them into space.*

Their main guide was a man, just turned eighty, named Norm. He had been with NASA since 1956. He got on the bus, cane in hand, and sat down in front, picked up the mic, and with a deep Texan accent he said, his voice cracking, —This will be my last tour, and I'm glad to be here with you.

Kit talked all the while, which she did when they were together. There were hours on buses, to and from the space center, to and from the launch-viewing site, maybe ten hours together on that bus, and they covered everything. She talked about the crazy roommate, the beautiful but uneventful campus, and how she needed to find some friends soon because she felt rootless and untethered. Alan tried to reassure her the same way he always had.

—I'm the eye in the sky, he said. I can see where you started and where you're going and it looks perfectly fine from up here. He had used this metaphor since middle school. *You're almost there. Almost there.*

Norm took them to the building where mechanics repaired and prepared the shuttles, pre- and post-flight. The *Atlantis* was there, being readied for its last launch, the last of all launches. There were bustling tours being given all around, but Norm was somber.

—I can't do these tours much longer, he said. I don't want to be the guy saying, 'We *used* to do this, we *used* to do that.'

Most of the NASA employees they met that weekend would soon be out of jobs. They were not the stuffy technocrats Alan expected. No, they were folksy, quick to muse, to drift off while talking about a certain flight, the weather a certain day when the shuttle shot through a hole in the clouds.

Something pierced Alan's chest. It felt like a railroad tie, thick and blunt. His body tensed.

—I'm sorry Alan, Dr. Hakem said.

The pain dulled. The movements returned to a certain rhythm, dependable in its order. There would be a scooping, a scraping, a pulling, then a moment of relief when Alan guessed some extraction had been made. Then the dab of the sponge, a pause, and more excavation.

It was interesting being this, a cadaver, an experiment. Who said *man is matter?* He felt like something less than that.

At night, in the Orlando hotel, he and Kit ate from the vending machines and watched movies, and tried not to talk about Ruby, or the future with Ruby, the past with Ruby, the wounds of Ruby.

In the morning they took a bus to Banana Beach, the closest site from which to view the launch. Everything there, everything associated with NASA, was stripped down, humble. The fences were rusted. The pavement was cracked. But then, across the water, there would be a spaceship leaving the Earth with manmade thunder.

While waiting for the launch they'd met an actual astronaut, Mike Massimino, there with his daughter. He was funny, candid, self-effacing. He'd been up in two shuttles, including the first one after the *Columbia* disintegrated on reentry. He looked like an astronaut, clean-cut and silver-haired and sturdy in his baby-blue jumpsuit, but he was taller than average, probably six-two, with a Roman nose and a thick Long Island accent. He talked about spacewalking to fix the Hubble telescope, about the eighteen sunsets and sunrises in any twenty-four-hour period up there, how it made it hard for certain religions — morning prayers, afternoon, evening, very difficult. But it's good for a Catholic, he said. They just want you to check in once a week or so.

Kit laughed. He talked about how the stars, seen from space, don't twinkle, that without the atmosphere, they're just perfect points of light. How his crew, during a rare hour of downtime, had turned off all the lights in the shuttle, to better see them. NASA was full of romantics.

Now Dr. Hakem was reaching further. Alan winced, his body jerked.
—Alan? Her voice concerned, surprised.
—I'm fine, he said.
—I'm going to ask Dr. Poritzkova to help steady you.

Alan grunted in assent, and soon he felt what seemed to be the entirety of a man's forearm on his head. The weight was great, far too much for the task at hand. Alan tried to shift underneath, to relieve some pressure, to no avail.

Dr. Hakem continued to scrape and pull, and the pain increased. What kind of idiot asks for less anaesthetic? It was too late to correct the situation. He would endure. He had to push through this. His father would laugh at his discomfort, and would want to show him the shrapnel still in his lower back, sixty years after the war. Alan could never escape the difference between what he had or would ever see or endure and what his father had. He could not even that score.
—Alan? Are you okay?
He grunted that he was fine.

And now he saw a night sky. Maybe he was dying. He was dying to the sound of the mad Asian humming. What was that tune?

The pressure on his head seemed to increase. The Russian wanted to make a point, it seemed. Let him push. Alan could handle this. He forced himself to disassociate, to leave the body under assault.

Alan had never been stabbed or shot or punctured or broken. Were scars the best evidence of living? If we have not survived something, and thus were certain that we'd lived, we could scar ourselves, couldn't we? Was that the answer to Ruby?

—Still with us, Alan?

—Yes, he said to the floor.

The forearm pressure increased. It was too much.

—Can you tell the man pushing me down to ease up? he asked.

And the pressure was released, the man making a sound of surprise. As if he had not known what he was doing.

The relief was great.

There had been delays with previous launches. People would come from all over the world and the launch would not happen for days, weeks. But this time, Alan and Kit were there, on the aluminum risers with a thousand others, watching the countdown and expecting it to pause. Expecting it to be postponed. We had made so many mistakes, the countdown seemed to say, we cannot make another. But then it continued. He held Kit's hand. If this happens, he thought, I am a good father. If I show her this, I have done something.

The countdown continued. When it dropped under 10, then 9, he was sure it would happen but could not believe it. Then 1, then 0. Then the shuttle, miles away and across the water, rose silently. Not a sound. Just a yellow light propelling it upward, and it was not until it seemed halfway to the clouds that the air cracked open.

—Dad.

—Sonic boom.

When the Shuttle disappeared through the canopy of white clouds, Alan cried, and Kit smiled seeing him cry, and afterward he looked frantically for Massimino, to offer himself to anything he needed. I sold bikes, he would say. I sold capitalism to communists. Let me sell the Shuttle. I will help you get to Mars. Give me something to do.

But he didn't find Massimino. The parking lot afterward was crowded with everyone so happy, so proud, so many people crying and knowing that it was over, and the highways back would be choked, and it would take all day to get back to their hotels.

—Alan?

He tried to say yes, but it came out as a wheeze.

—We're sewing you up now. Everything went well. We got it all.

XXX.

AN HOUR LATER he was in the same room where he had undressed, and he was retrieving his clothes from the plastic bag he'd stuffed them into. As he was tying his shoes, Dr. Hakem entered the room.

—Well, that was a bit harder than I expected.

She sat down on the stool opposite him.

—It's tough stuff. Do you feel better now?

—How do you mean?

—Knowing it's a lipoma and nothing else.

—I guess. You're sure it wasn't stuck to the spinal cord, anything like that?

—No. It's had no impact on any nerves at all.

Alan was relieved, but then his confusion deepened. If there was no tumor attached to his spine, dragging him to these recent depths, then what was the explanation?

—How do you feel? Any pain?

Alan felt feeble, dizzy, disoriented. The pain was sharp.

—I feel good, he said. How are *you*?

She laughed. —I'm fine, she said, and stood.

But Alan didn't want her to leave. It felt important to him to keep her close a few minutes more.

—The other doctors seemed to really respect you.

—Well, it's a good group here. Most of them, anyway.

—Do you do more operations now?

—Excuse me?

—Today. Do you do more of these, or…?

—You're full of questions, Alan.

He liked hearing her say his name.

—I just have a few consultations, she said. No more surgeries.

He looked at her fingernails, rough and short.

—Is the job stressful? he asked lamely.

He expected her to leave, finished with his inane chatter, but she softened and sat back on her stool. Maybe this was part of the doctor-patient relationship, something she realized she had to do.

—Oh, it used to be. When I did the ER. Now, only sometimes.

—When?

Again her face seemed to say, momentarily, *Are we really still talking?* —When? I guess when I think I'm at the edge of my abilities.

—Not with a lipoma.

She smiled. —No, no. More like a tracheotomy. I won't do a tracheotomy. I made some mistakes on one of those when I was a resident. And I get nervous generally. When it gets too bad, I spiral.

—You spiral.

—Just little spirals of self-doubt. You have these?

How far to go? He could go on for days.

—I do, he said, happy with his restraint.

—Do you need anything, by the way? For the pain?

—No, I'm fine.

—You have aspirin? Tylenol?

—I do.

—Use it for the swelling at least.

She stood to go. He hopped off the bed.

—I'm very thankful, he said, extending his hand.

She shook it. —Well, you're welcome.

He looked into her eyes, granting himself a moment there. There was something tender around the corners, a downward line that said she had seen terrible things and was prepared to see more.

—I wanted to say that I think you're very strong, he said. I know it can't be easy doing what you're doing, here in the Kingdom.

Her posture softened. —Thank you, Alan. That means a lot.

—So do I see you again? he asked.

—Excuse me?

—A follow-up.

—Oh. Sure, she said. She seemed to be recovering from a different train of thought. In about ten days, we can take another look at it. Make sure the stitches have dissolved, all that. If anything comes up in the meantime, you can call me.

She handed him a business card. On it she'd written her phone number. Then she backed out of the room on tiptoes, as if he were asleep and she was afraid to wake him.

XXXI.

EACH OF THE THREE days after his operation, Alan found himself awake at the required time, able to eat and dress in time for the shuttle, which he took to the site with Brad and Cayley and Rachel. They all waited each day, their presentation ready, and the young people passed the time on their laptops, or playing cards, or sleeping. Yousef phoned a few times from the mountains, where he remained, sure that his absence from Jeddah was doing some good. The threats were becoming rarer. Alan urged him to stay until the henchmen assumed he was dead or had left the country. And each day at five, Alan and the young people boarded the shuttle and went back to the hotel, where Alan ate and slept without struggle. Amid these days, though, new things happened.

One day, after spending an afternoon on the shore, Alan returned to the tent to find the three young people asleep, all on the long white couch, this time in a new configuration. Brad and Rachel were on one end, she draped on him like a thrown coat. Cayley's head lay on the opposite end, her hands together, childlike, under her cheek, her legs entwined with Brad's. He chose not to imagine what had happened or what might happen, and decided not to wake them.

One night in the hotel, knowing it was a terrible idea but he had nothing to lose, Alan emailed Dr. Hakem, thanking her. In a turn of events he thought impossible, she wrote back.

Dear Alan,

I was as happy as you to know that the lipoma was only that. I was sure, but not without a lingering question or two. Now that you are healthy and not facing imminent death, I hope I see you around Jeddah one of these days. I hope knowing you are not dying of a malignant tumor has your spirits high!

Ha ha,

Dr. Zahra Hakem

Alan spent the better part of the next day by the sea thinking of a response, something smart and witty and which might nudge things further. This, too, he assumed impossible.

Dear Dr. Hakem,

My spirits are high indeed — maybe too high? I'm feeling a little dizzy. The cause is mysterious, but I have felt a strange, new, lump in my back. I'm no doctor, but it feels like a rubber glove. Is there a chance you left one in me? Sometimes people leave things like gloves with someone they like, in hopes that the retrieval will provide an excuse to see that someone again.

Yours,

Alan

He knew it was bold, but as he wrote the words, he grew strangely sure that she wanted to see him again, and he was correct.

Dear Alan,

I actually might have left something. I'm thinking a sponge? Maybe part of a snack I ate during the surgery? We were all snacking, so I can't be sure. I think I need to see you again. Perhaps out of the hospital? We don't want to worry your insurers.

Dr. Zahra

This email came at night, too late to be vaguely professional in provenance, and so they continued to email for hours, until they had made a plan to see each other in person. Alan had no clue how this could be done in the KSA and left the planning to her.

I'll pick you up Wednesday, she wrote. I'll be there at noon. Look for an SUV. I'll write your initials on a card and put it on the windshield.

The next day, Alan could not sit still in the tent, and strolling the beach was not good enough. Instead he walked into the city's grid, passing the men in jumpsuits, nodding to them like a foreman. He walked for hours on empty roads, his energy rising with every mile. Finally he returned and found the canal he'd sailed. He walked a time along the canal, dumbstruck by its clarity and the color possible here. Amid the dust and the buildings that might never be, and the sand forever trying to overtake it all, there was this immaculate thread of turquoise, an irrational color, an unnecessary color. People had not made the color, but they had helped it to occur here. They had built something and the water had flowed and so people had brought bewildering beauty into a place in which it did not belong.

Alan took a long time along the needlessly blue canal, and when he returned to the tent, he was surprised but not so much to find Rachel sitting on Brad's lap, the two of them facing each other, soaked in sweat, their mouths trying to swallow each other, as Cayley worked away at her laptop, not twenty feet away.

Cayley noticed Alan in the doorway, and waved. But Brad and Rachel were not ready to stop. They looked to him, waiting to see if he intended to stay. He had no interest in what they were doing, and the next day was the weekend, when Zahra would be taking him to her brother's seaside home for lunch, so he found himself without any reason to interfere. He left the tent and continued to walk until the day was done.

XXXII.

AN ENORMOUS SUV swung into the Hilton driveway. It was gleaming, all the hotel's windows and lights reflecting on its obsidian exterior. Under the windshield Alan saw his initials, AC, as if the car was advertising its climate control. He smiled, and the back door opened.

Alan saw her legs first. She was wearing an abaya, but her ankles and feet, in strapped heels, were there before him. He looked up, and saw her smiling at him, her face alight in amusement.

He stepped into the car, in full view of a dozen bellmen and attendants, to all eyes a Western man invited into the car of a Saudi woman. How did it work?

Alan sat down and closed the door behind him and inside it was very dark. He greeted the driver with a smile and a nod, and they swung through the hotel turnaround, past the guard atop the tank, and out onto the highway.

Zahra wore a loose scarf over her hair, but her face was uncovered. In the golden light her eyes looked bigger and browner than they had in the hospital, and were lined with a tidy stripe of blue eye shadow. Her hair, with which she said she struggled, was so thick it seemed to have been not styled but carved. In the front, though, those curtains that needed parting. She did it again, using two fingers, revealing her face anew.

Alan wanted to say something significant. There were many things he wanted to say, but anything he might say needed vetting. What could he say in front of the driver?

—How is KAEC? she asked.

Like Yousef, she found it amusing how much thought and hope he had invested into the city-to-be. She said *KAEC* in a way that implied it was gauche and silly, a distraction from more essential things.

—Fine, I guess. They're making progress.

Her look was skeptical.

—They really are, he said. It takes time.

—*Lots* of time, she said.

They sped through the city, its glittering malls and high-walled compounds. The driver pointed out the window and threw a few words over his shoulder.

—He says that's the house of the Saudi Maradona. He thinks we care. Do you care? she asked.

Alan couldn't guess which home the driver was referring to, but they were in the middle of a strange but common sort of Jeddah neighborhood, where on one side of the road there were extravagant walled compounds, painted in pastels and worth millions, and across the street there

286

was a vast empty lot, where hundreds of trucks had dumped their construction waste. Tidy piles of rubble everywhere. Alan thought to ask Zahra about them but assumed it would be considered some kind of insult. He didn't know how proud or unproud she was of her country, presuming it was her country. He still didn't know.

—Water?

She had two glasses of water sitting neatly in the drink holders.

He took a sip.

—Good? she asked.

—Thank you.

She lifted her water glass to her lips, and seeing her like that, eyes closed, gave Alan a flurry of wild thoughts. She put the glass down, her tongue quickly catching a droplet.

—The drive is more than an hour, she said. By the time we get there we'll know everything important about each other.

And this was more or less true. She told him about high school in Geneva. A former boyfriend who was now trying to overthrow the government of Tunisia. The time she tried LSD. A stint with Islamic Relief, working in refugee camps in Kurdistan. A year in a medical hospital in Kabul. Listening to her, Alan felt like a less necessary species.

—So you're going to meet the King, she said.

He hoped she would be impressed. —That's the plan.

—So do you personally present to Abdullah, or...?

Alan wished he could say yes. But he was too well-practiced in self-deflation, so said, —I'll be part of the team. I really don't know much about the technology. I'm here because I know his nephew, or knew him.

—And who's the competition? she asked.

—I don't know. Right now we're the only ones in the tent.

—The tent?

—Don't ask.

—I won't.

She turned to the window, as if looking for inspiration. —It'll be interesting now that the Chinese buy more of the King's oil.

Alan had not known this.

—I wonder, she went on, if everything will follow that. I wonder if Abdullah and the whole crew will suddenly shift their allegiances. Maybe you're no longer the favorite.

Alan was suddenly transported far away from this car, from Zahra. Quickly he was in a room in Boston, meeting with Eric Ingvall, who was asking what went wrong, why he hadn't anticipated this, factored in that. And then Kit and her college. And then the money he owed to everyone he knew.

—I'm sorry, Zahra said. Don't worry. I'm sure you have nothing to worry about. I'm sure you guys have a *few* years left of preferential treatment.

She was smiling slyly, her forefinger tapping the rim of her glass. But could she be right? No one could beat Reliant on price or technology. Who else had a hologram? He didn't know, actually.

—I'm sorry, Alan. I've got you worried.

—No, no. Not at all.

—You seem distracted all of a sudden.

—No, no. Sorry.

—You have an in with the nephew. That's helpful, I'm sure. Abdullah is very loyal, I know. And anyone doing business in the Kingdom better know a royal or two.

They talked about Abdullah. Zahra liked him far more than the monarchs who preceded him. Alan said something about how it seemed good to have a reformer in the position of Abdullah, and soon found himself comparing Abdullah to Gorbachev and de Klerk. When he'd finished he knew he'd gone too far. But Zahra chose to leap over the mess of his misperceptions into a different topic entirely.

—I have children, she said.

—I assumed, he said.

—You assumed?

—Maybe not assumed. I assumed it was possible.

—I thought you meant you had seen something in my hips. You know, like the people who can tell from the way a woman walks.

—I'm not that clever.

—Well, they're teenagers now. They live with me.

—Their names?

—Raina, Mustafa. She's sixteen, he's fourteen. I'm trying to prevent my son from becoming an asshole like his father. Do you have advice?

—Does he tell you anything? Alan asked.

—Did you tell your mother anything?

Alan had not. Who did young men talk to? Young men have no one to talk to, and even when they do, they don't know what to say or how. And this is why they commit most of the crimes of the world.

—Get him alone somewhere. Something like camping.

Zahra's laugh cracked the air open.

—Alan, I can't take my son camping. People don't go camping here. We don't live in Maine.

—Don't you go to the desert?

She sighed. —I guess some do. The boys do, to race their cars. Then they wreck them, and they show up in the ER. I've saved two that way. But most of the time they die.

Alan said he'd heard something about this.

—From your guide?

—Yousef. He's a great kid.

—And he has nothing to do here.

—That's what he says, too.

Zahra thrust open the curtains of her hair and this time, because they were in her car, and traveling down the coast, and the sun was outside and there were stripes of sun within, he was momentarily breathless.

—What? she asked.

He smiled to himself.

—You're laughing at the thing I do with my hair. My husband used to make fun of me.

—No, no. I like it.

—Stop.

—I really do. I can't tell you how much I like it.

She twisted her face into one of guarded belief.

The road inhaled and exhaled, hugging the coast. He felt that the sunlight around them could be tasted, could be touched. He loved it all, the patches of empty land stacked with garbage. He loved the medical school featuring a Woman's College and a Man's College — two ends of the same building, looking vaguely like Monticello.

—It's almost comical, right? she said.

—There's a certain clarity to it.

She laughed, then reassessed him.

—You shouldn't be nervous.

—Do I seem that way? He was only ecstatic.

—You won't look at me.

—I was just watching the scenery. It reminds me of so many other coasts. The pink adobe on the water. The white yachts.

He sat back, watched the passing sea, the necklace of bleached homes strung beside it.

—Where are you from? he asked.

—You mean, where are my parents from? Their parents?

He knew it would be some unprecedented combination of peoples.

—I guess, he said. Is that a weird question to ask?

—No, no. They're from everywhere, really. Here, Lebanon. Some Arab blood, but my grandmother was Swiss. One great-grandfather was Greek. There's some Dutch in there, and of course I have lots of family in the U.K. I've got everything in me.

—I want that, too.

—You probably already do.

—I don't know enough about it.

—Well, you can find out, Alan.

—I know, I know. I want to find out where everyone comes from. Every side of me. I'm going to ask around.

She smiled. —It's probably time. Then, realizing that might have sounded scolding, she added, I mean, you have plenty of time.

Alan was anything but offended. He agreed with her completely.

—What do you think our kids would make of this? he asked.

—How do you mean? You and me? Because we represent some kind of big culture clash?

—I guess so.

—Please. We're separated by the thinnest filament.

—Well, that's the way I think.

—That's the way it is. She looked at him sternly. I won't let us play those games. It's so tiresome. Leave that to the undergraduates.

The driveway was interrupted by a steel gate, which the driver removed with a button somewhere in the visor. It slid away, revealing a modest ranch house of cream and white, with arched windows, pink doors and curtains.

When they entered, the driver stayed in the front room while Zahra led Alan to the back, to a room facing the water. She poured juice for the two of them and sat next to him on the couch. The sea outside was a raucous blue, dusted with tiny whitecaps. Across the room, a painting of what appeared to be the Swiss Alps.

—Strange in a beach house, Alan noted.

—Everyone wants to be somewhere else, she said.

They stared at the picture.

—It's horrible, isn't it? My brother buys paintings everywhere he goes. Every resort town. He has the worst taste.

—Have you seen snow?

Zahra turned to the ceiling and laughed, a burst of thunder.

—What? Alan, you are such a puzzle. You're so smart about some things, but then so oblivious about so many others.

—How am I supposed to know you've seen snow?

—You know I studied in Switzerland. They have snow there.

—Depends on where.

—I've skied dozens of times.

He didn't know what to say.

—Oh Alan.

—Okay, you've seen snow. Sorry.

She looked at him, closed her eyes, and forgave him.

She downed the rest of her juice, laughing into her glass.

—Time to swim.

—What do you mean, swim?

—We're going swimming. You'll borrow my brother's suit.

He used the bathroom to change into a pair of blue shorts, and when he was ready, he stood by the glass door that led to a small sandy beach and what appeared to be a ramp leading into the water. It was like an underwater concrete runway, from the back deck to the sea. It was as clean and geometric as a boat launch.

He felt a touch on his back.

—You ready?

Just her fingers, and he lost all composure.

—Sure. Let's do it, he said, loathing himself.

He didn't dare turn around. He would have time, soon enough, to see her in her bathing suit. She stayed behind him, and her fingers stayed on his back, and he chose not to move. She saw him looking at the odd ramp.

—My uncle liked to snorkel, so he made this for himself. It's cruel and indulgent, but it works. The fish are still here.

Her uncle had actually dredged the sea floor so there could be an easy way to enter the water, without having to walk on the coral.

—You go in, she said, handing him a snorkel and mask. I'll follow. I need to send the driver on an errand.

He opened the door, stepped out and made his way to the water. Here it was cooler than by King Abdullah's rising city. After the runway, the sea floor was rocky and dropped swiftly away.

Treading water, Alan fitted the equipment over his head. He pressed his face to the water and saw immediately that the sea was clear and the coral abundant. A flurry of bright orange fish drifted into view. He pushed his way out farther, following the line of coral underneath. It was gloriously alive and, though not untouched, it was thriving. Within minutes he saw a huge clownfish, swimming in circles, a pufferfish, puttering along with its undersized fins. A school of tangs, a rusty parrot fish. A roving coral grouper, with its look of perpetual dissatisfaction.

He went to the surface for air. There was too much to see, too many colors, the shapes irrational. Looking to the house for a sign of Zahra, he saw nothing. Not wanting to seem anxious, he turned from the shore, following the coral on the sea floor out, deeper, and saw the larger fish, those who traveled freely between the shallows and the deep. Ahead, the drop-off was extreme. The water below was inky, the bottom unseeable. A shape flew before his mask. It was bright, blinding, huge. He kicked and rose from the water, trying to see it from above.

The shape rose, too. It was Zahra.

—Alan!

His heart was hammering.

—I hoped to scare you, but not that much.

He was coughing.

—I'm so sorry.

Finally he could speak. —It's okay. I shouldn't have been scared.

He looked to her. He saw her head, her hair tied up, her jawline exposed — far more delicate than he'd imagined. She was beautiful wet, her black hair gleaming, her eyes alight.

But all else was underwater.

—I have to get back under, she said. Neighbors.

She nodded to the houses that ringed the inlet.

—I have to warn you, though. I'm dressed like you. If someone sees us snorkeling, they'll think it's two men. Just two backs uncovered, wearing men's trunks. You understand?

He thought he understood, but he did not understand. Not until he put his mask into the water again. Then he knew. She was not wearing a top. Her shorts were blue striped, male. He skipped a breath. My God. He followed behind her, watching her long strong legs, her long fingers trailing, the sun touching her everywhere, flashbulbs popping.

She turned back to him, smiling wildly around her mask, as if to say, Do I surprise you? She had some idea of how good she was, how much she pleased him. Then she turned back, all business, pointing below, to the thousands of fish and anemones of every improbable color, everything alive and grabbing upward.

He was dying to be closer, to have everything. He wanted to rub against her accidentally, to twist and roll in the water with her, to scream into her mouth. He settled for following her, ignoring the fish and coral below for a look at her breasts, descending from her, glowing, swaying.

She tried to get him to swim at her side, but he hung back, hoping to limit her view of him. They swam down the shoreline and he took a chance, grabbing her ankle, pretending to want her attention, to show her an oversized clownfish below. She came to him, and took his arm in her hand, squeezed. Finally his answer. He was sure. But what to do then? There were too many stimuli, in this water, under this sky, the light a latticework shifting over her bright flesh. He had never seen anything more beautiful than her hips rising and falling, her legs kicking, her naked torso undulating. She swam out farther and paused where the floor dropped precipitously into deepest blue.

She rose to the surface and he followed.
She took her mask off.
—Take a breath, she said.
He did. And she dropped, her hands stretched above.

He followed her down. She pushed the water so she sank, ten, twenty feet under. He met her, and when he did, she grabbed him, and he felt her against him. She kissed him, their mouths closed, and then kissed his chest, his nipples. He dropped to her stomach, kissing her there, rising to take her nipples in his mouth, one then the other as her fingers plowed through his hair. Then she was gone. She shot to the surface and he followed.

By the time he breathed the air and met the sun, she was off, her back to the sky, adjusting her snorkel. He followed her. They made their way slowly back to the house, again pretending to be men, friends. When they approached the ramp, she turned to him, indicating that he should stay. He hung back, watching her. She climbed up, threw a towel around herself and hurried inside.

He swam back and forth, pretending to be snorkeling but keeping an eye for any movement within. Finally he saw a hand emerge from one of the windows, beckoning him inside. He rushed up the ramp and opened the door.

—Over here, she said.

He followed her voice to another room. There, she was dressed, sitting cross-legged on floor, pillows strewn about. She was wearing shorts and a tank top, both loose, both white. The momentum was lost, at least to him, as he sat across from her, smiling stupidly.

—So, she said.

She took his hand, threaded her fingers through his. They both looked at their hands entwined. He could not build on this, didn't know what to do next. He found himself looking at a bowl of dates.

—You want one? she said, joking, exasperated.

—Yes, he said, having no idea why. He took one, chewed its flesh, feeling devastated, as always, by himself, his inability to do what he should do when he should do it.

When he was finished, and had delicately placed the pit back on the plate, she moved herself closer to him and reclined on her side. He did the same, mirroring her shape. She was so close he could feel her breath upon his face, could smell, faintly, the salt water on her tongue.

He smiled at her. He knew that she had intended this move as invitation, but he had not reciprocated.

—This is good, he said, unable to conjure anything more.

She smiled patiently. He collected himself. He knew he needed to kiss her. And then he would need to move himself atop her. He envisioned the steps, where he would set her shoulder, where he would put his hands. It had been so long. Eight years since he'd had to make decisions like this.

He glanced outside, at the sun-soaked sky, at the sea unknowable, and in their vastness he found strength. A million dead in that water, billions living under that sun, that sun a hard white light among billions more like it, and thus all of this was not so important, and thus not so difficult. No one was watching, and no one outside of him and Zahra cared about what would happen in this room — such strength born of insignificance! — so he might as well do as he wished, which was to kiss her.

He moved his face toward hers, toward those exuberant lips. He closed his eyes, taking the risk he would miss. She exhaled through her nostrils and the heat brushed his mouth. His lips touched hers. So soft, too soft. There was no ballast within — they were pillows upon pillows. He had to push harder to get some leverage, to press them open. She parted them, opened her mouth to him, and the taste was that of the sea, deep and cool.

He took her head in his hand, her hair more brittle than he expected.

It was not soft, no. Raking through it, he found her neck and cupped her head, bringing it closer. She sighed. Now her hand on his waist. Those long fingers, those nails. He wanted them to grasp and reach and pull.

He moved his mouth to her neck, ran his tongue from shoulder to jaw, and then moved atop her. That smell of hot flesh — this was reward enough. She murmured approval into his ear, her breath. She was either greatly forgiving or mercifully easy to please. His worries fled.

Her hand grasped above her, looking for a cushion. He found a throw pillow, placed it below her lifted head. For a brief moment their eyes met again, smiling, shy, astounded. Those eyes, as big as planets — he wanted them closed now, so she would not look upon him and reconsider. She would see his yellowing teeth, his fillings, his many scars, his ragged flesh, a patchwork of a life of disarray and carelessness. But maybe he was more than the sum of his broken parts. She had seen inside them, hadn't she? She had pulled dead stuff from within him, cutting and pulling and dabbing, and still she wanted to be here.

She pulled him down into her again and his mouth met her open mouth and now her movements took on new urgency. Her fingernails raked the hair on the back of his neck. Her other hand was grabbing the flesh on his back.

Across the room, he saw a mirror. They were visible in it, and he saw his arms around her. He looked strong, his arms tanned, his veins taut. He was not disgusting. *I don't want to have sex that someone wouldn't watch*, Ruby had said. She assumed it would all end at thirty-five. A sudden pain shot through him, a cold bolt of regret, everything they had done to each other, the primary mistake of his life, that time wasted hurting her and being hurt by her, the terrible things that take away the little life we have. He looked at Zahra again, into her dark eyes that forgave him and brightened when they saw him smile.

He pushed himself against her and heard himself moan.

—Thank you for that, she said.

He laughed into her ear and kissed his way to her clavicle.

—Are you stalling? she asked.

—No, no. Am I?

—Get inside, she whispered.

And he tried to, but found he wasn't ready.

—I want this so much, he said.

—I'm glad, she said.

But they found themselves apologizing for various failures, for parts of their bodies that would not cooperate, or did so only intermittently. When he was ready, she was not, and this sent him shrinking. Still, they caressed each other desperately, clumsily, with diminishing returns. At one point, trying to move behind her, his elbow struck her forehead.

—Ow.

He collapsed and looked at the ceiling.

—Zahra I'm so sorry.

She sat up, her hands in her lap.

—Are you distracted?

He had not been distracted, not at all. In fact, he had been so consumed in wanting her, enjoying her flesh, her mouth and breath and voice, that no other thoughts had entered his head.

—Maybe, he said.

He had no choice but to lie. He told her about the things weighing on his mind, the house that would not sell, its smell of decay, the man who had drowned himself in the lake, the money he owed to so many, the money he needed to do right by his daughter, his magnificent daughter who would not get what she deserved unless something miraculous happened out here in the desert.

—It doesn't have to be today, she said, though it sounded to him like, It doesn't have to *be*.

—Shit, he said. Shit shit shit shit shit shit.

—It's okay, she said.

—Shit shit shit.

—Shhh, she said, and they leaned against each other, tired as prizefighters, as they watched the sun pour into the sea.

XXXIII.

DUSK HAD COLORED the home's white walls blue, its pink curtains violet. The sea outside was restless and dark.

Alan and Zahra sat at the kitchen table drinking white wine. He had finished the dates.

—I have to go to Paris for a few weeks, she said.

Alan was ready for this.

—How long do you think you'll be in Saudi? she asked.

He didn't know.

They drank a bottle and opened another. They were so in love with the world, and disappointed in every aspect of it, that drinking another bottle while they sat at the kitchen table was the most obvious way they could honor it all.

Zahra poured him another glass.

Alan had the feeling that Zahra was waiting for him to leave. But he had gotten there with her driver so he could not leave until she sent him away.

—Can I tell you a story? he asked.

—Of course, she said.

—I have a story for your son. What's his name again?

—Mustafa.

—Mustafa, good. A good name.

Alan was drunk and wanted Zahra to know it.

—This is a good story for Mustafa.

—I'm glad. Should I take notes?

—No need. You'll remember the essence.

—I will try.

—Okay. My father and I went camping a few times.

—Ah, camping again.

—This is not about camping. Please listen.

—I'm listening.

He refilled their glasses. He could hardly see but felt very strong.

—I was around ten, twelve. And this one time he brought me up to New Hampshire. He drove into some national park. Just endless woods. And we parked, and got out, and walked deep into the woods. For at least four hours. We didn't see a soul the last three hours. We were off the map, basically. This was in the early morning. We started at sunrise. We had snowshoes with us, and used them when we got into some deeper powder. The walking was incredibly tiring. We stopped every so often for water and a snack. We ate beef jerky and nuts, that kind of thing. Then we would continue up the slope. Around three in the afternoon, the sun was already falling, so we stopped. We couldn't see any sign of civilization in any direction. I assumed we'd walk down then. It was getting cold and would get down to twenty or ten. And what we were wearing wasn't going to help us stay warm enough.

—What was he thinking? Did you have tents? Zahra looked aghast.

—I asked him that. 'Do we have a tent?' I thought he had some kind of plan. But he acted like he'd just realized the math of it all. That we wouldn't make it back before dark, and that the night would freeze us solid. Not to mention the prospect of wolves, bears.

—Wolves and bears? she asked. Her look was doubting.

—Believe it.

—I guess I have no choice.

—So he said to me, 'What should we do?' And then I realized this was some kind of test. There's something in his eyes that's testing me. So I thought about the Boy Scout stuff I knew and said, 'We build a shelter.' And that's what he had in mind. He opens his pack and he produces an axe and some rope. He's planning to have us make a shelter out of logs, tied like a raft.

—Oh no.

—'How long do you think we have?' he asks, meaning before the sun goes down and it drops below freezing. 'About two hours,' I say. 'I reckon you're right. Better get started,' he says.

—He was a tough guy, Zahra said.

—He likes to be thought of that way. So we got started. We took turns chopping and tying. We tied together two pallets of twenty or so thin birch logs. Once we had that done, we cleared a twenty-by-twenty square in the snow, and assembled it there, a pretty respectable A-frame. We gathered fronds from the pine trees and lined the bottom with them.

—Sounds comfortable.

—It was surprisingly comfortable. Then we built a wall around the shelter. Three feet, all around. To keep the wind out. We put snow on the roof, too, about a foot of it for insulation.

—And it wouldn't leak?

—Not when it's ten degrees. That's the best insulation we had.

—Did you have sleeping bags?

—No we did not.

—This man was a lunatic.

—Maybe. Then he asked, 'Son, what do we need now?' I knew. We needed needle and thread, or duct tape or something. So I tell him that, and he produces a roll of duct tape.

—For what?

—To make a sleeping bag out of our clothes.

—You're kidding.

—I'm not. We cut our jackets up, and taped them together to make a big wide sleeping bag. And then we slept there in our long underwear.

—You shared the sleeping bag.

—Yes we did. And I have to say, when we were all settled in there, it was very warm.

—You didn't have a fire.

—No fire. Just each other.

—And in the morning?

—We taped the jackets back together, went home.

—So you saved yourselves by building something. I get it. But he almost killed you both in the process.

—I guess, Alan said, and laughed.

—I'm allowed to laugh, right? Zahra said.

—You are.

—Good. Because I find just about all of it, she said — and swept her hand around the room, encompassing the house, the sea outside, all of the Kingdom, all of the world and sky —very, very sad.

XXXIV.

THE KING DID VISIT the King Abdullah Economic City, eleven days later. His visit was announced at nine o'clock that morning and his motorcade arrived just after noon. He toured the city's empty roads for twenty minutes, spent fifteen in the welcome center, then he and the entourage made their way to the presentation tent.

Alan and the young people were ready. The King sat down on a throne-like chair, brought that day, and his group sat on the white couches. Brad and Rachel and Cayley began the presentation, which went off flawlessly. Brad, wearing a sleek business suit, welcomed the audience, explained the technology, and then introduced another man, who was in London but then, aha, he was striding from the wings of the stage, wearing a thobe and gutra. He appeared to be in the tent, on the stage, walking and talking in both English and Arabic. He and Brad interacted for a while, emphasizing that this kind of technology was only one aspect of Reliant's vast capabilities, that they looked forward to much success together at KAEC. Then the man in London thanked everyone and left, and Brad thanked everyone, stepping off the stage and mouthing to Alan and the other young people his assessment of the performance: *Amazing!*

When it was over, King Abdullah clapped gently but said nothing. There were no follow-up questions. Neither he nor anyone from his entourage spoke to anyone from Reliant, though Alan positioned himself near the door in case anyone wanted to discuss the proposal. No one did. Alan had no opportunity to mention the King's nephew; there were four layers of men between him and the King, who left in minutes, along with all those who attended him.

Alan watched as they drove up the road, but not far. They disappeared into the garage below the Black Box. Outside the building, Alan saw three white vans parked in a tidy row. There had never been any vehicles like that parked outside the building in all the time he'd been there, so he went to get a closer look. On each van, there were two rows of type on the side, the first in Arabic, the second in Chinese. Alan couldn't read either.

He waited outside the building, trying not to attract notice, for almost two hours, until the King emerged with his men and a contingent of Chinese men in business attire. They all shook hands, smiling warmly. The King returned to the Black Box, and a few minutes later his motorcade emerged from the garage and left the city. The Chinese businessmen got in their vans and departed, too, leaving a wall of dust that took hours to settle.

When they were gone, Alan rushed up to the Black Box and found

Maha at her reception desk.

—Hello Alan, she said.

—What were those men here for? he asked.

Money. Romance. Self-Preservation. Recognition.

—A presentation for the King, she said. Same as you.

—You mean IT?

—I believe so.

—And they were in here? Inside the building?

Maha smiled. —Where else would they be?

—And how did they know the King would be here today? he asked.

Maha looked at Alan for a long while and then said —I guess they were just lucky.

That afternoon, the young people of Reliant dismantled and packed the equipment, then loaded all of it and themselves into the shuttle. They saw no point in staying, so they left Saudi Arabia the next day.

Alan remained. He returned to the tent each of the next three days, hoping to get a meeting with Karim al-Ahmad. Mr. Al-Ahmad had gotten very busy after the day of the presentations, Maha told Alan.

Finally, one day, as Alan sat alone in the tent on a white plastic chair, there was a knock on the door. Alan answered it. It was Karim al-Ahmad, who informed him, regretfully, that the contract to provide IT to the new city had gone to another firm that, he said, could deliver the IT far quicker and at less than half the cost.

—A Chinese firm? Alan asked.

—A Chinese firm? I'm not sure, al-Ahmad said.

—You're not *sure?*

Al-Ahmad feigned the searching of his mind.

—You know, I believe they might have been Chinese. Yes, I believe they were. Does that make a difference to you, Alan?

—No, Alan said.

It didn't really make any difference at all.

—Did he like the hologram at least? Alan asked.

—Who?

—The King.

—Oh he did, he *did*, al-Ahmad said, his voice full of feeling, something like compassion. He thought it was *very, very nice.*

Alan looked through the plastic window, at the blue water, the setting sun. —You think there's any reason for me to stay? he asked.

—Stay at KAEC?

—Yes. There are some other services I think Reliant might be able to help you with. And if not, I work with some other companies who could be very useful in getting this city off the ground.

Al-Ahmad stood for a moment, his finger to his lips.

—Well, let me spend a few days thinking about that, Alan. I certainly would like to help you.

—You would?

—Sure, why wouldn't I?

Alan could think of so many reasons. But he had to presume goodwill. He had to hope for amnesia.

—Then maybe I'll stay, Alan said.

He wasn't being sent away, after all, and he couldn't go home yet, not empty handed like this. So he would stay. He had to. Otherwise who would be here when the King came again?

ACKNOWLEDGMENTS

Always and most of all, VV.

Vast thanks to the staff at McSweeney's for their work on all aspects of this book. Thank you Adam Krefman, Laura Howard, Chris Ying, Brian Mc-Mullen, Sunra Thompson, Chelsea Hogue, Andi Mudd, Juliet Litman, Sam Riley, Meagan Day, Russell Quinn, Rachel Khong, Malcolm Pullinger, Brent Hoff, Sheila Heti, Ross Simonini, Heidi Julavits, Alyson Sinclair, Scott Cohen, Eli Horowitz, Walter Green, and Chris Monks. Em-J Staples and Daniel Gumbiner helped tremendously with myriad tasks, far-flung research and the difficult home stretch. Their enthusiasm kept me strong. Extra thanks to McSweeney's editors Ethan Nosowsky, Jordan Bass, Andrew Leland, and Michelle Quint, who had to read this book many times, and whose edits were surgical and brilliant.

This book grew out of a conversation I had back in 2008 with my brother-in-law, Scott Neumann, who traveled to the King Abdullah Economic City that year with a multinational corporation. Though this novel bears little resemblance to Scott's time at KAEC, I was helped enormously by his great generosity in sharing his insights. Vanessa and Inger, thank you, too, for friendship and family.

There are many friends in Saudi Arabia I would like to thank, first and foremost Mamdouh Al-Harthy, guide and friend, expert and philosopher king. His hospitality can never be repaid. Thanks also go to Hasan Hatrash, poet, troublemaker and friend, and to Faiza Ambah, courageous journalist and screenwriter. She read early and later versions of this book, and offered key comments and encouragement.

For their crucial reads of the book in various forms, profound thanks go to Noor Elashi, Wajahat Ali, Lawrence Weschler, Nick Hornby, Tish Scola, Alia Malek, Roddy Doyle, Brett O'Hara, Stephen Elliott, Brian Gray, and my brothers Bill and Toph. Heroic and repeated readings were done by the phenomenal novelist-editors Peter Ferry, Tom Barbash, and Peter

Orner. For their friendship, and expertise in matters of sales, manufacturing and consulting, vast thanks go to Paul Vida, Thomas O'Mara, Eric Vratimos, Grant Hyland, Scott Neumann, Paul Scola, and Peter Wisner.

For their guidance and advocacy over many years now, profound thanks to Andrew Wylie, Sally Willcox, Debby Klein, Lindsay Williams, Jenny Jackson, Kimberly Jaime, Luke Ingram, Sarah Chalfant, Oscar van Gelderen, Simon Prosser, Helge Machow, Kerstin Gleba, Christine Jordis, Aurélien Masson, the team at PGW, and the many other editors, publishers and translators who have brought books like this to new audiences.

At Thomson-Shore printers in Dexter, Michigan, thanks to the entire staff: Kevin Spall, Angie Fugate, Josh Mosher, Heather Shultes, Kandy Tobias, Sue Lube, Jenny Taylor, Mike Shubel, Rich McDonald, Andrea Koerte, Rick Goss, Christina Ballard, Frankie Hall, Bill Stiffler, Mike Warren, Anthony Roberts, Tim King, Tonya Hollister, Deb Rowley, John Bennett, Paul Werstein, Jennifer Love, Alonda Young, Sandy Dean, Matt Marsh, Renee Gray, Adnan Abul-Huda, Sue Schray, Jenny Black, Debbie Duible, Steve Landers, Connie Adams, Pat Murphy, Rob Myers, Al Phillips, John Harrell, John Kepler, Darleen Van Loon, Shannon Oliver, Diane Therrian, Mary McCormick, Dave Mingus, Sandy Castle, Sherry Jones, Steve Mullins, Bill Dulisch, Ryan Yoakam, Doris Zink, Ed Stewart, Robert Parker, Terri Barlow, Thoe Tantipitham, Cody Dulish, Dave Meacham, and Vanessa Van De Car.

Note: This book includes some of the history of Schwinn, an actual bicycle-manufacturing company based, for many decades, in Chicago. The basic dates and arc of the company represented herein are faithful to the historical record, though this is a novel, and a man named Alan Clay did not in fact work for Schwinn, and his experiences there are fictional. To read a fantastically well-reported and well-written nonfiction book on the subject of Schwinn, look for *No Hands: The Rise and Fall of the Schwinn Bicycle Company, An American Institution*, by Judith Crown and Glenn Coleman, published in 1996 by Henry Holt. My novel benefited greatly from that excellent book.

BOOKS BY THIS AUTHOR

FICTION
A Hologram for the King
What Is the What
How We Are Hungry
You Shall Know Our Velocity

NONFICTION
Zeitoun

FOR ALL AGES
The Wild Things

MEMOIR
A Heartbreaking Work
of Staggering Genius

ABOUT THE AUTHOR

Dave Eggers is the author of six previous books, including *Zeitoun*, winner of the American Book Award and the Dayton Literary Peace Prize. *What Is the What* was a finalist for the 2006 National Book Critics Circle Award and won France's *Prix Medici*. That book, about Valentino Achak Deng, a survivor of the civil war in Sudan, gave birth to the Valentino Achak Deng Foundation, which operates a secondary school in South Sudan run by Mr. Deng. Eggers is the founder and editor of McSweeney's, an independent publishing house based in San Francisco that produces a quarterly journal, a monthly magazine, *The Believer*, and an oral history series, Voice of Witness. In 2002, with Nínive Calegari he co-founded 826 Valencia, a nonprofit writing and tutoring center for youth in the Mission District of San Francisco. Local communities have since opened sister 826 centers in Chicago, Los Angeles, New York, Ann Arbor, Seattle, Boston and Washington, DC, and similar centers now exist in London (the Ministry of Stories), Dublin (Fighting Words) and in Copenhagen, Stockholm, Melbourne, and many other cities. A native of Chicago, Eggers now lives in Northern California with his wife and two children.

www.mcsweeneys.net
www.voiceofwitness.org
www.826national.org
www.scholarmatch.org
www.valentinoachakdeng.org
www.zeitounfoundation.org